USA TODAY BESTSELLING AUTHOR
ALISHA KLAPHEKE

FATE
of
DRAGONS
DRAGONS RISING BOOK ONE

PRINT book ISBN 978-0-9998314-5-8

❀ Created with Vellum

For Amelia and Aidan

Tidehame

Jade Caves

Silver River

Lapis Caves

Red Meadow

Bibotzetik
(Sunken City)

The Marshes

Dragon's Back

Forest of Illuviaurat

Lost Valley

The Great Sea

SUGARRABOTA ISLE

PROLOGUE

Four kynd dwell upon the world,
Water, Fire, Earth, and Air.
Flaws and power,
Magic and vice,
All these traits they share.
Then one breaks true;
Darkness to rise,
And the world begins to tear.

~a youngling's chant from the age of Matriarch Elixane

The dragon Matriarch flew as close to the sea as she dared, waves crashing against the island of Sugarrabota beneath her. Watching for swells of magicked salt water, she led her group above the coastline.

The humans, eyeing her from their settlement below, had first reported the signs of the Sea Queen's growing power. Rumbling earth. Beached sea life. Afraid and lacking the earth magic they once used to fight the sea, the humans had given the dragons permission to soar over their territory. Unlikely allies against a common enemy. When Matriarch Amona saw no further evidence of a coming flood, she banked away from the glittering ocean.

A human female ran toward her, holding a tiny bundle in her arms.

The way she moved caught at Amona's heart. So fierce. So determined.

She was fast. But the water was faster.

As she shrieked for help, the sea heaved, and a wave ten miles across exploded over the wall protecting the human city.

Dragonfire rumbled in Amona's chest, her blood racing.

She broke formation.

The other dragons shouted through the Bond, a jumble of confused and afraid voices inside Amona's head. They wanted to flee.

The spelled salt water, deadly to any dragon, cascaded into the streets and over the buildings, rushing to swamp the entire city.

The dragons begged Amona to leave.

But she was their Matriarch, and they could not stop her.

The water rose to the human female's waist as Amona reached her. The dragon extended her talons. Their gazes met. The human recognized that Amona was not attacking, knew the dragon was trying to help. Amona could see the knowledge in the human's round, brown eyes. The salt water rioted around them, splashing and full of spells.

If that water took Amona down, she would die. The human knew it. She lifted the bundle as high as her small arms allowed.

Amona grasped the baby in her talons, clutching on as gently as possible. The sea folk swarmed, arms and legs lined with fins, teeth like razors. The water bubbled to the human's shoulders as Amona rose into the sky.

"Her name is Vahly, *Blooded for the battle!*" the human shouted just before the sea folk pulled her under the vicious waves.

CHAPTER ONE

For the millionth time, Vahly reminded herself that she was no dragon. As the last surviving human—and possibly a future queen—hanging from the side of a cliff probably wasn't the best idea.

Muscles quaking, she blew the hair that had fallen from her braid out of her mouth and forced her body upward to grab a crack, her toe wedged into a tiny dish on the rock's face. Sweat trickled down her temple and wet the linen shirt she wore under her laced, leather vest.

No, this wasn't the best plan.

But it was thrilling.

A curling, violet fern the size of Vahly's fist appeared on a ledge not far from her right hand. Helena, the healer in the Lapis dragon clan, called it vivanias. She used it in medicines for the younglings. The stuff was rare as a cool day in summer, and Helena would pay handsomely for the small harvest. At least a ruby or a handful of old human coins.

With that sum, Vahly could enjoy several rounds of

dice at the cider house. Gambling was really her only true vice, and surely at least one such habit was permitted. Of course, she also did some thieving, but those days were seldom, and there was time enough to consider that when she wasn't hanging from a cliff.

She stretched to pluck the delicate fronds, but her short sword caught on a nub of rock and she nearly lost her hold.

"Stones and Blackwater," she snarled, trembling as she worked the sheath's loop to the back of her belt.

For all this trouble, she would demand three rubies *and* the coins from Helena. She tucked the valuable fern into one of the small bags at her belt. After all, no dragon could do this job. They'd never fly this close to the Sea Queen's realm. One splash of recently spelled salt water and a dragon was injured for life, or quite often, died from the contact.

As if the sea folk could read her thoughts, the ocean breeze blew in a rush of salty air that raked across one side of Vahly's face.

Shuddering, she imagined them far below, in the water, looking so much like humans, but with blue-green fins along their limbs and a taste for exactly her type of flesh.

During a sea battle that happened long before Vahly was born, the Sea Queen had proclaimed her intention to cover the world in ocean water, flooding this last island of Sugarrabota and killing every creature left on land.

Twisting, Vahly looked down.

Two hundred feet below, the sea surged and swelled like the back of a great watery beast.

Vahly's foot slipped.

Her fingers instinctively latched onto the mountain, and her nail ripped, pain searing her finger. Heart thrashing, she lifted her foot up and to the right, pulling up on a tiny crag.

A rushing sound of water filled the air and roaring waves crashed into the cliffs. Spray reached like a clawed hand into the air.

Vahly heard herself shriek.

She scrambled to lodge her hands into a long fissure that ran along the upper half of the cliff's face. The rock scraped at the back of her knuckles. Heart racing, she switched her feet, raising the left to stand on a higher divot in the rock. Her fingers numbed as she climbed, and with every breath, she feared the sea folk's spelled wave would thrash higher and drag her into the depths.

"This is not worth a game of dice," she hissed as she jerked her way, higher and higher, to another ledge, to the next lip of rock that might hold her weight.

The ocean roared.

The tip of a wave crashed against her leg, soaking through her boot and trousers. She had to fight panic, reminding herself that she was not a dragon like her family. The spelled salt water would not burn her flesh to black or eat into her bones.

But still, she could drown. Or the sea folk's needle-sharp teeth could shred her body. With perfectly evolved fins and powerful water magic that controlled the tides, they would have no problem introducing Vahly to a gruesome death, as they had the rest of her kynd.

From handhold to toe grip, with her torso and limbs

burning, she climbed along the fissure to the top of the cliffs. Using bruised and bleeding hands, she dragged herself the rest of the way to safety. She rolled to her back and gasped for air.

Once she could breathe normally, she leaned over the edge and glared at the rolling waters as they receded. "Getting a little out of hand, aren't you?" she said, wryly.

Had the sea folk been aiming for her specifically or was she in the wrong place at the wrong time?

A tall rock, not big enough to be called an island, stood about fifty feet offshore. This season's high water mark was nowhere to be seen.

The oceans were definitely rising. And fast.

Amona, Vahly's adopted mother and the Lapis dragon Matriarch, had told Vahly the Sea Queen had figured out how to multiply salt water. With that information plus what she'd seen today, Vahly wouldn't be surprised if the sea folk managed to overtake Sugarrabota in less than a season.

Vahly ran a finger over the Blackwater mark between her eyebrows. The shimmering circle of darkness, with its highlights of yellow, red, green, and blue, represented the Source's creation springs, the Blackwater. Born with the mark, the dragons considered Vahly as Touched and destined to become an Earth Queen.

Only an Earth Queen could shake the seabed, beneath the Sea Queen's wild waves, and drive the waters away from the land. If Vahly's powers had awakened upon her physical maturity, she could have raised mountains like the Earth Queens of the past. Vahly could have protected her dragons and all the simplebeasts on land as well.

But so far, Vahly had no power.

No earth magic whatsoever.

And at three and twenty, doubt swamped all hope of her growing into the Earth Queen everyone needed.

The summer sun warmed Vahly's blonde head and her tanned skin, the heat like a firm hand, steadying her. She didn't have the power to fight the Sea Queen herself, but she could at least keep her dragon clan informed. With today's ocean activity, they needed to clear the lowest levels of the palace. If the sea folk managed to flood the Lapis territory like they had the Lost Valley, the spelled salt water would kill thousands of dragons.

Pulse kicking in her throat and pain lancing through her ripped finger, she took off at a run, leaping over a small bush of bright yellow brazenberries and a patch of citrus-scented greenery before heading down the steep slope that led to the entrance of the Lapis mountain palace.

When she emerged from the narrow pass between the higher elevations near the sea and the lower region of Lapis territory, she remembered why she'd been off on a time-consuming, risky fern-gathering mission in the first place. Spending her day attending yet another dragon ceremony from the ground, as the only highbeast present without the power to fly or do any magic, was not her idea of an afternoon well spent.

High above the palace that had been carved inside a string of seven mountains, every dragon from the surrounding four hundred or so miles flew in concentric circles, fully shifted into their dragon forms for the Dragonfire ritual.

A rangy male named Xabier had reached maturity and had to go through the ceremony to receive his fire magic. After this, Xabier would be able to breathe fire from both his scaled human form and his full dragon form. Dragonfire was vicious. It burned through ground, through salt water—spelled or not—and made basic fire seem adorable.

Most of the dragons present had Lapis blood and therefore boasted scales of deep blue veined with a golden color, much like their lapis lazuli stone namesake. Even after a lifetime of watching dragons shift into full form, the sight stole Vahly's breath.

A coming storm's distant lightning flashed off the dragons' massive, sinuous bodies and their crystalline spikes. Light scattered like diamonds.

In comparison, Vahly was a slug.

Of course, she liked herself well enough. She was no lazy slug. Not an ignorant slug either. Good with bow and sword. Better with cards and dice. But a slug just the same—fleshy, and pretty much useless in a world where war was a constant. The dragons with Jade blood disagreed with the Lapis way of fighting the sea folk. Every season, sometimes every moon cycle, strategy talks erupted into battles of fire and blood. And of course, the ocean provided a hearty helping of disaster with its spear-wielding sea folk.

What Vahly wouldn't give for even a touch of the dragons' power. To stand as tall as two-and-a-half humans on end when in full dragon form. To breathe fire. To heal so quickly. To shrug off shell and coral blades like a mere splinter.

The dragons soared higher, their semi-translucent wings rippling in the wind and their Dragonfire crackling between bouts of thunder. Lightning branched between them, making Vahly jump. Raising their heads, they made sure to breathe their mighty flames above one another. The flickering orange, yellow, and blue joined to form a ring of fire so powerful that Vahly saw the waves of heat from the ground.

Her news about the ocean activity would have to wait. There was no interrupting a Dragonfire ritual. Fifteen-year-old Xabier would have his moment in the lightning storm, among his elders and their flames.

When Vahly herself turned fifteen, her body had no idea that humans no longer existed. It changed in preparation for procreation despite the complete and total absence of a potential mate. Humans could not make children with dragons for a variety of reasons, one of which was that they were physically incompatible with regard to reproductive organs.

But with these physical changes she went through, Vahly had hoped her powers would rise as they did in stories about humans, and in elves too, back when they had also roamed the island.

When her magic did not bloom in time with her body, Vahly had gone to Amona in hopes her mother knew of a human power ceremony similar to the Dragonfire ritual. But Amona knew of none and didn't believe such a thing had existed in the human culture.

Vahly had searched the dragons' records inside and out for any hint to discovering her earth magic.

But there was nothing.

ALISHA KLAPHEKE

When the Sea Queen flooded the last large city of humans, Bihotzetik, she'd also destroyed all of the humans' records. When Vahly was a baby, the sea's great maw had likewise swallowed the humans' final settlement in what was now called the Lost Valley.

The Dragonfire ritual ended, and Xabier landed to cheers from all the dragons in attendance. Unless he proved to be more suited to the kitchens or the smithy, the young male would join the other mature dragons in the fight against the sea. The dragons needed every warrior they could get.

With a bright flash of fire, the dragons shifted out of their full dragon form and into their scaled human form. Dragon servants came forward to hand out cloaks with large holes for their wings, dresses which were also sewn to accommodate flying, boots, trousers, and all manner of jewelry. Though the dragons were never ashamed of their nakedness, they preferred velvets, brocade, rubies, and gold.

When the dragons shifted to human-like forms, their scales diminished in size and grew delicate, curving around nostrils, ears, elbows, and eyelids not so different from Vahly's own.

The spikes faded in the fire of transformation, and the dragons now had long or short hair in shades of amber, chocolate, jet black, or flax like Vahly's own braid. Dragon eyes were not like a human's round version. Dragons' slitted, reptilian pupils worked far better in the dark. The dragons' fingers numbered five on each hand like Vahly's, but their scaled digits ended in talons, a far thicker version of human nails, capable of cutting flesh or stone.

Wings transitioned in a way similar to scales by simply decreasing in scale.

Most dragons in attendance were from the Lapis clan though a good number of clanless individuals had come. Amona tolerated their presence near the Lapis mountain palace during the Dragonfire ritual because the more dragons that participated, the stronger the maturing dragon's fire tended to become. It behooved her to welcome all, despite their defiance to her in the past.

Once all the dragons were in human-like form and dressed in their finery, Amona roared approval of the event. Her Blackwater mark shimmered in the uneven light, a near match to Vahly's. Just as Vahly's marked her as a potential Earth Queen, Amona's told the world she was meant to be a dragon matriarch.

Amona blasted a rippling stream of dragonfire into the steely sky.

She had been the one to rescue Vahly, the last of her kynd, when the Sea Queen flooded the final human settlement. Amona was scary, but she also had a good heart, and Vahly had grown attached to her despite their differences and Amona's oftentimes stoic demeanor.

Nix—the clanless dragon who ran the cider house as well as an impressive ring of smugglers and spies—was Vahly's only true friend. Nix slid away from the gathering as she fastened the last of her cloak's buttons—the dragons had openings in their cloaks, dresses, and tunics for their wings. Before taking off into the sky, she whispered to a nearby friend. The male laughed and reached out a hand to touch Nix's bright azure wings. She slapped his clawed fingers away and flew off as the male shook his head.

The cider house should be safe from flooding for the time being, Vahly thought. It was high on a ridge that overlooked the Lost Valley, and not prone to flooding like the lower levels of the palace might be.

"Vahly!" In the air, Nix twisted to shout through the chaos, her red hair tossing about and her bright green, quadrant-cut cloak flapping in the wind like an extra set of wings. "I'll need help at the cider house if Amona can spare you!" Dragons who bonded with the Lapis or the Jade, but then broke their bond gravitated toward the cider house for a variety of both honest and nefarious reasons.

Vahly waved and nodded. She hoped to escape after talking to Amona. A good game of chance at Nix's place was far better than sitting on an uncomfortable chair, smiling for Xabier and his new powers, and pretending she might still become the Earth Queen the Lapis hoped she'd be.

They had longed for a savior. Instead, they were stuck with her. In place of an Earth Queen to fight the sea, they had a powerless human with a faulty Blackwater mark and a penchant for gambling.

Amona came up beside Vahly, the matriarch's head tipping downward as she tied back her human-like black hair with a leather thong. More white showed in her tresses these days, but at four hundred years and counting, Amona still had the vibrancy of a far younger dragon. The breeze stirred the loose sleeves of her black, embroidered dress. The gold thread along the wrists glimmered in the shape of the Lapis symbol—dragon wings over a slitted eye.

"You will sit next to me at the feasting, yes?" Amona's voice brought drums to mind. There was an earthy beauty to the sound and a commanding tone as well. The matriarch smiled expectantly, her human-like red lips pretty against the deep blue of her scaled skin.

"I saw something." Vahly kept her own raspy voice low so as not to alert the entire clan. That was Amona's job if she saw fit to inform them.

Amona cocked her head. "I'm listening."

Vahly spoke quickly, relating what had happened off the coast.

Amona looked over Vahly's head, staring into the distance, in the direction of the ocean. As she glared at their ancient enemy, her pupils expanded and contracted in a way Vahly's never could.

"So the Sea Queen thinks to attack us here, does she? The Jades will need to know this too."

The other dragon clan, those with Jade blood, lived far to the north and battled almost daily with the Sea Queen's army in their colder waters. Sometimes it amazed Vahly that both clans were dragons. As the old saying went *Lapis hunt with their minds; Jades with their claws.* The end of the saying depended upon who was doing the telling. A Jade would conclude with *And see who has the blood of enemies between their teeth?* When the Lapis used the expression, they finished with *And see who has a full belly at the end of a season?*

Despite their frightening common enemy and the ever-increasing threat to their existence, the two clans fought almost as much with one another as they did with the sea folk.

"Vahly, are you injured?" Amona sniffed, then took up Vahly's hand. What was left of the ripped nail hung loosely and blackened blood surrounded the first two knuckles.

Vahly tugged away gently. "I'm fine. Would you like me to take a message to the Jades?"

Amona would say no, of course. The Jades openly hated Vahly for not growing into the great powers her Blackwater mark claimed she'd possess, but Vahly still wanted to offer help.

Heat crawled up Vahly's neck and spread into her cheeks, but she kept her chin up. It wasn't as if she hadn't tried to gain her powers. She'd imbibed nine kinds of potions Helena the healer crafted in the hopes of finding magic in her blood and bones. Vahly had scoured the Lapis library's scrolls. She'd even tried half burying herself in the earth of the Red Meadow, outside the Lapis mountain palace, praying somehow the earth would notice her.

Despite her determination not to hate herself, the pressure of not living up to everyone's expectations gnawed Vahly's heart and soul. Each day, the invisible beast of failure ripped another chunk of Vahly away and she found it more and more difficult to stand tall instead of crumbling into a mess of self-loathing.

"Thank you," Amona said, "but I think I'll send Lord Maur. He enjoys the shouting they call talking up there."

"So you believe the Sea Queen won't attack before he can get up there and back?" Vahly wanted to join Amona in gossiping about Lord Maur—he was a nightmare—but what she'd witnessed pushed everything else out of her mind.

"I don't know. There is no way *to* know. I'll evacuate the lower floors of the palace for the time being, but we can't scout or strike unless we have a plan in place. Like it or not, the Jades are my allies and I must make good use of their strengths. They must be involved in any aggression toward the Sea Queen. Not only because if we fail, the sea folk will strike the Jades next, but also because the Jades understand certain aspects of war in a way we Lapis do not."

This was why she was a great matriarch. All dragons were vain to a fault. But Amona never let those traits trip up her wisdom. Vahly hoped it would always be Amona's way to stifle her haughtiness in order to help her kynd. Amona was not perfect, but she was the best dragon Vahly had ever known.

"Do I truly need to be at the feast?" The Dragonfire ritual always included a massive concluding feast and Amona required all loyal Lapis to attend.

The crowd of dragons began the walk toward the entrance to the mountain palace, Vahly and Amona leading the way.

Amona's lips parted. She halted, sending several dragons into Vahly's back.

"What is it?" Vahly ushered her mother off to the side of the throng.

Murmured apologies and bows came from those who had bumped into their Matriarch, but Amona didn't seem to notice them. Her gaze flew to Vahly. A clawed hand shot out to touch Vahly's chest. Amona's orange eyes focused, pinning Vahly in place like Vahly had stolen the cookie jar.

"Daughter." Amona rubbed a circle over Vahly's heart and mimicked the movement on her own chest.

"Yes? What is wrong? Did I say something?"

"No." Amona smiled, and if Vahly had been looking at anyone but Amona she would have guessed those were tears forming in her eyes. But Amona never cried. Never. Dragons loathed weakness and what they deemed excessive emotional attachment. "You truly care about the flooding and the possible evacuation, don't you?"

"Of course, I do." What was Amona getting at?

"This is more," Amona said, murmuring to herself.

A buzz of excitement, or perhaps dread, ran through Vahly. Lightheaded, she blinked in the sun now piercing the storm clouds the dragons had called up. "It is?"

Amona nodded and walked quickly toward the front of the mountain palace. "You will attend the feast. By my side, in your proper place. Vahly, I have discovered something very interesting. About you."

CHAPTER TWO

I n the time before dragons recorded history, the
Lapis carved a palace into the eastern mountains.
The hard facade rose in stark contrast to the Red
Meadow's delicate grasses and the diminutive red hat
flowers that grew on the banks of the Silver River.

Above the entrance to the palace proper, numerous
windows carved in the shape of flickering flames, and
landings scored with claw marks from centuries of use
dotted the cliff face. Some windows were small, only
wide enough to grab a portion of the western light that
coursed over the distant western ranges and through the
meadow, or a bit of the eastern sunrises that glowed
beyond the coastal mountains where Vahly had collected
the vivanias plants. Other windows widened to allow for
a dragon's take off over the land in full battle form, or for
a group of the creatures to gather for a game of dice or a
meal and cider.

During a game on the nearest window's perch, Vahly
had won a fine bear pelt. Sure, she didn't have magic, but

she was no slouch with numbers or statistics. Sometimes, she thought she might have a touch of luck. That wasn't nothing.

Great steps of limestone, worn by weather and countless feet, reached wide enough to admit five full-sized dragons. An archway stood at the top of the stairs, its curve towering over Vahly's head. The sign of the Lapis marked the arch's peak—dragon wings over a slitted eye—and the lapis lazuli stone that naturally formed in these mountains glittered with stripes of golden pyrite and boasted the same blue as Amona's scales.

Inside, dragons had dug out massive tunnels and countless rooms. Sconces, as tall as Vahly and made of white crystal, hung at regular intervals down the main passageway. Dragons walked and talked, filling the corridor with smoky breath and the flutter of wings.

Amona kept Vahly close, expanding one wing—blue as the bottom of a flame—so there was only room for the two of them as they made their way toward the feast. Amona tried to be casual about her protectiveness, but for Vahly, such tricks didn't pass her notice anymore.

What was going on with Amona? What had happened outside, when she had stopped so suddenly? Vahly swallowed, her nerves on fire.

"Amona, you don't need to coddle me." Vahly gave her mother a questioning smile.

"I'm doing no such thing."

"Right." Vahly shook her head. "This isn't about new information on a human power ritual, is it?" Vahly whispered, not wanting the whole clan to hear the desperation in her voice.

Amona's eyes grew sad. "There is no ritual, Vahly. I have told you as much. We must simply be patient. Your power will rise, and we will fight the Sea Queen, and we will live."

So whatever Amona had learned about Vahly, it wasn't about a possible ceremony? Then what was it? Maybe she had discovered another way to wake Vahly's earth magic.

Vahly fidgeted with her sword hilt, clicking the end of it with a knuckle. Her mind threw ideas at her like a drunken juggler.

"There has to be a ceremony of some sort," Vahly argued. "Dragons have them. Elves, too, if the stories are true."

"Who has been talking about elves?" Amona sneered.

The venom in her tone surprised Vahly. Sure, she knew the Lapis were no friend to the forgotten kynd. They had warred in the past. But Amona sounded absolutely close-minded about the elven race.

"They were an arrogant kynd," Amona said, "and did nothing but hide their knowledge from us, age after age. Thankfully, I believe them to be extinct. Don't mention elves in my presence again. And, my daughter, if there had been a human power ritual, I would have heard of it long ago. I've told you this. We lived closely for a while. I would have seen the ceremony, heard the secrets."

Nix was the one who had talked about elves, but Vahly wasn't about to rat her out. Last night, during a heated round of Trap—a nine-player dice game in which

Vahly collected a lovely sum of coins—Nix had claimed elves had rituals for everything from gaining powers at maturity to taking out the rubbish bin.

Vahly's friend had also told her about a hidden chamber in the library where the dragons kept records concerning elves. The entrance was supposedly near a shelf of unlabeled scrolls. Vahly had originally waved off Nix's suggestion that Vahly find her way into that restricted area. She was sure Amona would have told her about it if the room did in fact exist. Or at least, Amona would have searched the scrolls there herself for anything that could be related to Vahly gaining her earth magic.

But now, with this strong, adverse reaction to Vahly bringing up elves, she wondered if Nix had been right to suggest sneaking into that hidden room.

If Vahly were caught violating the library's rules, she would be whipped. It was one thing to galavant around with Nix and the others and be a less than perfect daughter to Amona, but to directly disobey a written rule concerning official scrolls, here in the palace? The punishment would be steep. Dragons loved their scrolls almost as much as they loved their gold.

"If the humans held the ceremony in secret," Vahly said, "and performed under cover, then perhaps not?"

Dragons clogged the passageway, and Vahly, feeling hemmed in, unlaced her leather vest to let it hang freely over her shirt. Dragons never seemed to mind a crowd as long as it was made up of clan. Vahly, on the other hand, felt her differences keenly in such situations. Boots scraped the ground and wings shuffled. One male offered another a silver filigreed flask of firecider to a taller male whose laugh made Vahly's ears ring.

Amona let out a quiet, wry laugh. "And that is why I love you. You are not afraid to push me."

"Oh, I'm plenty afraid. Don't think that I'm not." Vahly held up her own hands, then gestured toward Amona's claws. "I'm no fool."

A smile graced Amona's lips as she ushered Vahly into a room off the corridor. Some dragon had stacked extra chairs along the back wall beside a row of wooden kegs. The rest of the clan streamed by the doorway, not noticing their Matriarch and her adopted daughter.

"No, you are not a fool," Amona said. "You are brave." *And I'm proud you're a Lapis.*

Vahly froze, mouth open.

Amona had used telepathy, known to dragons as the Call. Only when the matriarch of a dragon clan bonded with another dragon could the Call function.

A lump formed in Vahly's throat and tears blurred her vision. She had waited forever for this, thinking it would never happen. Vahly had all but given up on enjoying the closeness that this part of living with dragons allowed. She grabbed Amona's shoulders, not caring that dragons didn't like to show tender emotion.

Amona smiled genuinely and Vahly's heart soared. "You are now bonded with the Lapis, in every way, Vahly."

Amona collected a shocked Vahly into a rare hug. She smelled familiar, like the sandalwood she burned in her quarters and the sage-like aroma of a powerful dragon's blood. Vahly let herself be held until she could halt her tears. Amona was the only mother she had ever known.

"You are truly my daughter."

"Thank you, Matriarch. Mother. But how? What finally secured the bond?"

It was the highest honor for a creature not born into the clan. Vahly could think of only one other that had bonded with the Lapis—a Jade whose personality did not fit the Jade culture. She pulled back a little from Amona.

"You don't have to do this. I'm not your blood and I don't need your pity."

Amona straightened. A stab of fear shot through Vahly's chest.

"I am fully aware I don't have to do this, or anything." Amona's eyes blazed. "I do this because I want to."

Vahly couldn't believe it. She was bonded with the Lapis. A real bond she never thought she could have. She had long endured sly insults and the lancing pain of not belonging. Now, that would all change. Wouldn't it?

"When did you feel it? When did the bond hit you?" Vahly asked, a sour note wheedling into her voice.

Something was off.

When Vahly dreamed of being bonded, of hearing the Call, she'd thought her heart would fill. A glowing happiness did light her, but still, that same hollowness echoed inside her heart. That loneliness Vahly had always carried.

Surely, it was just shock. Once the truth of this set in, she'd feel satisfied.

Amona was practically glowing with pride. "Just now. After you warned me of the sea and what you saw. You must have been thinking of the clan, of your family," she stressed the last word, "and suddenly, the bond pinched me."

"Pinched?" Vahly had to laugh, even as she struggled with warring emotions, both good and bad.

Amona laughed too. "Yes. The bond feels like a pinch. Right here." She touched her chest. "It's not a dissimilar sensation to the one when we make a heart promise. But unlike a promise, a bond will not burn through your heart if you break it. Not that I have to tell you this." Vahly knew Amona was thinking of Nix and her Call Breakers. "If you feel the urge to leave us, I will fight it, but not more than I think is fair. I will respect your wishes and aid you in any way I'm able."

"I HAVE no desire to leave the clan." Vahly wasn't lying. She didn't. But she hoped the news of her bonding would bring her a true belonging and get rid of at least a few of the insults she had to endure every day. "If I did, I think the Jades would eat me for lunch."

The Jades were warlike and loud and did not pretend to be content with the way Vahly had turned out thus far.

Amona's laugh rocked the floor under Vahly's feet as they headed for the smell of roasted meat.

PALE SUNLIGHT FELL through the oculus set into the high ceiling of the feasting hall. Charcoal, deep red, and yellow ocher artwork showed age-old battles between dragons and sea folk. Wings unfurling. Jagged lightning. A long-dead Sea Queen brandished her coral spear, launching spelled ocean water through crashing waves. One of Amona's ancestors blasted dragonfire through the foam and burned a unit of sea warriors to ash.

Below, three large pits showed bubbling pools of earthblood. Similar to magma, though less hot and infused with magic, the golden substance gave dragons their energy. The pits belched a heat that slicked Vahly's face in sweat.

Once, when she was a third of the size she was now, she had gone past one pit's circle of high-backed chairs and stone table to look down and see what created those bursts of flame and that unrelenting temperature. Amona's own hand had snatched her back before she'd gone close enough to see more than a flash of earthblood.

Now, she stayed as far away from the openings as was polite.

The dragons didn't always open the metal grates that covered the pits. But when ceremonies required the entire clan to use dragonfire, the dragons grew tired and their magic withered inside the ovens of their chests. They needed to be near the earthblood's golden flow—its heat revived their dragonfire to full capacity. In such times of need, young dragon warriors would turn the pulleys and drag the great slabs of black iron along metal tracks to expose the earthblood.

The mood in the room would normally have been relentlessly celebratory, considering the ritual they had just completed. But the dragons' toasts to Xabier lacked enthusiasm. The scene of the heaving ocean, so near their home, had brought the knowledge that time was short to the forefront.

The clan's tension was a thousand pinpricks in Vahly's skin.

Servants brought out hundreds of glazed venison haunches—dressed in pickled onions—and laid them out on the circle-shaped, stone tables surrounding the pits. Every dragon took their seat, wings adjusting around slender chair backs that supported the spine. For a moment, the sound of flapping wings filled the room.

Vahly sighed at the relief of a breeze on her flushed cheeks. Then, resigning herself to at least one cup of cider and a small bite alongside Amona, with Maur on her mother's right, Vahly sat and tried to think of winter.

As they ate, Maur talked with Amona about the bear the Lapis believed was killing and leaving deer in the northern regions, past the Red Meadow, near Jade territory.

"We should send a hunter out. If left, that bear could offset the balance of the herd on which we depend for food."

"I agree. I'll see to it," Amona said.

Vahly glanced at Xabier's table. The newly matured dragon didn't seem overly bothered by the events of the day like everyone else. He downed a haunch of venison before Vahly could finish her cider. She smiled. He was a good dragon—simple and slow to anger—even if his appetite demanded a frighteningly high count of kills.

At a nearby table, Helena the healer held up a serving of venison. Vahly had shot one of the simplebeasts with her bow during her hunting yesterday. Most dragons thought one kill was nothing, but Helena grinned at Vahly in praise. "Very good meat. I think I have a portion of your kill!"

A few dragons laughed, thinking a hunting human was not much better than a soldier mouse. Would that change when Amona made the bond public? Or would the Lapis only become more hostile toward the failed Earth Queen?

"Thank you, Helena." Vahly managed a grateful smile. Then Vahly turned to those who had laughed and gave them a smirk. "I'd love to see you bring down prey without fire, wing, or claw. If I'm this deadly as a human, imagine how fantastically horrifying I'd be as a dragon!"

Most of her peers snickered at her bravado, but a few glared, smoke streaming from their nostrils in warning.

Just shut up, Vahly, she told herself. Another jab isn't worth losing your eyebrows.

At the high stone table, directly under the oculus, Lord Maur looked past Amona's outstretched forearm to eye Vahly. He had smoothed his brown-black hair away from his face, no doubt to show off his aristocratic nose. The noble's hunting grounds extended from the northern end of the Lapis palace, up into the northeastern mountains bordering Jade territory.

When dragons weren't fawning over Amona, they were at his heels even when said heels had been up to no good throughout the clan. Partly because idiots considered him handsome, but mostly because of his standing within the clan.

Nix had told Vahly to be wary. She'd said he gained much of his hunting grounds by using bribes to maneuver wealthy enemies' heirs toward the front lines of the war against the sea folk.

Amona tore a neat length of meat with a flick of three claws as Maur addressed Vahly.

"The earthblood has reddened your face terribly, Earth Queen." Maur scooted his platter toward a servant for a second helping. The young dragon piled another deer steak near Maur's seasoned mushrooms. "Do you find that since you matured," Maur said, "the heat here is too much for your quickly aging human flesh?" He said *flesh* like most would say *dung*.

She wanted to tell him where he could shove his platter, but she didn't want to ruin Xabier's special day with further bickering. Plus, Amona would probably announce the bond soon and Vahly wanted everything to go as smoothly as possible. "The heat is no trouble at all, my lord."

Thirsty, Vahly motioned to a servant for another drink. Some hated working for her, but she had won most of them over with humor that told them in not so many words that she did not see herself as above them at all.

The servant nodded his purple-blue head and brought over a bronze pitcher of dropcider. After setting Vahly's goblet in place, he lifted the pitcher high, then poured the amber liquid into the goblet. The distance and splash aerated the cider and made it even more delicious.

Amona leaned close, adjusting a velvet bag on the leather shoulder belt that most dragons wore tucked around their left wing joints. Smoke spiraled from her nostrils, a sure sign she was excited. "I'm going to announce your bonding unless you have an argument."

Vahly's heart beat stronger, and she tried to feel completely pleased about the prospect. Why wasn't she? "I have no argument," she said as the dragon in charge of the dessert trays walked by. "I just hope this doesn't end with me as dessert. I would probably be delicious in that vanilla bean pudding."

Amona stood and unfurled her wings with a loud snap. They stretched behind Vahly and Maur like a curtain. Her eyes took in the room, her gaze a sword point looking for a target.

Every dragon went silent, tucking their wings in tightly in submission to their Matriarch.

Vahly held her breath.

"Lapis," Amona said. "First, I offer a toast to Xabier."

Everyone lifted a goblet.

"May you become the warrior your father was," she said.

The room cheered as one until Amona set her goblet on the table, indicating she had more to say.

"We have a new bonding, Lapis." Amona's eyes glowed. The dragons regarded her curiously. "I know this is highly unusual."

Maur's head jerked. He stared at Vahly, understanding dawning over his features. "One of a kind, I'd say." His lip curled.

Amona silenced him with a glance.

He swallowed, dropping his eyes, but the moment Amona looked away, he glared at Vahly.

Vahly stared right back.

"Though this is unique," Amona continued, "it makes simple, good sense. Because the newly bonded clan member is of a different species, the bonding took far more time. Normally, we bond as younglings. Nevertheless—our Vahly, Touched and destined to rule this earth, heard my Call."

Shouts went up, along with a few blasts of dragonfire, but muttering and whispering behind clawed hands darkened the glad shouts.

Though she'd guessed most of the Lapis would not love this development, there had been a small, secret part of her that had hoped to see the entire hall welcome her.

Vahly's stomach turned, and she was glad she hadn't eaten any of the venison. She could guess what some dragons were whispering. That she didn't belong at the matriarch's side like an advisor. But Amona would never back down on the formality of Vahly's place as her daughter. They'd had the discussion too many times to count.

The room settled into more eating and even more drinking, then Maur's voice rang out. "Do you believe this change denotes an alteration in Vahly's condition?"

Condition. Like she had a disease. Stones and Blackwater, Maur was the absolute worst. She'd say he acted like this because he had low self-esteem and lacked properly sized reproductive organs, but she'd seen him naked, and he was definitely not lacking. Aside from his attitude, his words perked Vahly's spirit.

"I do," Amona said proudly.

Hope sizzled inside Vahly. She rubbed her hands together, feeling energized. "Maybe if we did our own ritual similar to the Dragonfire ceremony, my magic would rise. We could stand in a circle—as a clan—and…"

She bit her lip. Vahly couldn't fly. And being in the sky was definitely a key component of the Dragonfire ritual.

Maur's eyebrow lifted. "And what? Perhaps we could all jump so you would be off the ground with us for a breath?"

The hall broke into laughter, and Vahly felt as if her legs had been cut out from under her. An answer sprang to mind, her focus on defending the integrity of her idea. "I could ride on your back!"

Vahly's face flushed hotter than the hall's pits. She should not have said that. She couldn't believe she'd said it. It hadn't sounded demeaning and base in her head, but now that she'd suggested riding on the back of a dragon like it was a pony, well...

She grabbed an eating knife, readying to defend herself from claws and teeth.

Even Amona stared at Vahly in shock at what she'd said.

Maur's lip pulled away from his teeth. A growl purred in his throat. "Your kynd rode simplebeasts. Pack mules. Donkeys. We have never, and will never, lower ourselves to be your simplebeast, human."

Anger flared through Vahly. "So you prefer to drown in spelled sea water?"

Amona gasped.

One table away, Linexa, the lean dragon that kept the younglings called out. "Please, Vahly. Please. Not in front of them."

Linexa's kind eyes went to the circle of young dragons at the back of the hall near the pulley system. Most of them played, ignorant of the argument going on between the adults, but the eldest of the bunch, Ruda, blinked big eyes at Vahly. She'd always liked Ruda. In the healer's chambers, the youngling often padded around Helena's feet while they bruised lavender for sleep aids and chamomile for nerves. Vahly had taught Ruda where the best lavender grew in the Red Meadow. The youngling was a quick study.

Vahly's heart quivered with guilt. Although death was in sight, there was no reason to keep reminding them. "I didn't intend to frighten you."

Ruda's sky blue scales had paled to an icy color similar to Maur's.

Amona calmly wiped her hands on a towel provided by a servant like it was any regular day. "Linexa, please take the younglings to their rooms."

Once the young dragons were escorted out of the feasting hall, Amona stood and held her hands wide. "Today, the Sea Queen tested her power against our eastern coast."

There were gasps and hushed whispers of the Sea Queen's name *Astraea*.

Amona silenced them. "Vahly was on the cliffs gathering vivanias and saw the ocean heave and crash." Her eyes locked on Maur as if driving the desperation of their status home. "The salt water reached three-fourths of the way up the cliffs."

The arrogance on Maur's face flew away. He broke eye contact with the matriarch and leaned back in his chair. But he glanced at Vahly and his look said his anger burned still.

"We must evacuate the lower two floors of the palace

tonight. I hate to do this on such a special day for both Xabier and Vahly, but it must be done. We must be over-prepared for our enemy, in case she strikes. Tomorrow, I ask that Lord Maur take a message to the Jade clan concerning this development. We will confer with them, and I'll let you know what we decide."

Amona left the hall with two of her servants, presumably to craft her letter for the Jades and oversee the evacuation plans. Vahly knew she would want the story of the ocean's attack again in detail, so as soon as she had eaten enough to keep her stomach from complaining, Vahly left the hall, too, heading first for the closet of bandages Helena kept nearby. She cleaned her wounded finger with a pitcher of fresh water and a bowl, then wrapped the stinging digit in clean linen.

With an air of impending doom, the clan made their way through the tunnels. Each dragon and their mate, if they had one, possessed a den, forbidden to any other creature except upon invitation. Families gathered, rushing to secure their hoards. Ruda found her father and took his hand.

"Ruda?" Vahly swallowed, feeling bad about scaring her earlier. "Everything will be all right."

Ruda half-smiled and clutched her father's hand more tightly.

Vahly sighed, then hurried toward Amona's double chambers on the highest floor of the palace.

Around the third turn, something blocked Vahly's boot.

She fell hard on the rocky ground, hands out in time to save her chin. After years of dragons "accidentally" tripping her, she'd grown quite good at falling. It was tough to get the jump on Vahly.

When she gathered herself and looked up, Maur was there with a couple of his closest friends. Huge surprise, she thought wryly.

"My apologies, Earth Queen," Maur hissed. "I didn't notice you."

Vahly brushed herself off, doing her best to retain her dignity. "Listen, Lord Maur. I don't want to fight with you. Or to disrespect you. I truly don't. I'd be an idiot to try, and although I'm the incarnation of everyone's lost hopes for the future," she said sarcastically, "I'm no idiot. I realize what I suggested could be seen as insulting but—"

Maur was suddenly in her face. "Could be seen? Could be?"

The scent of dragonfire simmered from his partially open maw. It smelled like a mix of charcoal and something sharp like lemon. It wasn't unpleasant. Except when the scent preceded being scorched to ash.

Vahly held up her hands in defense, doing her level best not to tremble. "Lord Maur."

"You think," he said, "you are destined to save us all, and you parade around here like you are next in line to be matriarch."

Maur's own third daughter in fact was next in line. She had been born Touched by the Blackwater mark like Amona. For dragons that meant she was the next matriarch. No bones about it.

"I could never be your leader," Vahly said, "and well I

know it. I have no desire to take such a role. I'll fight the sea folk alongside—"

"Allow me to make your situation clear now that we're clan." Maur's words dripped acid. "You are nothing but a mistake."

Maur's claw darted out and jabbed Vahly's Blackwater mark. Pain burst to life, hot and bright. She held her ground and refused to flinch. Warm blood dribbled down her nose and fell into her mouth.

Okay. That was enough. She tasted salt and spit blood to the floor before stepping closer and raising her chin to meet his eyes.

"Are you so afraid of humbling yourself, Lord Maur, that you won't at least support me in trying to amend this… mistake, as you so aptly named me? One ride, one attempt at a power ritual—that is all I'm asking. If it proves worthless, if it fails to give me any magic, then you can rip me up all you like. For what difference will it make? We will all be dead by sea water in a month's time!"

She had backed the dragon up three steps.

Maur rose to his full height. The battle dragon's light blue scales blinked in the sconce's light and a deadly spark danced through his eyes. "If you think for one moment that any of us would permit you to—"

"Enough." Amona appeared. Her eyes were half-lidded. She clasped her hands gracefully and stared down her nose at both Vahly and Maur like the matriarch she was. "My daughter, I would bow my head, take you upon my neck, and fly you to the heavens right this moment if I believed it would help.

But it won't. Although the secrets of the human power ritual were lost—and I still hold that there never was one —in the great flood of Bihotzetik, our own dragon records are secure. Never once has there been an instance when a human and a dragon shared a ritual. But because you are sincere in your supplication, I'll consider taking you up."

"Thank you, Matriarch. We are the first to create a dragon-human bond through the Call, so perhaps we will be first in this as well."

Maur made a noise in his throat. "If the Jades hear of this, they will make war. They will attempt to absorb our clan and well you know it, Matriarch. The human spends half her days with Call Breakers at that cider house. It is shameful that she holds such a high place here."

Lapis and Jade clan dragons oftentimes called clanless dragons Call Breakers. Their matriarchs—Jade and Lapis both—had tried to bond with them when they were young; they had either fought the bonding and repelled it or they had broken the Call. They claimed to be the only free kynd in the land. Elves, if indeed they still existed, had their court. Jades and Lapis, their Matriarchs. But the clanless had *no leader and no leash* as they liked to say.

Vahly enjoyed their company. They didn't belong and neither did she. Even after her bonding, it seemed Vahly would never fit in.

Amona sniffed. "Lord Maur, I'm perfectly capable of handling my own reign. Thank you for your concern. Now Vahly, I believe you wished to speak with me?"

She had intended to do more planning and discussing, but now, now she only felt like doing *something*. Not running her mouth further to no effect. "Forgive me, Matriarch. I have a headache. I think I'll retire."

Maur huffed. "Matriarch, I'll await your summons in my chambers, if it pleases you."

"Of course," Amona said.

Maur bowed slightly, then hurried away with his cohorts. Vahly was glad to see the back of that dragon.

"You're certain?" Amona asked Vahly, her chamber door open behind her.

"Yes. I'll see you tomorrow."

Amona nodded. "Indeed. We have much to talk about." She disappeared into her rooms.

And Vahly headed straight for the library. If there was a hidden section, by Stones and Blackwater, she was going to find it.

It was time to stop avoiding possible strategies for survival simply because of age-old feuds or thoughts about what should or should not be a part of life.

If a ritual could be the key to unlocking Vahly's power, then it only made good sense to break the chains off the scrolls that mentioned the forgotten kynd who loved ceremony, who if Nix's stories were true, lived by such practices.

The elves.

CHAPTER THREE

R yton hadn't planned to be the Sea Queen's consort. Yes, he'd nearly worked his fins off to become the youngest commander of the Sea Army ten years ago. Yes, he'd wanted power and influence. It was the only way to survive in the underwater world.

Eat or be eaten, his brother used to say when he was alive.

And sometimes, that was not only a metaphor.

But he had not planned on getting this close to Queen Astraea. No one was fool enough to do that. Granted, despite her age, she remained shockingly beautiful. But she was also cruel. Even more cutthroat than Ryton, and he was no angelfish.

Inside the queen's multi-tiered rooms, deep within the vibrant, underwater walls of Álikos castle, Astraea walked along the pale sand floor. She idly touched her crown, which peeked through her blue-green hair. Gold made up the base of the diadem, the metal supporting five points of scarlet coral inlaid with pearls and shells.

A luminescent curtain of seaweed grew from the ceiling of her chamber. The leaves cast a bright blue glow over the queen's bare shoulders, sea tulip dress, and long, finned legs.

Desire bolted through Ryton and he pushed it away, wishing he could do so forever.

But it was complicated.

"If the Jades use dragonfire to melt our peak near Tidehame," Astraea said, bubbles rising from her lips along with the small waves of sound, "we will need a new strategy."

The queen kicked those lovely legs of hers, and the fins along the sides of her calves and thighs rippled as she swam to one of her many couches. This one was made of the same scarlet coral as the castle walls. A bed of salt moss covered the length of the piece. Astraea lifted a pearl necklace from a bright orange coral shelf and lowered the string over her head. The jewelry nestled in the intricately braided neckline of her dress. The queen's cheek dimpled as she looked down at herself.

Vanity aside, Ryton knew she worried about the Jades targeting their peak—with good reason. A cavern filled with Blackwater hid under that cone of coral and rock. If the dragons destroyed the Blackwater's undersea shelter, where it blended magically with salt water, the sea folk would lose their most significant source of magic.

"We could distract the filthy reptiles with a double-headed, straight-on strike from units one and two, then send in the third unit to spear the dragons while the fourth lures them near." Her soft, pink lips curved into a smile that gave Ryton the urge to check the shadowed corners of the room. Sometimes, she looked too much like an elf, the creature from which all kynds had stemmed.

Elves lived near the original Blackwater spring. Blackwater was in their very blood, and through it they had harnessed the power of the air, for all that was worth. Humans had embraced the earth's magic, moving rock and dirt like great insects, washing in Blackwater to wake their strength. The dragons were the warped kynd, the worst of all. They had lived too close to earthblood, magma infused with Blackwater magic. Those creatures had developed an entire second form, with massive, grotesque wings to flee their own fiery havoc. Couldn't they see their own foulness? None of the other kynd had two forms.

Ryton gritted his teeth, remembering the day of his sister's death. The smell of Selene's flesh burning under a torrent of dragonfire. The shrill note of her scream, cut off when the Lapis matriarch finished her with the swipe of a spiked tail.

Selene had been on her first mission. Her last mission.

And Ryton's brother, on his deathbed, had made Ryton swear to get vengeance for their lost sister. A part of that oath included doing exactly what Queen Astraea asked. Ryton's brother had meant well. Back then, none of them had truly known the queen.

Memories washed through Ryton's mind—Selene's sweet laugh and how her brown eyes had widened in fear when the dragons attacked. Bile filled his throat. She'd been too young to die.

In all the world, only the sea folk, his kynd, had improved with the combination of time and Blackwater sources. They worked pure water magic and had at last learned how to multiply salt water. Queen Astraea had developed the spellwork herself.

Now, Ryton rubbed his kelp-brown beard. "If we try that attack, we will lose two of our *best* units."

The queen tapped slim fingers on her chin.

"And we'll be left with lesser units to launch the full attack when the time comes," he said.

Arguing with logic and strategy rather than honor or emotion was the only way to win with her. She didn't care about the sea folk who died even though they were hers to care for. She wouldn't even blink when Ryton's only close friend, Grystark, led the first of those two doomed groups, despite the fact that Grystark had given his right arm, literally, to her cause already. No, the queen would only see the win or the loss as it applied to her realm and her quest to cover the entire world in salt water.

He wanted the same outcome. It was the only way to rid them completely of the dragons and protect his kynd. But Ryton hoped to gain the victory without losing the last of his loved ones.

For two cycles of the moon, the queen and Ryton had argued about a planned series of attacks on the remaining dragons. He was the only creature regularly permitted to disagree with her.

"Give me one more meeting with Grystark," he said, "and we'll come up with a better plan for you. In the meantime, we will create confusion and fear by launching a small attack on Lapis territory."

A smack of glowing jellyfish, white as moonlight, drifted past Astraea's circular window.

"You feel strong enough to manage that yourself?" Astraea lifted an eyebrow, the gills on her slender throat moving. "It will take a serious dose of magic to raise waves to a height that will actually do any damage. The Lapis aren't like the fate-tempting Jades. They don't spend time near the cliffs. You'll have to pull the water from the far eastern tides to have enough power to crash over the cliffs and then swamp even the lower levels of the mountain palace."

"I'm healed. I am ready." He'd taken a hit of dragonfire during a raid on Jade territory, but the flesh of his arm and the charred scales on his leg were fully back to normal, as was his power, healed by the very Blackwater they'd discussed. "Today we ran the most successful disturbance we've had yet below the Lapis cliffs, behind their mountain range."

"I heard about that. Ryton?"

"My queen?"

She was at his side in a second. So fast and powerful. His body responded to her closeness despite the revulsion he felt, his skin warming and his blood pumping. Her chest swelled under her pearls as she blew water past his ear. The scent of her magic rose, a natural perfume of salt, blood, and freshly bloomed sea lilies. His gills flared as the smell snaked through the deep blue water. Her delicate fingers ran down his triceps, then through his brown hair. Her round features were far too innocent-looking to belong to one such as she.

"Why do you follow me in this quest to pour my ocean across all the land?" She asked this question at least once a moon.

He always gave the same answer. His father and older brother had taught him the reason. But Selene's death truly motivated him. He would destroy all the Lapis matriarch loved before her very eyes. Matriarch Amona would learn about true loss before Ryton and the armies flooded her land and ended her kynd once and for all.

"Because dragons are joyless creatures," he said dutifully, "who destroy the beauty in the world and scoff at everything we hold sacred."

The answer to Astraea's question used to include *Because elves are soulless and would kill us all if given the chance.* But the queen had made a deal with Mattin, king of the elves of Illumahrah. Mattin had sworn to submit and render useless any human that managed to escape the flooding of the last of that kynd's settlements, in case the human turned out to be an Earth Queen. Astraea's one true fear was an Earth Queen.

In return for Mattin's heart-searing oath, the Sea Queen promised to allow the plateau that held the Forest of Illumahrah to remain dry.

Ryton knew that once she was certain of success, she would find a way to break that oath, a trick of magic to avoid the consequences of a promise like that, an oath that burned through lying hearts. Yes, she would dig up an ancient spell or resort to dark power from the unknown, break her promise, and swamp the elves.

Her grin flashed like a fish in the sun. "You may go." She waved a pale hand, dismissing him like he wasn't her consort, but just another warrior in her vast armed forces.

He bowed, hiding his delight. If she knew how he longed for the nights when she didn't require his company, she'd have him torn in two. She would think he wanted to go to another female.

But it wasn't that.

On his nights off, Ryton explored the far reaches of the ocean, places no sea folk visited, save him. In these lonely places, he'd glimpsed sunken cities of marble, built by the humans who were now extinct. The distant currents held evidence of former elven civilizations too—crumbling archways that hummed with magic and fine swords with odd symbols and markings.

Ryton walked calmly from Astraea's inner chamber and into the purple glow of the corridor that led to the descent to the first floor of the castle. The soft hairs of the luminescent seaweed growing from the walls brushed his arms and legs. One of Astraea's scouts, Calix, swam by, stopping for a moment to salute.

What would warriors like Calix think if they knew Ryton scoured other kynd's ancient sites?

Ryton's father had taught him to fight his curiosity. *A waste of time,* his father had said. *And potentially dangerous if the queen's spies see you skulking about.*

Sea folk elders trained the young to study only their own works and history. Tutors and instructors explained that the other kynd were lesser, low, and any influence from them degraded one's center of power.

But Ryton couldn't help himself. Truly, the risk made the adventure more exciting.

Four guards in silvery shell helmets stood watch at the door to the great hall. Ryton forced himself to walk instead of swim so he wouldn't appear too eager to leave the queen's home.

Tonight, he was headed to the Tristura Sea. As the last known dwelling of humans, it was off limits to all sea folk. Echo, another talented scout for the queen, had told him about it in passing. Spoiled human flesh, rotting bones, sharks, and foul magic tainted the waters there.

It sounded fascinating.

In the castle courtyard, emerald coral grew tall and wide. Yellow veil fish nibbled at the flickering light of the algae that hung from the coral's branches. The fishes' two-foot-long fins waved in the current, looking much like veiled brides walking down the mating path.

"Wait!" a guard shouted.

Ryton whipped his feet through the water, the webbing between his toes catching expertly, and faced the male. "Yes?"

"The Sea Queen says she forgot to tell you that she'll view the new recruits in three days' time."

Fuming, he bit his tongue. It was too soon. He'd have to spend all night and the next two training. The lack of sleep would weaken him. But if he argued more than he already had, he might end up with a spear pointed at his throat.

"Of course." He inclined his head respectfully.

The guard disappeared into the castle again, and Ryton swam off in a rush, no longer caring if anyone saw him in a hurry to leave. There would be no adventuring tonight. He had to fetch Grystark and get started on spellwork right away.

RYTON FOUND Grystark in The Rogue Wave Tavern. The owner had built the place to mimic the grandeur of the castle, but instead of using rare red coral to shape the walls, he had covered basic gray sea stone in fluorescent scarlet algae. Though the tavern brought the stories of red elf hair to mind, Ryton thought it rather homey. Its muted glow lit Grystark's narrow, lined face. Ryton's heart warmed to see his old friend.

"Ryton!" Grystark handed him a twist of spiced kelp.

Smiling, he pushed the offering away. He had to keep his head straight and spiced kelp, if aged poorly, could turn folk upside down with giddiness. "We have work to do, unfortunately."

A server, a pretty female with big eyes and a quick swim, asked Ryton what he would like. He ordered a net of mollusks and gave her three quality mother-of-pearl pieces. She tucked one into her sea linen chemise and brought the other two pieces to her boss behind the counter.

After Ryton informed his officer and friend about the recruits—keeping the information about the doomed attack to himself for now—Grystark put his own length of spiced kelp inside the bag on his belt.

"These recruits are fools," Grystark said. "But three of them show promise with the spellwork."

The mollusks were fresh and of nice texture. Ryton

polished them off quickly. "At least we have folk to recruit."

For years and years, his kynd had not been able to reproduce. A plague had swept through Ryton's generation and rendered many infertile. Thankfully, the next generation had been able to procreate in small numbers. Thus, this new group of young warriors recruited to refresh the queen's forces were about fifteen years old now.

Too bad most of them would die to achieve their goal of washing the world in salt water. He longed to see Matriarch Amona's face right before it was all over. When she had no place to land, when her loved ones burned like she had burned Selene.

"Our former Queen," Grystark said as they swam away from the tavern, "would have demanded that a third of the newly matured remain at Tidehame to help with the farming of seaweed, the raising of the young, and for further procreation."

"And dragons killed that queen."

Frowning, Grystark eyed the dark water and the pearl-white specks of glowing snails on the sand below. "Not because she cared for more than war."

"Be careful, Gry, She has ears everywhere."

"Not on my good friend's own head, I hope." Grystark slapped Ryton gently across the back of his skull.

"I have my own mind still," Ryton snapped, sounding angrier than he'd intended. "I believe in the queen's goal. The world will be ours and we will make it sing."

"With the screams of fifteen-year-old sea folk."

Ryton rounded on his friend. "Gry. You have to stop talking like this."

"No one cares what an old one like me says."

"You are a general in the queen's army. Everyone cares what you say. And she'll end you if you speak out against her." Ryton wanted to tell him that he was his last friend and that Ryton couldn't bear to lose him like he'd lost everyone else. But that smacked of a desperation Ryton didn't want to acknowledge right before entering the training grounds to command fresh recruits. "Please. Just … think before you open that big mouth of yours."

"For you, Ryton, I'll do that."

Grystark shook off Ryton's hold on him and swam through the archway of black dynami coral to the training grounds. The glittering edges of blackgold seaweed threw light over every face and weapon.

"One last traitorous thing," Grystark whispered. "Do you think the Lapis realize now how bloodthirsty our Queen is? Is that why they haven't called for a peace meeting in well over a year?"

"Perhaps they've teamed up with the Jades again," Ryton said. "Do you find it odd that the two dragon races are so different?"

Grystark looked over his shoulder and he was right to do it. This type of talk didn't make one popular. Two sentries zipped past, on their way to the boundary waters under the northern cliffs no doubt. "Both types of dragons want us dead. What does it matter which strategy they use?"

"It matters because it speaks of motivation," Ryton said. His lieutenant handed him a coral spear. Ryton ran a finger over the sharp edge. Water magic rushed over his hand, sending a rushing sound through the grounds, joining with the magic of the other warriors. "And if you know your opponent's motivation, you know exactly how to gut them."

"This is why you are High General," Grystark said, "And I'm not, despite my experience and additional years of service."

Ryton gave Grystark a playful shove. "Nah. That's because of your love for naps."

Grystark's mouth dropped open. "I use my off time to rejuvenate my power. No shame in that."

"Yes. Sure. An hour after mid-meal is one thing, but three hours? I'm surprised you manage to keep up any form of relationship. Why does Lilia put up with you?"

Grystark winked. "I'll give you one guess."

A new recruit swam up from the ocean floor with a training spear. He hovered, mid-depth, with Ryton and Grystark. "High General, would you like me to call the rest?"

"Please do. Anything to stop Grystark from continuing his little bragging session here."

The recruit nodded, then swam a few feet away. He extended his arms and spoke the spell to demand the presence of all new warriors in Grystark's and Venu's units.

The enlisted fell into proper rows on the pale sand, their coral and shell spears in hand and their eyes lifted to where Ryton, Grystark, and now Venu, swam.

Ryton returned Venu's salute, giving the black-haired

male a grim smile. Venu wasn't much of a conversationalist, but he was a great military leader.

Swimming forward, Ryton addressed the units. "Soon, we will launch attacks we never could've dreamed of in the past. You must rise to the occasion and become full-fledged warriors in less time than any that came before you. First, you must understand our enemy.

"Jades are aggressive and will sacrifice themselves to accomplish their army's goals. Never think a Jade dragon will shy away or say no to a risk. The answer for them is always raw violence, and their skill in the sky is unparalleled.

"The Lapis are another story entirely. Crafty. Cunning. Less physically capable than Jades as a whole, they use complicated strategy to win their battles. We recently downed one of their greatest generals."

A cheer went up, waves of sound echoing through the glowing water and rippling the blackgold seaweed.

"Yes. A massive achievement. Not only had this Lapis General killed scores of our kynd during his long career, he nearly destroyed our Blackwater source. His unit liquified the upper reaches of protective coral, blasting the salt water away and giving up their lives to do it. Thankfully, we stopped their progress with well-aimed and well-spelled spears."

Another shout rose and webbed fists waved.

Ryton raised a hand to quiet them as he swam low, nearing Grystark's unit specifically. "When next we fight these dragons, you must be ready." He longed to impart the importance of their commitment to excellence. If they failed, Ryton would lose not only them, but quite possibly the only friend he had left in this world.

A young female stared right back at him as he detailed the drills they would go through today. Her bright, brilliantly orange eyes filled with fervor. He blinked, realizing she reminded him of his sister Selene.

"What is your name, warrior?"

"Sansya."

"This one," he said, waving her to the front of the unit. "The tides are powerful in this soldier. I can see it here." He pointed at her face, and she straightened her back further, her feet eddying the water expertly and her spear held completely still. She was a natural in controlled swimming, not a float-about like so many of the younger generation.

Ryton addressed all. "Make it your aim to stand out when your brigadiers and captains are looking for a leader. Do not accomplish this on the backs of others. Achieve greatness by following your orders exactly, using initiative when necessary, and training with your whole heart, every second of every day. Then and only then, we will win this war."

The units called out as Sansya swam back to her place. The drills began, led by each one hundred unit captains.

Ryton, Grystark, and the quiet, but efficient Venu visited their brigadiers and then each captain's hundred, giving suggestions on spells to cast over their spears to make them fly through the water more quickly or to use the weapons to throw spelled salt water through the air. Grystark was especially good at teaching the magic needed to use whirlpools, unusual currents, and eddies to raise the sea level.

Ryton spent hours with the unit the queen herself had trained to multiply the waters. Ryton repeated the spell, careful to use proper vibration in the lips and tongue so the magic would wake and turn sand to water. The unit shouted at the mounds of snail-dotted sand and the sound rushed around their heads before blasting into the sea floor to create a new wave of salt water.

Ryton looked up, his sharp gaze on the distant surface of the sea. The ocean trembled with their efforts, the waves riotous.

It was a storm without rain or wind, and Ryton was proud indeed of his army. These were his kynd, and he would always be loyal.

For you, Selene, he said silently to himself. For you, I'll see them all die.

But his pleasure in a job well done was fleeting. Eventually, he had to talk to Grystark about Astraea's desire to lure the dragons to Tidehame again. They had to come up with a suitable strategy that wouldn't end with Grystark dead and Ryton mourning the last of a group of friends and the final stab to his already sorely wounded heart.

He had lost them all, one by one, to dragons.

But by the seas, he was not going to lose Grystark.

CHAPTER FOUR

Inside the Lapis mountain palace, a curved staircase of painted stone led up to the main library. The storm, called up by the Dragonfire ritual, had drifted away. Three arched windows spilled silvery moonlight across the ceiling and the nine dragon shapes burned into the rock high above Vahly's head. Tails and claws, long necks, teeth, fire, and twisting wings formed a pattern not unlike the one scored into the short sword Vahly kept at her belt.

These charred images lorded over a dizzying collection of scrolls housed on countless wooden shelves. The first Lapis had carved each shelf with art showing the rare finds they loved—lapis lazuli lined with golden pyrite, cliff owl feathers, the gold coins earth kynd used to bring to them, and stag antlers with twelve and fourteen points.

The librarians had doused the oil lamps hanging from the ceiling and left, off to help move those dragons whose dens were on the lower levels into temporary living quarters. The library was empty.

Or so Vahly thought.

As she went around a stack of newer scrolls, footsteps interrupted the silence of the room.

A dragon appeared on the first level, head bent to a partially open scroll she was reading by moonlight. Vahly didn't know this dragon well. Only that her name was Lys and she kept to herself.

Perhaps Lys would be so interested in her own research that she wouldn't notice Vahly.

Moving quickly, Vahly squinted in the weak light. Nix had told her the secret entrance to the restricted area— where the Lapis may have stored information about the now extinct elves—hid near a collection of unlabeled scrolls.

Vahly slipped behind a rock wall of tightly wound scrolls. There didn't seem to be any labels in this area of the first floor. A violet wax seal closed each roll of parchment.

The first one Vahly picked up had a seal with the shape of a mountain. She held the scroll up to the moonlight coming through the high windows and tried to see what information sat inside. Lines crossed and circles twined around what might have been lettering. One word showed clearly. *Eneko.* Ah. He was a noble dragon who lived in the far northeastern wing of the mountain palace, with lands extending alongside Maur's. This scroll held a map of territories and holdings of the nobility then.

The scroll scraped lightly on the shelf as Vahly slid it back into place. She held her breath, waiting to see if Lys noticed the noise. But no voice interrupted, so Vahly continued her search, moving past that series of shelves. The wax seals served as labels so it wasn't the place Nix had discussed with her.

Scouring the entire wall of shelves, Vahly read label after label. *Dragonfire and Its Uses. The History of Our Matriarchs. Herbs A-C. Herbs D-F.* And so on. She searched every shelf on the first floor, except those too close to Lys.

Vahly licked her dry lips, wishing libraries weren't so opposed to having drinks around.

It was time to ascend the steps to the second tier.

Walking on the sides of her boots, heel to toe, she hurried along the iron railing. A square of moonlight illuminated her path.

Vahly ran a hand over the nearest scrolls, eyes scanning the labeled shelves for one that remained unmarked. This particular section of the second tier featured information on simplebeasts—hawks, eagles, rabbits, that sort of thing.

She crouched to look over the bottom row. But the dragons had labeled that one too.

Maybe the scribes had changed the set up since Nix heard the stories about the hidden room. Vahly went over what Nix had said.

Supposedly, the dragons who had designed the restricted area had attached a mechanism to a particular shelf, and when manipulated properly, said mechanism opened a small chamber that held writings on subjects the dragons weren't too keen on. Subjects like matriarchs who had sullied their dragon honor by taking mate after mate with no regard for bonding. Stories about the Jades being the first dragons and how the Lapis truly evolved from them and not the other way around. And of course, elves.

The reason dragons hated elves was still a mystery to Vahly.

Yes, they were clever and arrogant. But so were dragons. Sure, the elves were secretive. Who cared?

Vahly's best guess was that their magic made dragons sweat. It wasn't a straightforward magic like dragonfire, the only magic dragons possessed.

Elven magic, the power of the air kynd, had blurred boundaries much like the power of the earth kynd—well, back when they'd still had earth magic. But the humans had met with the dragons, had worked with them. And the elves had kept to themselves. The elves' blend of unpredictable power, exclusivity, and arrogance rubbed dragons—fire kynd—the wrong way.

Dragons had their own huge egos, and elves didn't bother to stroke them as the dragons thought they should have.

Yes, Vahly thought, perhaps that along with the fear of their power was the reason any scrolls that mentioned them in earnest were held in the hidden, restricted chamber.

Labels with full titles and subject lined the entire bottom row of shelves.

Vahly stood and put her hands on her hips. "Where else to look…" she muttered.

Lys appeared.

Vahly jumped.

"What are you doing?" Lys tucked her own scroll under her arm.

Vahly's heart skittered inside her ribs. "Research. On … stag beetles. I think my kynd once ate them and—"

"Ugh." The dragon held up a hand. "Enough. Fine. Do as you like. Put that candle out when you go, all right?" Lys jerked her head toward the one flickering lantern in the main room.

"Will do."

"Thanks. Oh, and Vahly, welcome to the clan." Lys still looked slightly disgusted at the stag beetle idea, but her smile was genuine.

Guilt tried to breathe down Vahly's neck, but she shook it off.

The moment Lys left the library, Vahly took up her search, this time going to the end of the shelving. The structure was partially cut from the mountain itself, with wooden planks set into the spaces. Thousands of clawed fingertips, used gently and gracefully, had worn smooth the place where wood met stone. Vahly's own unclawed hands grazed the surface, top to bottom.

Next, she brushed a palm under the triangular slice of wood tucked into the corner between two shelving areas. The surface had served as a place to write or read as needed, complete with inkpot and quill. No luck.

A shuffling sounded from the corridor downstairs, outside the doorway to the main floor of the library. A head appeared. Lys again.

"Maybe I can help you finish up, Vahly?" she called, her voice grating and too loud in the library's quiet atmosphere.

"No. No, I'm just fine." Vahly grabbed a random scroll and waved it in the air. "I found one on the nutrients of a stag beetle's innards. Finally." She blew out a dramatic breath. "Really interesting stuff right here. In fact, I have an extra beetle here in my pocket. Want to taste?"

Lys grimaced. "Uh, no. I'm quite full. Don't stay all night, okay? Draes will have my tail if I leave that lantern lit." She glanced over her wings as if the dragon himself might be on his way to the library.

"Understood."

With Lys gone, Vahly put her hands on her hips and looked over the whole area. She'd searched the entirety of the section, down to the underside of the tables.

Where could this legendary restricted section be hiding?

Shaking her head, she noticed the moonlight catching on a spot between the last two shelves. Hurrying over, she bent to examine the knee-level space between wood and stone. She hadn't even realized this shelf was actually two shelves. The sides fit together so neatly. All except this one space. The scrolls beside it were labeled, but the ink was far darker than the labels around it. Nix had said the shelf near the secret entrance was unlabeled.

But this label was new. Perhaps someone had realized the scrolls were not categorized and fixed the problem.

Or there was a dragon who specifically didn't want this room found.

Vahly wiggled her first finger into the space. The stone tore at her nail bed as she pushed her finger further in. The way her day had gone so far, she'd be all stumps by sunset.

Something cold, and possibly metallic, hit the end of her finger.

Voices trickled from the corridor and into the library. Lys and Draes.

Sweating, Vahly pushed harder. Her skin ripped. The pain of the deep scrape burned like fire, and she blinked watery eyes.

She had to hurry. If she were caught doing this, breaking into this restricted area, she would be flogged in front of the entire clan. Brought low. It was the punishment for any Lapis who broke a rule. The dragons normally flogged a dragon's wings with a leather strap, sometimes grounding them for a day or more. With Vahly, they would most likely strip her vest and shirt off and come within inches of accidentally killing her. Well, this little slug wasn't saying hello to a strap anytime soon.

Shuddering, she gave the metal knob one more poke.

The floor under her feet moved.

She leaped backward as a half circle opened up.

A spiral staircase led into the wall, then dropped behind and below the shelving of the second tier. The steps ended on the same ground as the first floor, but the walls kept the whole thing from view. Completely tucked away inside the walls of the library, the hidden chamber released the scent of dust.

Vahly wasted no time rushing back to the first floor to blow out the lantern. Then, she hurried back up the stairs to the second tier, walked onto the spiral steps, closed the secret door behind her, and pattered down, into the darkness.

Fumbling in the dark, Vahly reached into one of the

bags on her belt and pulled out a handful of distura feathers. The finger-length glowing plumes came from the birds that lived near the Fire Marshes beyond Nix's cider house. Vahly had found these on the ground where a fox had obviously enjoyed two of the creatures for dinner. She held them up and tried to get her eyes to adjust to the low light. The glow of the feathers wouldn't last long, but it was bright enough.

She rotated slowly, studying the small chamber. Floor to ceiling shelves covered the walls, but they differed greatly from the ones in the main library. These were made of, what was it? Vahly walked over to one and gripped its edge, holding the distura feathers up.

They were made entirely of lapis lazuli. Vahly blinked. The shelves were worth a fortune, and here they were, hidden away where no one would ever see them. Shaking off the puzzle of why an ancient dragon had decided to waste the beautiful stone on a room no one saw, she counted the scrolls. She gave up at one hundred nine.

None of these writings were labeled, but they were each enclosed in a leather case with a symbol burned into the bottom end. Perhaps the symbols indicated what was inside?

Vahly started with a set of scrolls closest to the stairs so she could keep an ear out for Lys and Draes. The first of the set of four had a case that boasted a sunburst symbol.

Setting the feathers on the step that was head-high, she slid the scroll from its case and set the container on the ground by her boots. She opened the scroll slowly, careful not to crack or tear the vellum.

Faded writing started in the center of the piece and spiraled out. It was written in the dragon language and spoke of a battle against the elves. There were place names—Birne, Typeth, and Grigain—that she'd never heard of.

This one was no help although it did offer an explanation about why dragons hated elves. They'd been at war ages ago. Though the battles weren't recent, many dragons made it to four hundred years of age, or more, and their memories were long.

She went through the rest of that set, only to find more detailed accounts of battles with sea folk, but no more mention of elves or anything about ritual practices. So most likely, the sunburst symbol indicated battle history.

The next set also showed sunbursts, so Vahly moved past them to the third collection, stowed on a lower shelf. The image of stag antlers marked the end of the first two scroll cases and an acorn showed on the smallest of the bunch. Vahly read through the first two. They were dry accounts of hunting grounds and who owned what. Lord Maur was mentioned in these, but she wondered if the writing was actually talking about another dragon with the name. Maybe an ancestor of his?

The final scroll didn't look like much before she unrolled it. Tattered edges. Small. Reeking of decay.

But when Vahly spread the vellum, she had to stifle a gasp.

Braids and leaves in gold powder ink framed the faded writing. Small illustrations decorated the left side. A rabbit danced with a frog. A gryphon, thought to be extinct, flew over a trio of mountain peaks. Humans with several different skin tones laughed and raised toasts in large mugs as simplebeasts—a small bear, two wolves, and a rather fat beaver—gathered in peace around their legs.

Under the weakening light of the glowing feathers, she tried to read the minuscule lettering. Many phrases were so worn, they were completely illegible.

But two words caught Vahly's eye.

Earth Queen.

She read as much as she could, murmuring to herself. The scroll detailed a meeting between an Earth Queen and the matriarch that had come three generations before Amona.

Vahly mumbled the words to herself as she scanned the parchment. "... *under the Sacred Oak...*"

The next section had faded into nothing. Then, later it read, "... *to lay out negotiations between Jade and Lapis concerning hunting grounds made fertile by earth kynd and air kynd...*"

So the humans—*earth kynd*—and elves—*air kynd*—had worked together?

That was new.

The scroll under Vahly's bunched fist had one last paragraph. Controlling her frustration, she read on. There had to be something here.

"*Because the land in question is the birthplace of an earth kynd, it must be protected. Hunting should be limited to...*"

Why would the birthplace of a human need to be protected?

Another set of lines ran along the bottom of the scroll.

They were written in elven language, brighter than the

brown, inked letters on the rest of the scroll, as if the elven had been added later. Beside them, an illustration of a woman with pointed ears and a pair of vicious-looking throwing knives rose a few feet above a field of brazenberry bushes.

Vahly cursed herself. Why hadn't she taken the time to learn the elven language? Did Nix know any?

There was a bump outside the room.

Someone was coming.

Pulse ticking, faster and faster in her neck, Vahly rolled the vellum and tucked it into its leather case. But they would notice if she attached the case to her belt or held it in her hands.

Eyeing the various hiding places on her person, she took the scroll back out of the case, set the case back into its place on the shelf, then loosened the front ties of her vest to make room for the scroll between her shirt and the leather.

Squeezing her eyes shut, she hoped with all she had that her actions wouldn't completely demolish the beautiful scroll or its potentially key information. She hurried up the steps, just then realizing she'd let the feathers drop.

A rumbling voice Vahly was almost sure belonged to Draes echoed through the library, followed by something Lys said. Vahly heard her own name.

The glowing feathers lay in a scattered heap near the base of the stairs. But there was no time.

Well, she had to make time or the next dragon in here would know someone had been in the room.

Holding her breath, she leaped down the steps, then

shoved the feathers down her shirt. Pulse racing, Vahly vaulted up the last three steps, then reached across the opening to push the mechanism that would seal the chamber.

Draes and Lys were coming up the main stairs from the first floor.

Vahly was trapped on the second tier.

She grabbed the nearest scroll, sat abruptly, and threw the writing open on her lap. Lys and Draes would find it incredibly odd that she was reading by moonlight, but that was fine by Vahly. Odd worked. Breaking into highly prized and restricted scrolls did not. One ended with a shaking head or an eye roll, the other concluded with a whipping.

But then another voice joined Draes' baritone and Lys's alto.

"If it's her, I'll deal with her infringement. I'm here on the authority of our Matriarch."

It was the deep bass of Lord Maur.

Vahly swore silently, her palms sweating. He would never swallow her little act.

The window bled moonlight over her shoulder.

Vahly winced, knowing what she had to do.

Getting to her feet, she faced the window. In one movement, she jumped and grabbed the window's stone ledge. As she hauled herself up—smashing the stones out of the poor scroll she'd stolen and probably ruining everything—the footsteps closed in, coming around the corner. Maur would see her.

The leaded glass pane opened with a squeak. She latched it on the hook above, then on her belly, she edged out of the wide, rectangular window. She let her feet drop away from the opening, on the outside of the palace.

Night air rushed up the mountainside and tangled her hair as she flipped over carefully and slid lower, using her hands to hang from the outer ledge. Her two injured fingers were quite insistent on this caper not lasting long. She had to find a foothold or she would topple and plunge into the dark drop.

Turning to peek at the elevation, she heard the voices as if they were right above her. The amber glow of a lantern reflected off the window glass.

Had they noticed the window was open?

It was impossible to know exactly how far Vahly was above the forest that surrounded the mountain, but she had a pretty good guess. The library wasn't on the highest level of the palace like hers and Amona's chambers, but it was only two levels below. Still very high.

"Nice work here, Vahl," she whispered to herself.

In a second, Lys would look out here to investigate. Draes would've noticed the night air, surely. And Maur would *accidentally* shove her off the edge. It would be the perfect solution for him. Vahly would be out of the way. He didn't believe she would ever have the power to save them anyway. Maur stubbornly refused the idea that the sea folk might win the war.

Hands shaking, Vahly tried to still her brain.

The voices faded. The light from their lantern disappeared.

Vahly had no energy to celebrate that. Her fingers were giving out.

One by one.

First, the one she'd injured on the seaside cliffs. Then the two beside that one. Next, the one that she'd ripped getting into the chamber.

Panting with the effort not to fall, she moved the flexible soles of her boots right and left, up and down, desperate to find a foot hold.

At last, her toe found purchase on a tiny ledge. She put her weight on it.

"Please hold me, rock," she whispered. "I'll never step on you again if you keep my arse in the air for a minute or two longer."

The rock did hold. She moved each hand to a new hold, ignoring the pain in her fingers. When she thought the dragons had moved far enough from the library, she dragged herself back up and through the window. Panting, she slumped against the wall.

Her gaze went immediately to the place where the floor had opened earlier.

She blew out a heavy breath.

It was still closed.

No one knew she had been in there.

After closing the glass over the window, she crept down the second tier stairs and slipped out of the library.

It was late, but Nix and the Call Breakers would still be up. Vahly touched her chest and felt the scroll under her vest. If anyone could help her translate the elven words at the bottom, it was Nix.

After a stop in the dark kitchens to grab a loaf of bread and a crock of cider, Vahly walked the labyrinth of passages to the palace entrance.

She handed the cider to the taller of the two entrance

guards. "Big day, huh, Rip?" The taller of the two was infatuated with Amona and he knew that she knew. It was enough to keep the male on her side. "I thought maybe you had missed out on some of the festivities, this being your watch and all. Ty?" She handed the second guard the bread.

The guards accepted her offerings, nodding.

"I'm going for a short walk. All this attention is a little much for me, you know?"

"I can imagine," Ty said.

With a wave, she made her way into the night and headed straight for the cider house.

CHAPTER FIVE

At the edges of the Red Meadow, a ridge rose steeply, rocky and covered in nettle one had to avoid or resign oneself to a sennight of fierce itching and burning. Clanless dragons had tunneled a veritable city inside the ridge.

Voices, the clanging of pots, and all the sounds of living life flowed from the numerous doorways. Lit by torches, stone stairways ran up and down the ridge like uneven seams in a poorly tailored cloak. Two dragons in their human-like form argued over a basket of bread on a high stair on the eastern side of the makeshift city. Another dragon hurried down the lowest outer staircase, a sword glinting from the creature's belt.

Dragons tried to avoid using dragonfire on one another. If at all possible, they settled arguments with blades that hardly ever brought blood and only injured their pride.

Atop the high land formation, the windows of Nix's

three-storied cider house glowed—a welcome beacon in the night.

Boots crunching over sand and stone, past Nix's chaotic apple orchard and its glorious smell, Vahly wondered what her friend would think of the bond Vahly now had with the Lapis.

Well, she didn't exactly wonder, she thought as she leaned on a tree to take a breather. Nix would be far from elated about the bond. Vahly picked at the tree's papery bark and sighed. Nix didn't trust Amona or any of the Lapis clan. But Vahly wasn't sure how Nix would actually react. Would she remain a close friend, or would she want to distance herself somewhat from Vahly now that Vahly would have to answer Amona's Call when or if she was summoned to action?

Stomach twisting, Vahly hoped the Call Breakers wouldn't ban her from the cider house. That would put her in a dung position. It wasn't as if Vahly had a choice whether to bond with the Lapis. Amona was, for all intents and purposes, Vahly's mother. She had saved her life. And continued to come to the rescue when Jades ran into the lackluster Earth Queen and decided to show exactly what they thought of Vahly.

Nearly there now, she plucked a pepper from a head-high plant and sniffed its pungent aroma before moving on, a habit she had picked up years ago.

Vahly wanted to be bonded with the Lapis. She was glad of it, proud and pleased at the unexpected development. But she still felt the same connection to the Call Breakers and her friend Nix. No matter how Amona claimed Vahly, she remained an outcast like the kynd that spent their free hours at the cider house.

Besides, their dropcider had a much better kick.

Inside the carved, wooden door, Nix's establishment was packed to bursting with dragons.

Sitting at one of the many round gaming tables, Dramour adjusted his eye patch. The lean Jade-blooded dragon had seen his fair share of war, but the horrors hadn't stolen his ability to see the joy in life. He noticed Vahly and winked.

"How are pickings?" he said over the din of coins and stones exchanging hands, raucous laughter, and the bang of mugs on wood.

Dramour wore his usual midnight blue cloak. Slits for his bright green wings boasted pewter buttons and blue embroidery in patterns of cracked dragon skulls and curling flames. His white shirt, shockingly clean compared to everyone else's clothing, fit snugly over a frame built by years of training with the Jade battle dragons and more than one horrible feud with the Lapis that Vahly called family.

At some point, he'd realized how ridiculous it was that the creatures that should have banded together to fight the murderous sea folk were killing one another instead. He'd left the Jades and their feud, broken the Call, and come to work for Nix.

Thankfully, the Jades and the Lapis had agreed on peace for the time being. But everyone knew it wouldn't last.

Vahly often wondered what Dramour would do if his

former general marched in here and demanded his return.

Normally, the clan dragons shunned the clanless, but with the approaching threat of the rising ocean, would they continue to do so?

Vahly flipped the pepper she'd nicked into the air, catching it neatly before tossing it again. "Pickings are slim, my friend. Slim, indeed. Though I did snag some of that rare fern I told you about."

At the same table, Ibai and Kemen joined Dramour's game. The mixed Jade and Lapis-blooded dragons worked as healers for Nix's small army of spies and smugglers.

Ibai rolled a pair of black dice, and Kemen finished his cider before throwing a wave at Vahly.

Ibai sniffed, his gaze darting around the room. Sometimes he reminded Vahly more of a bird than a dragon. But he didn't have the brain of a sparrow. That dragon held worlds of knowledge in his shifty little head. Ibai had healed Vahly more than a few times after a fight.

"Did you find the fern on the sea cliffs?" Dramour rolled his own set of dice, then leaned an elbow on the table to watch his luck spill out. "Can't get enough of danger, can you?"

Kemen gave Vahly an approving nod. Kemen and Vahly were well known for daring one another to steal from the Lapis treasury. Kemen had been caught attempting the foolish deed, forcing Vahly to make up a wild excuse for the dragon, claiming he'd been looking for her because of an emergency outside Nix's establishment. The excuse worked only because the guard that had nabbed him was a complete idiot and allowed Kemen to escape with his life.

Vahly snorted at Dramour. "Don't worry, mother. I have been climbing those cliffs since I was a babe." Her hand darted in front of his nose, snatched his cider, and then downed the rest of the cold liquid.

"How dare you?" Dramour held a hand to his forehead like he was going to faint.

Vahly's gaze flicked to Ibai. "You should thank me, Dramour. I just saved you from being too drunk to notice Ibai is about to turn that second set of dice to match his first throw."

Dramour's eye widened. "What?" He turned, then lurched forward, jostling the table and spilling Kemen's drink. He snatched Ibai's hand. "I thought you used that brain of yours to win."

Ibai laughed nervously. "Sometimes only luck can grab a win, Fine Eye."

Fine Eye was Dramour's nickname. He'd been a handsome dragon in his youth, or so they claimed. Vahly was not attracted to dragons. The scales didn't do it for her. She knew well that even if she was interested, she could never mate with one. Her body was not set up to handle dragon mating; the parts involved were all wrong and they tended to breed in full dragon form.

"And by luck you mean cheating," Vahly said to Ibai. She patted Dramour on the back. "Let him go. Whatever coin he wins he'll use to buy some fine salve that you'll most likely need in the future if you keep annoying his rather large brother." Vahly nodded respectfully at

Kemen, who almost smiled in return—that was the most anyone got out of him.

Dramour released his hold, a wry grin pulling at the green scales around his mouth. "All right. But you're rolling again, Ibai, and this time, I'm watching."

Kemen threw a small chunk of jade into their piles of old human coins and glittering stones while Dramour shouted to Baww, the cider house's chunky barkeep, for another cider.

Oil lamps hung from the rough hewn timbers of the ceiling, and smoke rings issued from the nostrils of a narrow-eyed male named Euskal and a bald female named Miren, who were obviously having a contest of sorts. Beyond them, five dragons—all newer Jade smugglers that Vahly couldn't keep straight—threw bones on the chalked floor, amid a scattering of coins and precious stones. The largest of the bones landed in the chalked twelve-pointed star. A big win for that fellow. An even bigger loss for the others.

Vahly stepped quickly around them, knowing a fight was coming.

One of the losers slammed a fist into the winner, and chaos ensued, nostrils smoking and talons slashing.

A chair flew backward.

Vahly, snickering, ducked to keep from being hit. She headed for the bar where countless glass liquor bottles in every color of the rainbow perched precariously on a wall of wooden shelving.

Thankfully, Dramour and Kemen hurried to drag the new Call Breakers apart before the fight escalated into a bout of dragonfire. Nix would have murdered any survivors if they burned her cider house down over a game of bones.

One of the Jades pulled a knife.

Kemen kicked him in the gut, throwing off the other dragon's balance. Then Kemen stole the knife in one quick movement.

Dramour held another male dragon by the scruff of his black tunic. Releasing his grip, he shoved the male into his fellows. "Leave off, fools. If you want a proper fight, you can find me outside in an hour."

Narrow-eyed Euskal broke away from his smoke ring contest with Miren and shouted to a group hanging halfway out the side door. "Dare you to fly over the Lost Valley! I'll give you five rubies and a jade piece if you go beyond the peak."

"I'm not that stupid, Eus!" It was Aitor. He drank from a dented mug, then wiped a blue-scaled hand across the burn scars that marred his mouth.

The scars were shocking. It took a lot of dragonfire to scorch a dragon's scales. Normally, it was only seen when dragons asked an artist to mark them with a symbol or design. He must have been tied down by an angry Jade and tortured. Vahly was selfishly glad she hadn't been around for that one.

"You've been trying to get rid of me since that fouled up robbery on the Jade blacksmith's guild," Aitor added. Vahly remembered that heist. A fun night. "I won't be downed that easy," Aitor said.

Euskal worked his way through the crowd to the bar where he stuffed his mouth full of pickled scorchpeppers, a snack Vahly was sad to say she could not handle. She tried them once. That afternoon had not been pleasant.

"Coward!" Euskal shouted at Aitor around his mouthful.

"Don't be so hard on yourself." Aitor laughed at his own wit. "Vahly, buy the poor dragon a cider. He shouldn't be talking down to himself like that."

"I'll buy that drink," Vahly called out, "but don't come crying to me when he's off his head and clips you with that jab of his."

The cider house filled with laughs. Euskal was well known to be terrible at boxing, a pastime dragons loved. The sport had all the fun of fighting but didn't use up their dragonfire magic. They could box for hours on end.

"You're kind of an arsehole, Vahly." Euskal grinned and shook his head.

"But you love me." Vahly gave him a toothy smile.

Small platters of venison sat beside the goodies covering the stone bar top. Vahly took a bright yellow brazenberry, ready to enjoy the kick they gave to one's energy levels. The sour-sweet fruit exploded on her tongue. Then, leaning over the bar, she grabbed the wooden mug she kept there. Flashing a chip of lapis between two fingers, she ordered a pint of cider from Baww, who'd returned from filling Dramour's mug. Baww's wings fluttered as he took payment for her drink and Euskal's.

"I wouldn't pay for that Blackwater-cursed fool's drink." Baww lifted his bronze pitcher and let a stream of cider flow into her mug. Little drops of the chilled drink fell onto Vahly's forearms.

Euskal shoved his mug forward. "She didn't ask your opinion about it, keep."

"It's not the best of times, my friend," Vahly said. "No matter how many females he has stolen from you, we must stick together."

The cider went down, nice and cold. Stones, she was glad the Breakers felt no need to open great pits of golden earthblood. They rejuvenated themselves and their dragonfire magic by lounging near a crack in the ground where the Fire Marshes began—a far better system than the Lapis's smoking pits of painful heat at the palace. Far better to the last human anyway.

Baww secured Vahly's lapis lazuli chip inside the jewel box sitting beside a set of shelves. Crockery and glass jars of fermented eggplants crowded the space. "I know we're all nigh on doomed, but is there something else wrong?" he asked.

Vahly had to keep the new developments quiet for now. A full-scale alarm wouldn't help things. Not yet. "It's nothing Nix can't fix."

"And here she is now." Baww grinned, looking over Vahly's head.

There was a shout of greeting, and Nix sauntered down the wide, stone steps from the second floor.

The room exploded into toasts to the cider house's owner and operator.

Nix's ample hips and bosom, the complete opposite to Vahly's lean build, had most of the males drooling as she dramatically entered the common room where she pretty much ruled as Queen. A red and gold brocade pouch fixed to her belt shifted as she walked. The bag held precious stones for bribing members of the Lapis and Jade clans. Nix never let laws get in the way of collecting secrets for this or that lord or lady.

"To Nix!" Dramour called out. His lean face drew up into a lopsided grin, his river-green scales shining. "The only matriarch we'd ever answer to!"

Nix's laugh bubbled out of her throat as she slid gracefully to the bar top to take up her bookkeeping ledger. She wore a gold ring on every finger. "If I were your Matriarch, you'd all be hiding in Jade and Lapis treasure rooms waiting on my Call to clean those lofty lizards out."

Laughter shook the stacked rock walls and mortar plumed from the larger cracks around the windows.

Body swaying, Nix winked at the crowd and they cheered for her again. "I'm sorry they're being so ridiculous," she said to Vahly while writing five quick tallies inside her ledger. Her long, white writing quill bobbed near her apple-shaped cheeks.

"They're always like this for you, and you know it," Vahly said. Nix deserved the adoration. She'd given these kynd a place to feel welcome no matter what. "You make this house a home. Plus, there's the cider." She held up her mug and Baww refilled it.

"Don't let Amona hear you talk like that, calling this place a home. She might decide you have too much rebel in you."

"No leader! No leash!" Ibai and Kemen shouted from the other side of the room.

The rest of the crew took up the chant.

"Speaking of Amona," Vahly said, leaning over to

whisper into Nix's ear. "We need to talk. Can we go to your rooms?"

"Of course, gorgeous."

"I'm not gorgeous. I'm human. And a plain one at that." She'd seen enough illustrations of humans in scrolls to know.

"I'm not talking about looks, dear. I'm talking about soul. There is nothing plain about you in here." She pointed her quill at Vahly's heart.

Vahly rolled her eyes. Her soul was far from gorgeous. She'd broken as many laws as any dragon in here and she was younger, by decades, than almost all of them. "Beauty, in all its forms, is subjective."

"Why can't you just say *Thank you*?"

"Thank you."

"Let's go to the storage room," Nix said. "I have guests lounging in my upstairs room."

"And by guests, you mean a crowd of male admirers ready for you to finish work."

Nix gently tapped Vahly on the nose with one clawed fingertip. "You are quite correct, darling."

The storage room had one narrow door Nix barely fit through and no windows. Because of the protection from the sun, and the fact that it was partially underground on the backside of the cider house, it was chilly. Vahly wished she had a room like this back at the Lapis palace. It was glorious after feasting near the pits.

A while back, Nix had invited Vahly to live at the cider house. But Amona had railed, recounting the many reasons Vahly should remain in the Lapis palace. Being one of a kynd could be dangerous, Amona had stated, and Vahly was safer near the Lapis who had adopted her.

Well, Amona had been right. Vahly had been safe. But after her trouble tonight with Maur? Now, she wasn't sure there was a safe place for her to live anywhere in the world.

"Today when I was climbing the sea cliffs there was a disturbance."

Nix froze.

"The sea folk used their magic on the water and raised the largest wave I've seen yet."

Nix's gaze roamed Vahly's face. Her pupils shrinking, then expanding. Nix clicked her blue tongue against her teeth, a common dragon habit. Their tongues weren't quite forked, but the end was less rounded than Vahly's. "How bad is it? Your face says it is dire."

"I won't lie."

"Please don't." Nix set her ledger on a shelf beside a crock of butter and lit a large candle.

Vahly explained what had happened in detail as Nix listened. "And now, the Lapis are evacuating their lower two floors. I think you're safe up here on this ridge, what with how the land lies now, but our time is running out. My time. I have to figure out how to get my powers going, Nix."

Nix took a moment to absorb the idea that the sea folk seemed ready to strike. She pressed her red lips together and took a slow breath. Then she opened her bright yellow eyes. "What's the plan?"

The scroll slid easily from Vahly's vest. "I stole this from the hidden chamber you told me about."

"Nicely done, thief." From Nix, that was a compliment.

"It talks about the Sacred Oak, mentions earth kynd's birthplaces, and even has a line about humans and elves working together."

Nix's eyes widened. "Now, that *is* interesting." She held out her hands. "Don't hold out on me, woman. Let me see this shocking text."

Vahly watched her carefully unroll the delicate strip of vellum. Nix read it over, her tongue clicking again.

"Can you read the elvish at the bottom?" Vahly pointed at the darker ink near the elf holding the daggers. "It would be fantastic if it said something along the lines of *Here's how earth kynd gains magic. Step one,* and so forth," Vahly said wryly.

Nix snorted. "Right next to the line about the exact location of Matriarch Elixane's lost hoard of cursed gold coins."

"Yes, exactly. Considering she stole them from my kynd—the first and only crime committed by a Lapis matriarch—there should be mention of them in every important document."

Nix shook her head. "Humans stole the gold to make the coins."

"No, no. I think you are mistaken, friend. The legends say the people of Bihotzetik mined that gold all on their own, eons before Elixane was even alive."

"You have only read that in one single scroll. It is a lie. And you know it."

This was their favorite argument. There wasn't a

meeting that went by when they didn't badger one another about the lost hoard.

"And this is just one single scroll. But still, it says something important, doesn't it? Please say *yes*." Vahly's joking tone slipped as hope sizzled around her heart.

Nix raised one eyebrow. "I knew an elf once. A long time ago. He was a wonderful kynd. Honorable. Wise. Quick as a wink. I like elves. Well, I've only met the one, but he sealed the deal. I like them. I don't care that everyone else claims they're pretentious. They have cause for their arrogance. They have kept their secrets for all of time. Impressive."

Nix dealt in secrets so that was no surprise. Vahly had witnessed countless such exchanges during her two years of friendship with the vivacious female. The first exchange she'd witnessed dealt with Vahly's clan.

The Lapis carvers' guild had needed to know the new drilling methods of the Jade carver's guild, and Nix had provided the information. Now, where she'd gained the knowledge, Vahly wasn't sure. But she'd never ask. Nix protected her spies like a mother hen did her chicks. And so, Vahly would not dare question Nix about befriending an elf nor how she'd made contact with a kynd so reclusive most believed they were extinct.

"This," Nix said, pointing, "this says that earth kynd, humans, visited the Forest of Illumahrah. I'm almost certain."

Fire rushed through Vahly's veins. The forest was the home of the elves, high on the plateau, beyond the Fire Marshes' long stretch of inhabitable land. "Was the visit tied to the ritual?"

"That, I can't tell. I only know the words for visit and the phrase the elves use for their forest."

Vahly's fists clenched in frustration. "This is going to sound obnoxiously pert, but I don't understand how you and many other dragons could have lived alongside the human clans for so long and not picked up anything about their power ritual."

Nix touched Vahly's arm gently. "The humans did a good job keeping secrets. Not as good as elves, but still, good."

Nix studied Vahly's face, and Vahly ignored the look of pity in her friend's eyes. Normally, she would leave off this type of talk, but the time for pride was long past. She had to find answers now.

"Did you ever have someone search the Jade library?" Nix asked. "Probably a waste of time, but you never know."

"Amona tried that years ago. She says they only have one set of scrolls anyway. They're all battle histories. Nothing in depth."

Nix carefully closed the writing and handed it back. "What are you going to do, Vahly? Because I can see those wheels turning in that head of yours."

She needed more information. Elven information. But she couldn't seek them, could she? Amona would never allow it. They might not even exist anymore. It could lead to death through the Fire Marshes or by elves if they were indeed still around. They might decide Vahly's head looked best on one of their enchanted platters.

"I should try to visit the elves. If I don't take risks and gain information soon, we'll all be dead."

"If it helps," Nix said. "I'll go with you."

Pressure built in Vahly's chest like her heart wanted to shout. "You would?"

"I could use an adventure." Nix shooed Vahly back through the narrow door. "I need more stories to tell while I pour cider."

"Nix." Vahly put a hand over her heart. "Thank you." Vahly was honestly shocked. Nix had a love for sleeping in and for the first fruits of any hunts her employees went on. A trip through the Fire Marshes would be the furthest thing from pleasurable. "But what will the other Call Breakers think when you tell them you're off to visit elves?"

"Hush, please. They don't need to know what we're up to. We could just be on our way to scour the western lands for early cave paintings near the ruins of Bihotzenik."

"Amona herself ran a full search of the area years ago, then again two seasons ago."

"The Breakers won't know all of that. They won't care. It'll be enough to have an interesting lie for them to chew on while I'm gone. Now, let's have a meal and talk on the balcony upstairs."

CHAPTER SIX

The common room was still packed and noisy. Peering through green and blue wings, Vahly could see empty bowls, more dice games her fingers itched to play, and a slew of swaying dragons. Several stools lay on the ground, evidence of another tavern fight. Vahly's boots stuck in a puddle of spilled drink.

At the dark, hand-hewn wood of the bar top, four Call Breakers played Waterfall. The race to finish one's cup of dropcider started when the youngest of the bunch began to drink. If any dragon stopped drinking before the youngest, said dragon would have to buy the next round.

Beside those fools, Dramour slumped onto the bar. He lifted his black eyepatch to scratch underneath. When he saw Nix, his good eye brightened and he attempted to stand straight. The effect was comical. Like a sapling in a strong breeze.

Nix walked around the Waterfall players and past the large copper sink where a pile of dirty dishes sat ready for

Baww to wash. Amid the colorful display of bottles, Nix's jewel box sat on a dusty shelf.

Vahly didn't know who had made the box. Nix pushed the question aside whenever Vahly asked about its creator. The craftsman had carved lapis lazuli stones into circles and set them into the sides and top. Everyone knew that Nix only permitted Baww to touch the box. It held the night's take.

Nix opened it, threw in a pocketful of coins, then shut the lid. She had to have enough gold in there to buy a whole new tavern. Nix removed a large and tightly rolled scroll from the shelf that held the jewel box.

Dramour, swaying on his feet, accidentally knocked one of the Waterfall players' drinks over with an elbow.

Nix glanced at Dramour. "Best sit down, Fine Eye. You're about to greet the ground, my friend."

Nodding at his nickname, he took a stool, resumed his position on the bar top, and promptly began snoring.

"Baww," Nix called out. "Bring a good meal to the balcony. And don't let anyone else come upstairs for tonight, please, darling."

Baww nodded, then shouted in the direction of the kitchen.

Nix brought Vahly up the stairs and through a round door embellished with wrought iron red hat flowers.

Four males waited in Nix's rooms.

One lounged on a four-poster bed, his chest bare. The scales over his heart bore the scorched image of a flame hovering over a single claw. It was the symbol of the Call Breakers. The other three males sat in the plush velvet chairs scattered around the room in no semblance of order or arrangement. A large scarf in shades of amethyst and emerald stretched across the ceiling. The thin fabric caught the glow of several oil lamps that hung from chains near the center of the chamber.

"You'll have to wait for me downstairs, my dears." Nix swept through the room, toward the double doors leading to her balcony. "I have business with our Vahly."

The males grumbled, but started out the door.

"Save some of your energy for me!" The bare-chested dragon grinned at Nix before shutting her door.

Nix waved a hand at him, then proceeded to stroll through the double doors. She pulled two chairs up to a table.

The balcony, closed in with an intricate framework of iron flowers that formed a barrier, overlooked the broken ground that eventually sloped downward into the Lost Valley. Saltwater waves rippled across the area like snakes. In the moonlight, the water took on a wine color that reminded Vahly of the place's history.

The flooded valley had once been Vahly's home.

A collection of two-story stone houses, taverns, workshops, and a marketplace used to thrive in the place where the ocean now ruled. The settlement hadn't been there too long, built by those pushed out of the West by the tragedy of the main human region near Bihotzetik. They'd never even given it a name which Vahly saw as a clear statement of their mindset then. The sea folk had beaten the humans, nearly wiped them out. And the humans were numbly going about the business of surviving by the time Vahly was born with her Blackwater mark.

ALISHA KLAPHEKE

Amona had told Vahly the story. The humans had informed their neighboring dragon clan, the Lapis, about the child who'd been born Touched. The earth kynd anticipated Vahly's future as an Earth Queen, hoping she would gain the powers that had grown weak and oftentimes unseen for far too many generations. The last Earth Queen before Vahly had died in the Bihotzetik flooding three generations ago, and she'd never been powerful to begin with.

The Lost Valley settlement had thought they were safe from the sea, there on the eastern coast, protected by the wall that mirrored the one holding Nix's cider house and the clanless city. Besides, the sea folk had never attacked this side of the isle. It was believed their powers waned as they left the western waters.

But the humans had been wrong.

Vahly took a shuddering breath and faced the rippling waters covering her birth mother's final resting place.

"Vahly?" Nix came to stand in front of her, face filled with concern. "Are you all right?"

"I was remembering my biological mother. She had some guts to do what she did. I wish I could thank her."

"You just did." Nix's yellow eyes reflected the moonlight. "I think the dead can hear us if they so choose."

"We'll find out the truth sooner rather than later."

"Not if you have anything to do with it." Nix took a seat and pointed to the other chair. "I have a good feeling about this plan of yours."

She spread the large scroll across the table. Green

88

stretches lay against gray mountains and a long, branched strip of silver crossed the length of it.

"I didn't know you had a fine map like this." Vahly scooted to the edge of her seat and ran a careful finger over the Red Meadow.

"How else would I help my smugglers find new routes to escape those we aren't able to bribe?"

"Nix, you don't have to help me. Let me be clear. I would never hold it against you if you took the wiser route and stayed out of this."

"You've been dealt a dung hand in life, Vahly. You may have bonded with the Lapis—"

"You can tell?"

"I can feel the bond on you. I'm far more sensitive than most dragons. If they paid any attention to those other than themselves..." She waved a hand indicating they would hash that out later. "So yes, you are bonded with the Lapis, but the Call Breakers bonded with you long before today's event. Not in the same way, but it is a bond nonetheless."

Baww brought a tray of herbed venison, olives, scorchpeppers, and apple slices that showed the slanted markings of a dragon's claw. He then set two mugs of cider in front of them.

Vahly couldn't believe Nix's reaction. The bond with the Lapis was no small thing. Amona could potentially sway Vahly's mind and force her to do her will.

It was a threat to Nix's operations.

Once Baww left, and they were alone again, Vahly voiced that very concern.

Nix sipped her cider. Her hyssop-blue scales glittered

in the moonlight as she turned a gold and lapis lazuli ring around her finger and tapped it against her mug. "You and I both know that what you witnessed on the cliffs means I can no longer allow my business to come first." Her reptilian gaze locked onto Vahly.

Vahly reached across her plate to grip Nix's forearm. "I vow, as far as I am able, I'll never allow my bond with Amona to endanger you or any of the Call Breakers in any way."

"I accept your promise, Vahly of the Earth."

A tingling rose in Vahly's fingers as the vow encircled her heart, warming her chest.

Could Amona feel her promises now that they were bonded?

Nix pointed to the Fire Marshes on the map. "Obviously, we need to find a way through here."

Vahly thought of how Amona had rescued her and had an idea. From the trouble she'd had with her suggestion of riding a dragon's back, she knew better than to bring that up, but perhaps it was less appalling to think of carrying her in another fashion. "Could you shift and carry me in your claws like you do a kill?"

She wasn't keen on being hoisted up by full-sized dragon claws like a sheep headed for the roasting pits, but both her fear and her pride would have to stand down in this situation.

Nix tilted her head. "Yes. I could do that."

"The marshes are extensive." Vahly bit her lip. The map showed the scorched and smoking ground reaching for miles and miles. "Do you know of certain spots that are safe enough to land?"

"None that I know have ever tried to enter the marshes in full. Of course, we enjoy the earth's break and the earthblood there at the start of it, but the wind clears the air. Further in, well, breathing will become rather difficult."

"So we'll have to move fast or die."

Nix jabbed a claw into an apple slice, then chewed it noisily. "That should be my motto."

Vahly touched her sword hilt, the sword Amona had given her. "I think we should ask Amona to help us get there. To the elves."

"But she loathes their kynd. What am I missing?"

"She is wise," Vahly said. "Surely she can get past old hatred to see the sense in my seeking them."

Nix ate another apple slice. "Doubt it."

"But she could order a troop of dragons to get us across the area. Three, perhaps, that could trade out so that we would always have a strong retinue." Vahly didn't love the idea of including Amona, but she didn't want to risk the lives of Nix and the Breakers more than was absolutely necessary.

"Too bad we can't simply signal the elves and ask them to come to us. You know, I honestly thought they'd come for you at some point in your life."

"Why?"

"They can sense great events. Like your birth and who you are meant to be. The elf I knew claimed the wind and shadows sometimes told him stories."

Vahly frowned. "Right." When she had been a child, she would've loved this idea of what elves' mysterious magic could do. But now, after years of magic not doing what every text and creature claimed it should be doing to her, she was less than amused by whimsical stories about vague elven powers.

Nix shrugged. "I think we should go. Now. Under the cover of darkness so there are fewer eyes watching us traipse into the marshes like fools."

"I don't know. I could be leading you to your death."

"Death is breathing down our backs already, wouldn't you say?" Nix jerked her chin at the Lost Valley and the salt water covering its former understated glory.

"I should talk to Amona. I don't want to, but I should."

"Why don't you sleep on it? No matter what you decide, your body needs rest. Take the couch in my room where you won't be bothered." Nix pushed away from the table. "I need to meet with Aitor, then I'll be back shortly. We will discuss your decision over breakfast."

With the balcony doors closed, Vahly was alone in the night.

What was the best choice? To ask Amona for help or not?

The entire idea was three jacks shy of a full deck.

Heading into the Fire Marshes to meet with elves who might very well be extinct. Insanity.

She stood and began to pace, drawing her short sword and her cleaning cloth. Walking the length of the balcony, she ran her cloth over the etched wing and flame pattern of her blade, the familiar job easing her nerves somewhat. The ivory hilt warmed under her grip.

Amona had ordered the weapon made for Vahly long ago. She'd harvested the tusks from a sea beast that beached itself when Vahly was still toddling around the mountain palace and drooling. *Fight the sea with the sea,* Amona had always said of the sword, smirking at her own little joke about the ivory.

Vahly loved the sword. It was part of her. She'd perfected an array of seamless moves made with her weapon side forward. Nothing that would take down a dragon set on killing her, but enough to drive away the ones who merely wanted to bruise the failed savior of the dragons.

Rubbing at a particularly stubborn smudge near the hilt's scalloped guard, Vahly's mind whirled.

What if Amona refused the trip to the Forest of Illumahrah? What then? Vahly was definitely going. No doubt. But it would prove far more difficult if Amona knew the basic plan. She could Call Vahly back with a word and it would be impossible to disobey unless she was able to Break like the dragons here had. There would be no going back to the Lapis if she did that.

What were the chances that Amona would help Vahly and Nix cross the marshes? From the way Amona had acted about the elves today, gaining her support was a long shot with odds too rough even for underdog-loving Vahly.

No, she couldn't tell Amona. She had to come up with a reason to be gone for a while.

In the past, Vahly had traveled with Helena the healer, Xabier, and a few others to treat a disease in the goats that grazed the Red Meadow. At Xabier's feast, Maur had voiced concern about the bear that was killing all the deer. Maybe Vahly could tell Amona that she would gather the

Call Breakers and head out to slay the bear. Amona would fight the suggestion, but Vahly could persuade her, noting the recent excursion's success. Then, she'd have an excuse for her absence.

Sighing, Vahly finished polishing her blade. She hated to keep the real plan from Amona, but it couldn't be helped.

Vahly sheathed her sword, tucked her cloth into one of the many small bags at her belt, and went to bed.

CHAPTER SEVEN

The next morning, Vahly found Nix at the front door of the now empty common room where she was watching Aitor slide into the orange light of dawn.

"Off for a stroll, is he?" Vahly hitched up against the doorframe.

"A stroll that ends with details about a certain male noble that will make Amona very happy."

There were rumors that Amona was considering a relationship with the reclusive Lapis named Eneko, who lived in the far northern wing of the impossibly huge mountain palace. He was bonded with her, as all Lapis were, but he didn't attend events like Dragonfire rituals. For some reason, that only piqued Amona's interest further.

"And keep Amona blissfully ignorant that her adopted daughter is headed for a chat with the elves she loathes so completely?"

Nix's eyes found Vahly's. She smiled. "Honey keeps the bees busy."

"I have another idea along similar lines." Vahly shifted her weight from foot to foot, Amona's stern face flashing through her mind. She filled Nix in on her idea to pretend as if they were headed out to hunt the troublesome bear.

Nix led Vahly to the bar where Baww set out a plate of hardboiled eggs and two cups of lemonmelon juice. They sat on the stools and ate in the special silence that descends on those who make dangerous plans.

Finally, Nix wiped her mouth with a folded cloth and met Vahly's gaze. "Do you believe Amona will allow this feigned hunt?"

Vahly finished her water and gripped the wooden cup's deep grain. "She is distracted by the sea folk and the message to the Jades."

"And she does indeed have a problem with that simplebeast. I've heard of the bear too and the ones that go off like that have to be put down," Nix said.

Sliding off her stool, Vahly chewed the last of her eggs. "I'll be back by sunset. Can you get a group ready by then?"

"Yes."

"You know," Vahly started, "We are slightly cracked for even considering this trip."

Nix smiled at Baww as he collected their plates. "I prefer the term *adventurous*."

Vahly waited to speak until Baww had disappeared into the kitchen. "We could bring Dramour, Ibai, and Kemen. What do you think?"

"Dramour hates elves. Well, they all do, but he does especially. Why him?"

"Because he is in love with you. He'll risk all to keep you breathing if we get into a rough spot."

Nix touched Vahly's cheek gently. "My sweet. You are a good one."

Vahly smirked. "Not exactly. I'm about to lie my tail off."

Nix's eyebrow lifted as her hand fell away from Vahly's face, then she turned to look at the front door as if their friends might arrive simply because Vahly had said their names. "Ibai is an obvious choice, with his healing knowledge. He'll want to bring half his stores though. Why Kemen?"

"He's big."

Nix laughed as they walked toward the front door of the cider house. "That he is. A nice, scary dragon to spook the elves if needed, hmm? All right, Vahly. I think you have chosen wisely. Shall I inform them or will you? This is your quest and you will take the lead on all decisions from here on out."

"Can you tell them while I'm gone? Get them ready?"

Nix nodded. "You handle the biggest dragon of them all and I'll set things right here." She shooed Vahly into the daylight.

As she walked back to the mountain palace, she had to laugh at herself. This slug was about to make history, one way or another.

~

97

SMALL BIRDS DASHED into the blue, midmorning sky as a group of Jade dragons descended into the flowers and grasses near the front entrance of the Lapis mountain palace. One dragon near the back of the group dropped a pile of bags.

Vahly's heart puddled between her ribs and fell into her stomach. "Great," she muttered. "They packed to stay a while."

She fought the urge to draw her sword. If she did, they would see it as a sign of aggression and burn her down where she stood. With this many Jades so close, she didn't have a chance. Her best choice was to show confidence and respect, all rolled into one. The respect wasn't so tough. After all, they were dragons. But the confidence? The sweat pouring down her face made that act difficult to pull off.

The twenty green dragons focused their eyes on her.

It was disconcerting, to say the least.

Especially considering the emerald dragon leading the group was Zarux, a real piece of work.

With a sizzling flash of fire, they transformed and began to dress. Zarux wore a cloak so green that it was nearly black. His tailor had embroidered the edges with the Jade sigil in golden thread. The symbol showed the profile of a dragon's open mouth and the long teeth designed for tearing.

The dragons walked toward Vahly, teeth bared and nostrils smoking. Vahly frowned, noticing several bled from what looked like fresh wounds.

A blotch of blackened scales marred his right arm. A

spelled salt water wound. If his body didn't fight that off, he would lose the arm. Maybe his life.

The dragon beside Zarux had an ear wound. Blood pooled over the blackened scales near the lobe and dribbled down the side of his angry face.

A sour taste hit the back of Vahly's throat. Dragons with wounds like that didn't last a day. She had no love for these Jades, but no one deserved to die like that, watching the black of the wound spread day after day until breathing was impossible and pain dragged the victim under.

Zarux's dark green head rose high above Vahly. "What a wonderful conclusion to our last twenty-four hours, to be greeted by the sight of Sugarrabota's greatest disappointment, Vahly of the Lapis." He sniffed, and Vahly fought the urge to flinch. "Ah. So it is true. You have finally heard Amona's Call. How sweet. Were you all celebrating while we were at war with our common enemy?" He spat the last two words as if they tasted foul on his tongue.

Every muscle in Vahly's body argued as she gave Zarux a bow. "The Lapis battled the sea folk one moon back."

"Isn't that nice?" Zarux smiled at his cohorts. "They take a moon cycle off to rest. Must be lovely to live so far from Tidehame and remain so ignorant of the rising waters."

"We aren't ignorant."

Zarux stepped closer, the smoke from his nose increasing.

Vahly held out her hands. "We spotted activity off our

own cliffs yesterday. That's why Matriarch Amona has called you here."

Zarux let out a short stream of dragonfire and Vahly jerked, wanting to run but forcing herself to stay put. "Called us? She is not our Matriarch! We are here because we chose to come."

Vahly bowed. "Of course. I was only talking about the message she sent to your clan."

"How many of your precious Lapis have you lost this past sennight? One? Five? Guess how many dragons the Jades have sacrificed in as many days."

Vahly held her tongue.

"No idea? Allow me to inform you, Earth Queen," he sneered. "Fifty-two. Perhaps we should just eat the Lapis for extra energy before we head back into battle. That way, your blue friends would actually be of use. Fifty-two dragons lost to the sea folk while you and your precious strategists hole up in your southern mountains, far from danger. Give me one reason why I shouldn't gulp you down right now, human. I'm hungry from risking my life and ruining my arm to try and save the land we're standing on."

"Zarux!" Amona's voice boomed down the palace steps and across the waving grasses. "Stand down. You are in my territory now, and two thousand dragons wait for my Call if you break our codes of conduct."

Vahly released the breath she'd been holding.

Zarux snarled and tossed his head, but he turned away from Vahly.

The sun cut over the rise of the mountains and veiled Amona's black hair with light as she approached them.

Her blue-scaled cheekbones sat high in her regal face and she looked at Zarux like he was a biting fly she simply needed to swat away.

Vahly smiled. Stones and Blackwater, she loved her mother.

"Do not speak down to me," Zarux snapped. "My Matriarch has had enough of you and yours. She sent me to tell you exactly that. If you don't join us now, in the attack set for the coast nearest our territory, we will consider you full enemies and war with you as we do with the sea folk!"

Did he truly have to shout everything?

Zarux's hand shot out. He swiped a talon under Amona's wing joint, one of the only sensitive spots on a dragon.

Shock held Vahly in a vice grip.

Amona grunted, then blew dragonfire into Zarux's face.

Panic hit Vahly like she'd fallen from a tree. She had her short sword out before she knew what she was doing.

Amona and the rest were fighting in truth now, wings flaring, fire blazing, claws ripping.

Lapis poured from the palace and swarmed around the Jades, bumping Vahly outside the action. The Jades saw how outnumbered they were and stopped fighting. They never did that against the sea folk, not when Vahly had watched them in battle. The ceasefire gave her hope that they did at least want to talk even if they started the conversation with blood and fire.

Go, Amona said through the bond to Vahly.

Vahly looked to her. "But—"

Go. The command pushed Vahly's feet into a jog, going back the way she'd come, toward Nix's. *Stay in the forest or the city of thieves with Nix if you have to. Stay gone until we sort this. The Jade Matriarch has decided you are the target of her ire.*

Vahly's heart pounded in her temples. She gave Amona one last look, then ran to the cider house, her head full of worry.

CHAPTER EIGHT

With her heart beating in her teeth, Vahly crossed the cider house threshold and pushed through the crowd to find Nix at the back, talking quickly and quietly to Baww.

"You'll open tomorrow at regular time. It'll be fine. You don't need me."

"They do." Baww glanced over Nix to scan the room of Breakers. He saw Vahly. "Hi, Vahly. Are you all right?"

Nix swiveled, eyes wide. "What is it? What's happened?"

"Jades. They attacked the Lapis."

Baww rolled his eyes. "And ice is cold."

"No, Baww," Vahly said, "this was different. It wasn't on their territory. They came to the Lapis palace and Zarux attacked Amona."

Nix hissed. "Stones and Blackwater. The gall of that dragon."

"But she trounced him, aye?" Baww looked hopeful.

"She did. But she commanded me to flee. She said the Jade Matriarch decided to blame me for everything."

"I thought she already did," Baww said.

"Me too, but when Amona said it, the declaration sounded more official. I think she heard from Lord Maur. She had sent him to the North."

"Bloody Jades." Nix walked into the kitchen and Vahly and Baww trailed her. The scent of chocolate filled the air. Rows of chocolate dipped scorchpeppers lined a metal tray. With two dainty fingers—well, as dainty as a dragon's can be—Nix lifted one and popped it into her mouth. "Don't panic. There is dessert."

Vahly found a bowl of unmelted chocolate discs beside the tray and gobbled a handful.

"Baww, can you give us a minute, darling?" Nix asked.

Baww dipped his head and hurried out the back door with a wicker basket.

Nix put her head near Vahly's. "Dramour, Kemen, and Ibai have all agreed to go."

Vahly breathed out slow, relief rushing through her.

"I have put Baww to the task of packing our bags with fresh water, food, and various other items. Now, you eat, drink, and enjoy yourself. We leave tonight."

"Perfect." Vahly put a hand over her heart. "Thanks, Nix. Really. You're taking a tremendous risk for me."

"It's not as if we have a thousand options. You're the hope of the land. And I am your friend."

They embraced, then Vahly left the kitchen to find a game to distract her from what was to come.

· · ·

By DUSK, Vahly's whole body simmered with the need to get going. She was afraid she'd lose her nerve if this took much longer. Dramour had fallen asleep in the orchards and had to be found. Ibai had insisted they wait until his latest wound treatment had been chilled for three full hours.

Kemen threw the bones into the chalked circle at Vahly's feet. "I don't have any more lapis to give you, Vahly," he mumbled, shaking his head.

She clapped him on the shoulder. "Don't chew your talons off about it. I'm only playing to keep from screaming in panic."

Kemen snorted a weak laugh.

"I'm going outside. Tell Nix if she asks."

Not much for words, Kemen jerked his chin in agreement.

With the starry sky stretching across the Red Meadow, Vahly's feet took her toward the Fire Marshes, toward the elves' homeland.

The night crawled from the shadows, bringing the chirrup of insects and the *coo-coo* of the distura bird with its glowing feathers. Vahly stepped over a tumble of stones that had once served as a marker for her kynd. A rise of ground led her past the marker, then back down again as the earth presented a low-lying area veined in glowing lines of golden earthblood.

Smoke rose from black cracks in the ground. The heat intensified as she neared the marshes' border. The air here was not unlike dragonfire, charcoal and that lemony-tang scent that cut through any other smell. No trees grew in the marshes of course, and few animals lived in the awful place. Just the rock lizards that reminded Vahly of wee dragons, not that she would ever say that in earshot of a dragon.

In this first part of the marshes, one could see the remainder of the path humans and elves had worked together to build centuries ago, back when they first ventured from their towering forest atop the plateau to meet with the dragons and the Earth Queens of the ages.

The marshes had absorbed the rest of the pathway, but the beginning was clear enough. Boulders and patches of earth marked safe spots to stand, mostly undeterred by the steaming pools of murky water and their accompanying streams of golden earthblood.

Vahly said a quiet thank you to her own evolutionary ancestors, the humans who'd risked coming to this island and adapted to the heat by way of guided procreation and earth magic, which created skin that didn't burn like it once had long, long ago.

She wished magic would ooze from the ground like her forebears had. If she could sense the earth's heartbeat, maybe then she wouldn't feel so alone, so separated from her own kynd.

A voice broke into her thoughts.

She looked up from the smoking ground at her boots, but couldn't spot a dragon anywhere.

Had Euskal decided to make good on that play bet to fly over the area?

Straining her neck, she stared into the night sky, but she caught no glimpse of wings or dragon shapes. Maybe it was only a distura bird. Or even a rock lizard. She had never been out here, this close to the marshes. Perhaps they made such a noise after sundown.

But then she heard it again. A male voice. Low, strong. But the words…

It almost sounded like another language.

The voice echoed across the simmering marshland once more—just a weak shout.

A hissing started near Vahly's boot.

A plume of acrid smoke blasted from the ground. Vahly leaped back, boots crunching on the uneven ground. Stumbling, she landed on her backside. Thankfully, she hadn't been burned. But that creature out there, it was surely in trouble.

She would at least go as far as the remaining path allowed. Then, if she couldn't go any further, she would return to Nix's and get help.

The old path wound through pillars of curling gases and past black and crusty ground. Vahly's throat burned, and a coughing fit stalled her progress. The path was nearly gone and now she second-guessed this rescue mission. Once she had stilled her struggling lungs, she walked a few more steps.

There, on the ground, was a shape that was not rock or smoke or golden earthblood.

Or dragon.

Her lips parted in a silent gasp.

Two arms. Two legs. Supple flesh instead of scales.

Crouching by the body, Vahly moved a curtain of obsidian hair away from the creature's face.

A pointed ear.

Vahly's tongue didn't want to work.

ALISHA KLAPHEKE

It was an elf.

She shook him hard, finally forcing her mouth to make sounds. "Wake up, fool! You're going to die out here and I'm not about to go down with you. I thought your kynd was known for wisdom. Why in the world are you out here by yourself?"

He could have asked her the same thing.

The elf was nothing like she'd imagined. Yes, he had the glowing elegance of the illustrations she'd seen from the library scrolls. His exposed arms showed powerful muscles and his features were just as chiseled as recorded in dragon history.

But there was an age to him, a feeling of having weathered many storms, a burnished look to his fine, clear skin and proud, beardless chin. His presence weighed on her like a winter cloak, heavy but somehow comforting.

A line between his sharply slanted eyebrows made her think he had experienced great frustration in his lifetime. She hadn't thought to see that in an elf. This wasn't the picture she'd cobbled from her research.

He was so much … more.

Grabbing the sleeveless, black surcoat he wore, she shook him hard. Dirt fell from his front, but his inky lashes remained closed and resting on his sharp, moonlit cheeks. Silver embroidery sewn to resemble small oak leaves decorated the shoulders and breast of his surcoat as well as the outside seam of his travel-stained trousers. An image covered his heart, perhaps a half moon, half sun, though it was difficult to tell in the dark.

A quiver was attached to his belt, its details echoing

those on the surcoat, and a bow showed behind him, its tip touching his head. On his belt, he wore two knives with hilts of silver and blades of swirling steel—similar to the throwing knives the elf on the scroll held above the brazenberry bush.

The moonlight seemed to be playing with the shadows around his mouth, as if with a word, he could make light and dark dance to his tune.

She couldn't stop staring. So still. So lovely. Like marble or glass, with the tiny scratches that time wore into such surfaces.

Except in illustrations, never had she seen a form so similar to her own. Her entire life, Vahly had known only dragons. Claw and fang, scaled bodies and translucent wings. She lifted his hand to study his fingers, marveling at their slender strength. They were larger than her own, but smoother. He had no scars whatsoever though he appeared roughly her age. Though she should have expected that part, it was still astounding to see with her own eyes.

A hiss sounded beside his left leg.

Panic needling her veins, Vahly put arms under him and attempted to move him, but he was too heavy.

The hissing grew louder.

She was going to watch his flesh, so similar to her own, boil in front of her eyes. Adrenaline pumping through her body, she moved herself over the hissing spot and rolled the elf onto his side, then to his stomach, avoiding the dangerous area.

The ground popped. The fire marshes' deadly clouds reached out of the ground like claws.

Only a small area of the elf's upper arm had suffered from the heat. The flesh was darker than the rest of him, but she couldn't quite see the extent of the damage.

She had to get him out of here. Now.

Like so many times before, she wished she were a dragon with powerful wings. A dragon could easily save this elf. But she was a lowly human with a faulty Blackwater mark between her brows. A cruel joke.

She collapsed, her lungs beginning to clog in the foul air again. Soon, she'd be on the ground with him, well on her way to death.

"Nix!" she called out, knowing the only chance she had of being heard was if the dragons had already set out to meet her. "Dramour!" Stones, why had she wandered out here by herself? Her nerves had trumped her good sense.

The elf stirred, and his fingers twitched. He moaned a word or what she guessed was a word. It sounded like *Etor*. A name? She reached for the opposite hand and found a circlet of leather on his wrist. Tiny silver bells rang out as she shifted his arm.

The elf said the word again.

"Are you saying *Etor*? Is Etor a friend? Does that mean *help*?" Vahly cursed her own ignorance. Granted, no one besides Nix had seen an elf in an age. But still. She should have at least studied the basics of their language just in case. This was twice now it would have come in handy. "We need to get you out of here or we're both destined to be a fine, steamed dinner for the marshes. Does this have magic to it?" She shook the bells.

A black and white horse with a curved neck pranced out of the darkness.

Vahly stood. "Etor?"

The horse clomped forward, then skittered at the nearest vein of earthblood.

She held out a hand. "It's all right. Just stay on the path. Let's get your master on your back."

"Etor." The elf's luminous, black eyes opened briefly.

Vahly shivered. "We need to go," she said, hoping against everything that he might understand.

The elf nodded doggedly and hauled himself to a seated position. Vahly crooked an arm under his and helped him to his horse. She put a steady hand on the simplebeast. The animal's coat was finer than Amona's best velvet.

The elf coughed out words in a language that wasn't elven or dragon. She shook her head, fearing the hiss sounding right behind her.

Dropping suddenly, the elf called the horse's name. Vahly caught him, and he seemed to fade away for a moment before rousing himself again.

He managed to stand, leaning heavily on Etor. With a shove, she aided him in working his way onto the horse. It wasn't easy. His sword's sheath—pale bone tooled with a riot of symbols Vahly had not the time nor the will to study—stuck her in the side once. His boot caught on the horse's saddle as she tried to get him settled. With his feet in the stirrups, she had done all she could do. The elf's eyes remained shut. He swayed like a drunk, his hair falling in front of his face and his pointed ears catching the moonlight.

She took Etor's bridle and headed quickly down the winding path of rock and earth, toward safety. Seen only through the haze of gases released by the earthblood cracks, the sky was starry bright. Using the constellation of Goat's Horn and Wolf Pack, she determined she was heading the right direction.

Another hiss and a blast with no pause between sounded behind them.

Etor startled, jingling his reins. The elf pitched to the side.

Vahly spun to catch him. The gas burned her leg. Her trousers smoked in one spot and agony crawled up her limb. The pain was red-hot, and it pulsed slow and strong, taking her breath and making her shiver. Coughing, she forced the elf to his seat, then took up the bridle.

Her body shook as she guided the horse through the fire marshes. One more step. Just one more. One more. She took up the phrases and turned them into a chant to keep her going despite the pounding pain in her leg and the intense heat soaking through her linen and leather clothing. The soles of her boots softened in the extreme temperature and sweat pooled between her toes. The fire marshes were going to eat through the bottoms of her boots.

She glanced back at Etor and his master. The horse's white mane trailed low, to the simplebeast's knees and he nickered in Vahly's direction.

"Yes, Etor," she croaked. "This isn't my favorite day either."

The elf kept his seat. His fingers curled loosely around

the reins, but his feet hung free of the stirrups. His cheeks looked hollow and unhealthy and his color had faded further. If they didn't get out of this foul air soon, he would surely die.

Finally, they breached the last stretch of fire marsh and felt solid earth under their feet and hooves, respectively.

She tied the horse to a tree at the side of the cider house and hurried inside the kitchen door. She found Nix with her crew huddled around her like disciples.

"Vahly?" Nix hurried to meet her, mouth drawn.

She winced at her own injury, the pain lancing through her in time with her heartbeat. "I found an elf. In the marshes. Just now. He's wounded."

CHAPTER NINE

D ramour's eyes slitted. "Are you joking? You are, aren't you, Vahl?"

"I'm not." She pointed to her burned leg. "I do love a good laugh, but I wouldn't scorch my leg off to sell a prank, my friend."

Ibai hurried to check out her leg. She waved him away. "The elf needs your help more than me. Come on." She limped out the door and pointed. "He's there. Hopefully, still on the horse."

She followed Nix and the rest toward the spot where she'd left the elf and Etor. "Stones."

The elf lay sprawled on the ground, unconscious, and all that was left of the horse was a torn bridle.

"Horses don't love dragons," Nix explained.

"I suppose losing a horse is the least of his problems," Vahly said. "What would push an elf to brave the marshes?"

Nix rushed inside to close the cider house down. Her coaxing and singing rang through the night.

"Spend a night or two without her,
See your love grow harder … "

Dragons poured from the door, laughing and shouting praises to Nix. A few voiced their willingness to test Nix's song upon return.

Ibai and Kemen stood shoulder to shoulder to block Vahly and the elf from view, even though most of the dragons leaving wouldn't be bothered to check the far side of the cider house. They headed for their hideouts in the city of thieves—tunnels and homes carved into high ridge.

When the place was cleared, the dragons helped Vahly to one of the gaming tables. Then, Kemen hauled the elf inside and plopped him on the bar top.

Nix rubbed her hands together. "We are going to find out what made this elf risk the marshes. And maybe, if we're lucky for once in our Blackwater forsaken lives, he'll know all about your scroll and your dozing powers."

Ibai was already emerging from the storage room with a mortar, pestle, and three bunches of herbs. "We don't know that anything we do will work on this thing."

"He is not a thing." Vahly winced as Kemen poured clean water over her burn.

Kemen snorted. "I didn't know you were into elves," he said, his voice nearly too low to be understood.

"I'm not into elves. But I'm not an arse. He is a highbeast like me and like you."

Ibai shuffled over and handed Kemen a small crock. Kemen's scarred fingers were gentle as he applied a paste of honey, aloe, and brazenberries on Vahly's wound.

"I respect that runaway horse more than I do his master," Kemen mumbled.

"Just because dragons warred with elves ages ago? Or is there another reason?" Vahly honestly did not understand their prejudice.

"Wait until the creature opens his mouth. Then you'll be on our side again," Dramour said, bringing Vahly a cup of water to drink. "Now, why did you leave without us? Nix has told us everything and we are behind you, Vahly. Although we do wish it had less to do with those." He snarled in the direction of the elf.

The water cooled Vahly's scorched throat. "I didn't leave without you. I just heard the elf calling out. I went to help."

The corner of Dramour's mouth lifted. "A queen indeed."

"What do you mean? Nix, what does he mean?"

"None of us," Nix said, fingering the ruby necklace at her throat, "would head into the marshes to rescue a creature shouting in a foreign tongue. We are good to our fellow Call Breakers. That's it."

But they had accepted her, a human, into their makeshift clan. Vahly decided not to push it. They would care for the elf because he might be able to save them a trip to the Forest of Illumahrah. It didn't matter what they would have done under other circumstances. Finding the answer to Vahly's power was all that mattered. If they ever subdued the Sea Queen, then they could argue about the rest of it.

Ibai stuffed a woven sack with the herbs he'd crushed, then held it to the elf's nose.

Nothing.

"He might be dead," Nix said.

Kemen crossed his arms and clicked his tongue. "No. His chest moves. Wait. No. Yes, he is dead."

Vahly came out of her chair, her wound forgotten.

Dramour snatched the herbs from Ibai and sniffed, his green nostrils flaring. "I would die too if you stuck your sack up my nose." He lowered the bag. "Someone, please. Make a joke about that. Come on. You cannot let that one pass. Anyone?"

Vahly grabbed the elf's surcoat and shook him hard. This elf could be the answer to everything. "You are not allowed to die, elf. I saved you. You have to get my permission to die!"

Dramour leaned on the bar and pointed a thumb at Vahly. "I love her more every day."

Ibai clapped his hands, startling Vahly so that she jumped. "I have an idea," he said. His mottled, blue-green wings fluttered behind him as he rushed into the storage area. "No one do anything. Keep your hands off."

"Still begging someone for a joke, here." Dramour blinked pleadingly at Vahly. "You know you want to."

"Want to what?"

"Keep your hands *on*—"

"Shut up, Dramour," Nix and Vahly said in unison.

Banging sounded from the room, then Ibai ran out, holding blacksmith bellows. "Hold his mouth open and his chin back, Kemen."

Ibai fit the end of the bellows into the elf's mouth, then compressed the goat skin contraption.

The elf was standing, and the bellows—as well as Ibai

and Kemen—were on the ground before Vahly could blink.

He was magnificent.

His black eyes scanned the room and took in each of them, including Vahly. He uttered a phrase in what Vahly guessed was elvish, his bow-shaped lips quick. His voice was dark and melodious, like the six-foot high stringed instruments the dragons played when battle units returned for respite. A well-worn bow strapped to his back, painted in charcoal shades of gray, peeked from the top of one shoulder, and his quiver remained on his belt. Five black and silver fletched arrows sat inside.

Nix held back Ibai and Kemen. The males were a touch unhappy at being flung to the floor. Nix kept a hand on each as she said three words to the elf in his language.

The elf's arms fell to his sides. His posture relaxed somewhat.

"I told him we are friends," Nix said, "not foe. And that I don't speak his language past this."

He bowed to Nix, then to Vahly, and Vahly almost missed his next words as she marveled at his movements. It was fascinating to see a creature so like her speak and gesture. Though he was an elf and had flesh far stronger than her own, he still appeared incredibly fragile compared to dragons. She couldn't even guess how terribly weak she seemed—and indeed was—when studied by dragons.

But seeing this elf, so like her in ways that dragons were not...

"My name is Arcturus," he said in dragon. "Please tell

me what is happening. My mind is addled, from injury or foul play, I don't know."

Vahly coughed. "I found you in the Fire Marshes. You passed out. From the gases, most likely. I'm pretty sure you died."

Dramour held up his first two fingers. "Just a little bit."

"And you helped me regain my consciousness?" Arcturus watched Ibai and Kemen as Nix let them step forward.

Vahly worried they might decide they liked him better dead, so she got between them. "Yes, they did. These two are healers. Well, Ibai is and Kemen is his helpful brother. Would you like to sit down?" She gestured toward the chair she'd been sitting in.

He nodded and took the seat. "I can't remember why I went into the marshes. You're quite certain you found me there? Is your mind addled as well?"

"I'm fine. And yes, it was in the Fire Marshes. I don't think I could mix that place up with anywhere else." Vahly fought the urge to glare.

Dramour elbowed her. "Now you're seeing the parts no one likes. Supreme pigheadedness. Ultimate arrogance. I remember an elf I met during a trade when I was five and fifty."

"Shut it down, Fine Eye," Nix barked.

Dramour nodded. "No problem."

Arcturus looked at the open door, then lifted his head and cocked his sharp chin. "Someone tricked me. Someone close to me."

Ibai made a face. "The gases of the marsh took you down. That's why your head's not straight."

"You are wrong. This feeling is more than natural injury."

"Super delightful, aren't they? Still taking his side?" Dramour whispered.

"I apologize for my tone, Healer," Arcturus said.

Ibai stuttered, obviously flustered at the show of respect.

"Do you think you were followed? Should we guard ourselves?" Vahly put a hand on her sword hilt. If a band of elves stormed the cider house...

Nix slid a mug of cider in front of Arcturus, then glanced at the side door. Smoke spun from her nose in warning.

"I don't think so," Arcturus said. "The wind only hints at foul play." He scooted away from the table and headed toward the door. "Thank you for rescuing and healing me, dragons, Earth Queen."

He didn't know anything about the current problems on the island if he was calling her that.

She pointed at her Blackwater mark. "This is a mistake. I don't have any power. The Sea Queen is actually about to take over every bit of land and kill us all. That's why I was in the Fire Marshes. I was planning a trip to visit your kynd to find answers. I thought maybe you would know about human rituals of power."

Arcturus furrowed his brow. "I ... I don't know. I can't remember..." He looked up, suddenly fierce like he'd been when he first awoke under Ibai's ministrations. "You see? I should know all about my kynd and this threat to all of us. But there is a blank place in my memory, and what is there … it's twisted. A strong elf has set foul magic upon me. I must leave and attempt to discover who wishes me ill. If I recover my full capabilities, I can perhaps fight the sea folk and aid you, Earth Queen." He stopped at the door and whispered elven words into the air.

"What are you doing? Ibai, maybe he needs another herbal remedy to clear his head."

"I'm calling my horse."

"Oh, Etor took off, into the forest beyond the Red Meadow. He didn't like the scent of dragons. You mentioned his name when I found you."

Arcturus turned. "Thank you for being kind to Etor. He gives you great praise. Once I untangle the wrong that has been done to me, I'll do my best to return and give you the information you require, Earth Queen."

"Please call me Vahly. We'll save the impressive title for the day I can do more than win at dice."

"Winning a hoard of gold out of me isn't nothing," Dramour said, a bite to his tone.

"You practically told me what tallies you were going for. If you'd cease your bragging for a minute while you gamble, you'd be doing a lot more taking than giving."

Nix clicked her claws against the table. "So. We're just going to let Arc leave, are we? Without gaining any info?"

"Did you give him a nickname?" Dramour looked offended that someone else might have the honor that Nix had previously only bestowed on him.

"What do you think we should do?" Vahly asked.

"Ask our new friend here to stay the night. Once he's

rested, perhaps his mind will return to normal and he'll be able to shed light on the scroll."

That was a sensible idea.

But here was a guide that could help them get to King Mattin, king of the elves. Arcturus might prove to be the only opportunity to enter the Forest of Illumahrah without force. If he left, that opportunity would be gone. Dragons were indeed formidable, but Vahly had no doubt the elf had the ability to sneak out while they slept.

"With respect," Vahly said, "I say we leave for the elven lands tonight. Now. Arcturus might not know his arse from a hole in the ground, but he is far more likely to be accepted into the elven lands than we are. We can use him to gain entry."

Arcturus leveled his gaze on Vahly. "I'm not quite that addled."

"Sure, the elf would be a help. Unless someone is trying to off him," Ibai said, holding two satchels and a bow. "Then we'd all be salted."

Arcturus glanced around the room. "The Healer makes a fine point."

Vahly took a steadying breath. She was ready to stop being the slug and move toward becoming who she was meant to be. "These dragons have agreed to shift into full dragon form and carry me across the marshes. They will carry you too. Wouldn't it be much easier for you to return home if you didn't have to cross the marshes on foot?"

Arc's mouth twisted, his fingers curling into fists before relaxing again. He looked to the dragons. "Are you truly willing to take me as well? And Etor if he returns before our departure?"

Dramour walked past Arc and began to undress outside. "I'm not carrying the elf." He shoved his clothing, boots, and eyepatch into his satchel, then handed the bag to Vahly, who'd followed him out. "I say we burn our way to King Mattin."

"There might be an army of elves there," Vahly said.

"And we'll make toast of the lot, leaving one to tell the story you need to hear."

Everyone gathered in front of the dark windows of the cider house. The smell of the ocean lurked in the occasional breeze.

Nix put a hand on Dramour, visibly calming him. "If there is an army of this kynd, we would be wise to use great caution. They can fire large arrows into the sky with great accuracy. We are only four dragons."

"So we're doing this?" Dramour's eye studied Nix's face, then he looked to Vahly.

"We are." Vahly tried to put more confidence into her voice than she actually felt.

With a flash of blue-orange fire, Dramour shifted.

Vahly jumped back as his wings unfurled, emerald under the moon. The scent of fire magic, sage-like, wafted through the air, accompanying the power's crackle and snap.

Nix pulled her dress off. "Yes, elf. We will carry you, but the horse is on his own. Vahly is taking the lead here. What she says goes." She tucked the dress, along with her rings and ruby necklace, into the bag Vahly held. Ibai and Kemen didn't even try not to stare at her lovely curves.

"Dramour," she said, "if you continue being rude to our elven guide, I'll never invite you to my quarters for conversation ever again."

Dramour growled quietly, but he bowed his head. Vahly was fairly certain he would mate for life if she asked. Of course, so would half the Breakers.

Arc whispered into the wind, presumably calling Etor again. Moonlight danced around his fingers as they twitched by his sides. He stood so straight, so sure of himself and who he was, and he didn't even remember why he'd left his homeland to go traipsing about in enemy territory. His fingers moved again, stirring light and shadow until Vahly was almost certain the shape of a horse had formed in front of him. The illusion disappeared before she could be sure, and then his fingers were still.

Nix raised her arms, ready to shift. "Wondering what he can do with those hands of his, Vahly?" Her laugh disappeared inside the fire she called up.

Vahly blinked in the sudden brightness, and when she opened her eyes, Nix was a battle dragon, complete with talons the size of Vahly's forearm, crystalline spikes from her brow to her tail, and starlit wings of a deep blue that was nearly the color of amethyst.

Ibai and Kemen shifted then too. Arc and Vahly took the three satchels of footwear, weapons, jewelry, and clothing.

"I never thought I'd ask a fully shifted dragon to please take me into their claws, but here goes," Vahly said to Arc.

Despite being so obviously ill at ease with everything

about this night, Arc smiled wryly. "It's not something I would've planned as a part of my evening either."

Nix's wings flapped, and she lifted from the ground. Her claws curled gently around Arc's middle, allowing his hands to be free to hold two of the satchels. She beat her wings with more force and flew into the sky.

Dramour rose next and took up Vahly. His claws were firm on the flesh around her ribs, but not overly painful, more of a cage to set feet and hands on than a tight grip. His wings whipped air around her face, tugging her hair from her braid and making it difficult to hold on to the one satchel she was in charge of. As they soared into the sky, she found she could put her feet on the lowest claw and easily look out over the highest talon.

They grouped close, the moon shining above, and headed toward the spiraling gases and golden rivers of the Fire Marshes.

CHAPTER TEN

T he ground flew by under Vahly's feet, the combination of moonlight and dragon wings casting disorienting shadows.

Golden threads of earthblood shot through the blackened ground, large boulders showed fragments of the old path, and thinly leafed bushes grew here and there—the only thing that could possibly grow in such an environment. Thin plumes of white smoke twisted into the air like spirits.

Vahly's throat burned with the vicious gases that the Fire Marshes put off, and a coughing fit pressed her ribs painfully against Dramour's hind claws.

Arcturus seemed well enough tucked away in Nix's careful grip. The wind flew through his jet hair as he glanced at Vahly, his face possibly showing concern, though it was difficult to tell in this light. She coughed again. The elf had no trouble with the gases and that made her pause. He had definitely struggled to breathe when she'd found him, stranded and barely conscious.

She determined to ask him about this when they took their first rest. If she could get her wounded throat to work. Too much time spent in this kind of air, and Vahly would be mute or dead, neither of which allowed for the questioning of elves or the saving of dragons.

"We should fly higher." Arcturus's voice rang out like a large bell. Was that also elven magic?

Vahly nodded in agreement although she wondered how much the air would improve. Surely they would have to travel quite high indeed to avoid these noxious fumes.

Nix turned her huge dragon body toward the heavens, capable of understanding everything going on between Vahly and Arcturus. The rest of the dragons followed suit, gaining altitude at a speed that took what little breath Vahly had. A chill permeated the air as they climbed, but Vahly did find she could breathe without coughing up here.

"Much better!" she called to Arcturus and Nix. Dramour growled, the sound vibrating Vahly's bones. "And thanks to you as well, Dramour." Vahly shook her head. Dragons.

They flew for hours before Nix gave her a look that said it was time to stop.

Squinting as they glided away from the stars and into that horrible miasma, Vahly spotted the place Nix had shown her on the map at the cider house. A stretch of earth, not marred by cracks or gases, spread out before the group. A line of impressively hardy bushes marked a natural boundary. Vahly thought perhaps it would be a good idea to gather leaves and stems from the bushes.

They could prove useful to Helena, if Vahly ever did make it home.

The only way to land without experiencing the full weight of a shifted dragon was for Nix and Dramour to open their claws and let Vahly and Arcturus fall to the ground. A clacking sort of growl sounded from Nix's throat, and Vahly took that as the signal to prepare for the drop.

Dramour's claws opened.

Vahly bent her knees and tucked her chin, rolling as the ground rushed up to meet her. Grit scraped her forearm and her knee bumped her cheek. But aside from that, she was well enough.

Arcturus was already on his feet—for all she knew, he'd landed that way. He extended a hand, but she hopped up and waved it away.

The dragons landed in a circle around them, breath puffing out and heavy feet shuffling.

Vahly gave Nix a bow. "Thank you, friend."

The dragons nodded in response, then settled down to soak in the energy the earthblood gave them. They spread their great wings over their bodies like the thin walls of a summer tent.

Nix's eyes glowed like coals through the translucent color of her wing.

Arcturus walked out of the circle of resting dragons, his gaze flicking from the way they'd come and toward his homeland. He adjusted the bow slung across his back and met her eyes. The first violet light of dawn seemed to gather around his temples and his long fingers. Placing the bag of Kemen and Ibai's clothing and footwear at his feet, he looked to the West. She wished he would have kept the eye contact, but she wasn't sure why.

"Rest if you like," he said, staying quiet and not disturbing their fellows.

"You don't need to take a break, do you?"

"Not yet."

The air bit at Vahly's throat and she coughed, touching the cheek she'd knocked during landing. It wouldn't be bad to be an elf, she thought, with skin nearly as strong as scales and energy to spare. Both physical traits would have served her well when fending off sea folk spears near the Jades' coastal territory or during the Jade-Lapis feuding that went on for months last year.

"May I ask you a question?"

"I love questions. I specialize in alchemical sciences so curiosity is key to my study. Plus, I owe you a life. The least I can do is satisfy your inquisitive mind. I might even beg an answer or two from you if you'd allow it."

This elf continued to surprise her.

"Why did the Fire Marshes' gases seem to bother you before, but now you're standing there like you're fresh from a pristine forest of dreams?"

The corner of his mouth lifted. "I am far from fresh." He held out his hands and dusted black grime from his fingers.

"But seriously. I could tell the air had injured your lungs."

"Only because of the foul spell one of my kynd placed on me. It hinders my healing." His lips tightened into a line. "It damaged my body as well as my mind. The bent magic sticks to my thoughts even now." He looked up, sincerity widening his hawk-like gaze. "I do hope it does not affect you. Or the others."

Vahly swallowed against the fire in her throat. "I feel nothing strange. Just the pain of being in this awful place. I think I'll take you up on that whole you guarding while I rest thing. I'm merely human and need a nap."

"You are not merely human. You are the epitome of human strength and capability." He gestured at her Blackwater mark.

"How many times do I have to explain this? I have no power. Not a blink of it. That's why I'm helping you get back home—so I can find out if your kynd know of any rituals my kynd used to perform to gain their magic."

"Forgive me. My mind remains hazy."

"No, forgive me. I shouldn't bark at you when you've been through so much. I apologize."

"Where were you born?"

"My family lived in what is now the Lost Valley. The Sea Queen flooded the area, but my mother held me up to Amona, the Lapis matriarch, before she was dragged under. Amona took me in, hoping I would save the dragons and balance the world. But so far, I'm not the creature they were counting on."

"But the dragons," he opened a palm in the direction of Nix, "they follow you. You do have power, Vahly. These would never listen to my commands nor my suggestions."

It was kind, the way he tried to make her feel

important. But it was unnecessary. They either would or would not find the answer to her questions in the Forest of Illumahrah. It made no difference what she felt about herself otherwise.

"I'm going to rest now."

Arc nodded. "As you wish."

Vahly made a pillow of Kemen's trousers and shirt, knowing the dragon wouldn't care as much as the other three if she dirtied his clothing on the ground. She closed her eyes, thinking there was no way she'd sleep here, half choking, but before she could form another thought, dreams took her away.

MIDMORNING LIGHT SEEPED through Vahly's eyelids, and she sat up quickly, panicked. "We should go," she tried to say. Most of it ended up as sputters and coughing. Her entire esophagus was a column of pain.

Arc was talking to Nix. He was apparently able to communicate telepathically with dragons.

His surcoat did indeed feature a half sun against a half moon and she wondered at his powers, the magic of air.

He glanced at Vahly and switched to speaking aloud, most likely for her benefit. "Yes, I do think we should stop closer to the boundary. It would be good if you were rested in the case that my welcome is less than positive."

Vahly stood and hacked up at least half a lung.

Ibai nudged the nearest satchel with his smoking snout. Vahly opened it to find a large water skin. Thank the Stones, Ibai had thought to bring it. Wincing, she managed five good gulps before pouring the rest down Ibai's throat.

"Leaving now, yes?" she croaked. "Because I'd like to be *not dead* when we finish this trip."

Nix gave a small roar to wake Kemen and Dramour, and after a few morning ablutions, they sailed into the golden sky.

VAHLY ENJOYED THE RIDE, breathing normally again. Her throat still throbbed along with the fingers she'd injured during her climbing and thieving escapades, but it was all so much better than being down there in that nasty mess of horrible.

Vahly's cheeks and ears grew numb from the wind buffeting her flesh. Her stomach growled too. At least she was standing in the comfort of claws. She snorted at herself. If only her kynd could see her now.

Did something entertain you? Arc said from Nix's clutches.

I didn't know elves could do this. Could speak telepathically.

We can. And no, I cannot read all of your thoughts. Only the ones you project to me like your previous question and phrase.

Arc's telepathy felt different from Amona's. Hers held a command, a force. Arc's words were simply communication.

Vahly wrapped her hand around Dramour's first claw. The ridges were like wood grain on an ancient tree. *All right. You can speak like a matriarch into my head. That's . . . unexpected, but not bad.* She took a deep breath. There were sure to be more surprises as this journey continued. *I was laughing because I feel better in the claws of a dragon than on the earth at the moment. Pretty ironic from someone who is meant to be an Earth Queen.*

Arc raised a black eyebrow. *No one could love that stretch of earth.* Arc eyed the smoke curling from the black ground below. *Even the fire kynd hate it.*

The dragons did gain strength from the earthblood. Vahly supposed that was why they hadn't needed to hunt. The proximity to the golden fire kept them going.

Well, too much of a good thing and all that, Vahly thought to Arc.

Our friends are no gluttons then.

Vahly felt herself grin and was surprised by it, considering the circumstances. *They are the finest dragons.*

Her own words also shocked her. She'd always said Amona was the best of dragons. But it was true. Nix, Ibai, Kemen, and Dramour had agreed to follow her despite their misgivings about elves. They'd been good to her and to Arc. Amona would not have done so. It was a safe bet to say the matriarch would have fried Arc the moment she laid eyes on him.

They share no bond with any matriarch. Arc's phrase held a question.

They refused the Call when it was offered, or broke it after the fact. They lay claim to the name Call Breakers *and act much like a clan themselves.*

But you are bonded with the Lapis.

I am. She could see the confusion in his graceful features, in the line of his strong brow and the narrowing of his eyes. It made sense that he wondered at the workings of this group and their split loyalty.

The veined ground of the Fire Marshes was slowly but surely fading into a greener landscape. Vahly was almost certain the movements she glimpsed far, far below were large rock lizards, creatures who could live on the edges of the marshes.

"I wonder..." Arc's voice startled her. She'd grown used to his voice inside her head. Nix had flown close to Dramour. Their wings fitted like puzzle pieces, and Arc was just behind Vahly, not too far away at all. "I wonder what the Lapis matriarch would think if she knew her human was soaring above the Fire Marshes and headed into enemy territory."

She ignored that comment. It was none of his business.

The synchronized movement of the dragons' wings mesmerized Vahly. The muscles and bones worked the leather-like skin. Sunlight passed through the emerald wing above her and made her feel like she was under the fresh water of the Silver River, peaceful and cool.

The idea of peace made her twist to face Arc. "Are the elves truly enemies of the dragons still? They've had no interaction in ages. Why have your kynd hidden away?"

The elf closed his eyes in obvious frustration, his head giving half a shake. He switched back to using telepathy. *I wish I could tell you, but that part of my mind is cloaked by the spell. It makes me rather curious about what I'll find upon my return.*

Well, tell me about yourself then. What does your average day look like?

Arc leaned back, resting on Nix. *I study alchemy. Specifically, I experiment with how magic interacts with gold. The research has wandered into the study of the four types of magic and how they might work together. Fire, Air, Earth, and Water.*

Vahly raised her eyebrows. *How do you experiment with magic you don't have?*

I simulate it in my laboratory. He bent forward. *Do you think perhaps Nix would be willing to help me by donating some dragonfire?*

Somehow I don't think asking for a dragonfire donation would be a great idea.

Arc's shoulders dropped, but then he laughed. *Good point. I'll wait until she trusts me. I appreciate candles, but I do not want to become one.*

Do you believe a dragon could ever trust an elf?

The concept has not been tested under these conditions, so we shall see.

Vahly grinned. *You are an optimist.*

I am an alchemist.

In the distance, a plateau reached from the end of the glowing, smoking marshes all the way to the isle's sea-foamed edges, along the western coast, covering the entire peninsula. Dramour and the rest soared closer to the ground, to better view the plains and the plateau.

The green of countless ancient oaks cloaked the stretch of raised land, miles upon miles of velvety color. The image stirred Vahly. Her feet itched to walk the legendary forest's ground, to smell the earth there—

A flash of black zipped past her ear.

Dramour jerked forward and down and nearly lost

hold of Vahly. Heart in her mouth, she gripped the dragon's claws and turned to see Nix spiraling out of the sky, a massive arrow shaft sticking out of the spot under her wing joint.

Dizzy, Vahly looked down.

Arcturus was a spot, falling, falling toward the earth.

CHAPTER ELEVEN

Vahly held on, gasping as Dramour banked left and dove toward Nix, Ibai at his side. The wind whistled in Vahly's ears as Dramour swooped under Nix and put a wing under her body. Ibai did the same on the other side. Then, extending the wings that weren't supporting Nix, they soared toward the earth. Vahly tried to see what happened to Arcturus. She assumed Kemen had gone after him, trying to catch him before he hit. They'd been roughly one hundred fifty feet in the air.

Could elves survive such a drop?

The world was a blur of green and gold and Vahly fell, rolling on the ground until she came to a stop, panting.

Dramour and Ibai shifted immediately, and Vahly shielded her eyes from the light before running forward to bring them the satchel with Ibai's medicinal items.

Nix lay on one side, chest shuddering. A massive arrow shaft sticking out of her side. Her wing sat at an angle that was all wrong. It was broken. The worst kind of injury for a dragon. Worse than the arrow.

Vahly was numb. Who had shot her? And why? Who even had arrows like that?

Ibai, naked, face drawn with worry, dumped the satchel and rummaged through their things. "Don't shift, Nix. The wound will be too large for your kynd form. Where is Kemen? Did he save the elf from the fall? He might be able to help here."

The scales around Dramour's temples and mouth paled. "It was his kynd that shot her! If he arrives safely with Kemen, I'll see that he learns what an arrow feels like under the arm."

But then Kemen was there, rushing toward the ground in a full dive. He shifted before he even hit, his magic crackling.

"Any sign of the elf?" Dramour asked him. "Splattered fancy blood? Please tell me he suffered."

"It's not anything Arcturus did," Vahly snapped.

"No sign of the elf." Kemen sounded more troubled than Vahly would have guessed he would be. He quickly pulled on his wrinkled clothing. "Vahly, you all right? That was a rough tumble."

Vahly's mind was finally catching up. "I'm fine. Thank you."

She hurried to Nix's side and put a gentle hand on her head. Nix's pain showed in her half-lidded eyes and the wrinkle between her eyes. The sun glinted off the glassy spikes near her ears and down her back.

"That was a bit dramatic, don't you think?" Vahly's voice cracked despite her determination to stay positive.

"If you wanted our attention, you could have just asked."

Nix's mouth lifted at the corners, showing white teeth the size of Vahly's hand. Moisture gathered at the edges of Nix's eyes before she shut them. Nix never cried. No matter the fight, the hurt, the loss. She joked and continued on. The tear that wove its way down Nix's snout before dropping into the tall, dry grass panicked Vahly more than the ruby red blood streaming from the wound or the cracked wing.

Ibai applied a greenish white poultice to Nix's wound, then joined Dramour and Kemen behind the broken wing, hands on their knees, studying how far in the arrow had gone.

"I think we should push it through," Dramour said. "Remember Baww's run in with the bald pine? Same spot."

Ibai clicked his green and blue mottled tongue against his teeth, his copper eyes over-bright. "I agree."

"Truly? Because you never agree with me." Dramour was trying to joke, Vahly could tell, but he also looked like he was about to vomit.

"I'll keep a watch out for Arcturus. And for any further company we might receive."

"Receive into our flaming maws," Dramour muttered, rage ringing through his words.

Vahly ignored the fact that her own bandages were hanging loose as she drew her short sword. A scant number of trees grew along the uneven ground; the land not quite free of the marshes' heat and poison fumes. The slender oaks spread deep green leaves to block a few rays

139

of the powerful sun. There were no paths here, no obvious sign of elves or any other highbeast.

If the elves could see well enough to hit Nix in one of her rare soft spots why hadn't they noticed their own kynd rode with her? Or had they actually aimed for Arcturus? He had, after all, been left in the Fire Marshes with his memory wiped and his magic dampened. Was this attack aimed solely at Arcturus or was this simply the age-old elf and dragon feud?

Vahly didn't know which truth to prefer. Neither helped Nix. Neither meant their entry into the Forest of Illumahrah would go smoothly.

A branch snapped in the distance. Vahly held her weapon at the ready.

She lifted her gaze to see the plateau where the elves' great forest thrived, but the surrounding trees and the slope of the land blocked her view. They were close though.

If a load of elven warriors rushed her, she was toast. Well, these weren't dragons, so maybe not toast. Perhaps more like a pincushion for their throwing knives.

A subtle breeze drifted by, tickling Vahly's cheek, and a tingling sensation touched her back like eyes were on her. She turned to see three elves walking out of the trees, one with an arrow nocked and aimed, two with knives drawn.

Fear tried to grip her arms and lock her down. Amona would not appear to save her here like she had so many times. Vahly lifted her sword and set her jaw. The vicious drive to live flooded her veins as it did during battles and feuds. Her body was used to the adrenaline rush, the fear, the counterbalance of courage.

"You shot down one of your own kynd. Did you realize that?"

The three looked somewhat like Arc, tall and ethereal in appearance, with pointed ears and that burnished skin that looked more like brushed metal than flesh. Their presence didn't shake Vahly like Arc's did though. Was that only because he had been the first elf she'd seen?

Her throat squeezed. She hoped he lived. Pushing panic to the back of her mind, she studied these potential enemies facing her.

The one with the bow had red hair like Nix, although the shade was more poppy than copper, a color she'd only seen in illustrations of elves. The first knife-wielder was thinner than Arc, less muscular in the arms and shoulders, while the second, a female, was far older, with silvery hair and wrinkles around her eyes and mouth. It had to take ages for an elf to show age. She must have been around when the Source brought the world into being.

"We have none missing. The dragons carried deer or some such kill." The female's gaze traveled the lines of Vahly's face. "The wind tells me you are what you cannot be."

None missing? Did they not know Arc? Elves only lived here, as far as Vahly knew. How could they not realize he was missing? Perhaps the same elf who had spelled Arc had spelled them too and their minds no longer held the memory of him.

The red-haired elf glanced at her. "What is she, old mother?"

The aged elf shifted her long legs and pointed a knife at Vahly. "Look at her forehead. Do you see the mark?"

The elves' eyes widened.

"She is an Earth Queen," the red head whispered, lowering his bow a fraction.

Vahly breathed in and out, keeping her wits about her. They could strike her down at any second. She longed to spill her tale and beg them for help. Nix and Arc could be dying right now.

"It can't be," the thin elf said. "All humans died."

Vahly made a show of sheathing her sword. It had to be her best bet. They hadn't killed her right away so there was a solid chance they would listen to reason. They were all on the same side. The Sea Queen was after the entire island—the only land left in all the world. She'd made that clear with her declaration. Vahly had read all about it in the dragons' scrolls.

"I'll tell you everything, but first, will you consider helping my friends heal?" she said, trying an angle that didn't involve the mention of an elf they couldn't remember. "You shot them down."

The red-haired elf gave a shrug. "Well, only a human would befriend a dragon so at least that much rings true. Maybe she is what she seems to be?"

Vahly smeared a hand across her Blackwater mark. "No magic could make this."

The old mother nodded and jerked her pointed chin toward Nix. "We are no friends to dragons, but since you are what you are, we will consider it."

Nix's eyes were closed when Vahly escorted the three elves into the clearing. Vahly's heart constricted at the sight of her friend, lying there in a pool of blood. Tears burned her eyes.

Ibai and Dramour had clothed themselves while she was gone. Dramour held a cloth against Nix's wound while Ibai and Kemen worked to bind Nix's broken wing to a tree branch. Nix's breath shuddered in and out as they approached.

Ibai froze. "Vahly?" he said, not turning to see them. He had smelled them.

Dramour turned his head to look, then drew his blade, keeping one hand on Nix. "Which one wants to die first for this crime?" he snarled. "I'll be merciful to the first. The second two, not so much."

Murder filled Kemen's face, but the dragon stayed where he was, where Nix needed him.

Vahly heartily approved of their fervor, but the end game was what mattered here. "Dramour. Stand down, please. They are here to mend what they have broken as best they can."

Ibai's face was icy when he did finally turn. "Why would you do that?" His slitted eyes focused on the red-haired elf.

The old mother spoke up. "Because she is an Earth Queen. And I thought we had no chance of seeing another."

Some of the fire left Ibai's glare. He stepped around, took Dramour's place, then explained Nix's injuries.

Dramour kept a hand on his hilt as he walked to Vahly. "Did you find Arcturus? Is he good and dead?"

"Dramour. I want him alive. And no. I should go look for him, but I can't leave Nix. This is awful."

"I'll go with you if it's what you want, Vahly. Don't they," he jerked his chin at the elves, "want to help us look for their own kynd? Did they say why they shot at Nix considering she was carrying one of theirs?"

"They thought we were deer."

Dramour coughed a laugh.

"Shut up."

"Sorry." Dramour held out his hands, smiling sadly. "So much for elves having good vision, eh?"

"I think someone spelled their minds too. They don't even remember Arc."

The elves had removed all bandaging and splinting. They placed their hands on Nix and whispered words in elvish. Their lips moved quickly and their own flesh seemed to glow in the rising sunlight. Small globes like tiny suns bloomed around their fingertips before soaking into Nix's body.

The sound of wind in the trees echoed like music the day had just remembered. Vahly thought the rushing might have been related to their magic. The dragons' magic crackled like fire and lightning. Perhaps each type of power had its own sound.

Ibai stood back, his mouth pulled into a grimace and his kynd form wings shivering every so often like he was trying to shake a burr off. A low growl rumbled in the back of Kemen's throat. They truly did hate one another.

Nix's eyes opened briefly and Vahly dared to hope.

Could they actually heal her?

She realized she'd left Dramour and was standing right beside Nix's head. "Be well, my friend. I can't run that cider house for you, you know, and if you leave it to Dramour, he'll gamble all the house winnings away in a day."

Tears leaked from Vahly's eyes then. She couldn't hold them back anymore.

Ibai let out a short roar and the elves lurched back, weapons aimed in a blur of movement. Ibai bowed his head and tucked his wings in submission. "I was only registering glad surprise, friends."

Dramour's mouth hung open. "Never thought I'd see the day Ibai submitted to elves."

There was a flash of fire, then Nix was sitting on the ground in her human-like form. Her face was paler than Vahly had ever seen it and blood still flowed from a small gash in her side. Her injured wing hung at a poor angle, but no bone showed.

Ibai and Kemen rushed to wrap both her injuries again. Ibai's hands lingered for a moment on Nix's shoulder, a subtle show of deep feeling.

When Nix was ready, Vahly helped her up. "Never thought I'd see the day elves saved my life."

Heart full to bursting, Vahly looked from elf to elf. "Thank you for your work."

"She isn't fully healed. Not at all," the old mother said. "That wing will take a long time to mend and she has lost a great deal of blood."

"Now, we need to find the other friend of ours you shot down."

"Another human?" the thin elf asked.

Should she lie? Yes, perhaps this was a good time for lying. "Yes."

The old mother tilted her head. She definitely wasn't buying what Vahly was selling, but the group followed Vahly quickly enough when she started out of the clearing and toward the area where she guessed Arc had landed.

Vahly looked to Nix and Ibai, who were working Nix's dress on, the wing-slash buttons glinting in the sun. "We will return shortly to figure out a way to transport you, Nix."

Dramour spoke quietly with Nix, and she nodded before he joined Vahly and the elves.

A stand of beech trees led them to a rippling creek of fresh water. Vahly followed the creek up a small rise and tried to listen for Arc's voice.

But there was no need.

Arc walked around a silver-gray tree trunk and held his hands out, unarmed.

Once again, his presence hit Vahly like a strong drink. Her skin tingled with the knowledge that he was near and a completely ridiculous desire to bow her head—a subtle movement, like an acknowledgement—came over her.

If she looked out of the corner of her eye, she could see movement around him. Swirling rays of light in sunset orange, midday yellow, and sunrise violet danced with purple-tinged shadows around his cheeks, hands, and head. His eyes were pools of glittering black, and they touched Vahly with a look she felt in her chest.

"Thank the Source." Vahly bent over, putting her hand

on her knees to support herself. She let the worst of her fear wash over her. He was alive. This kind elf who had agreed to help her. This good elf who had been wronged and sought to do what he could to aid Vahly and her dragons despite his own problems.

"Do you not know me, Vega?" The pain on Arc's face as he looked at the old female elf cut Vahly more sharply than she would have guessed it could. "You knew my mother…" Shoulders dropping slightly, he turned to the red-haired elf. "Leporis? I taught you how to use that bow one hundred years ago. And Pegasi? When did King Mattin assign you to this post? I congratulate you on completing your training. It is Arcturus, my kynd. Please, try to remember."

Vega's forehead wrinkled and she lowered her knives. "Arcturus, you say?"

Arc moved his hair away from his ears to show his points. "Yes." The smooth column of his throat dropped as he swallowed.

"Some magic has been done here." Pegasi's young voice was almost a whisper, distrust breaking the syllables at odd points. His black eyes, a match to Arc's, were wide as platters as he studied the light and dark curling around Arc, a sight that Vahly could barely see.

"Yes, Pegasi." Arc's tone curled around the name like a protective hand. The young elf was obviously important to him. "I was there when your dear parents birthed you. Your father, Rigel, swiftest elf in all of Illumahrah, traversed the entire forest in four days to tell everyone of your arrival."

A sad smiled painted Arc's mouth, and Vahly had to

go to him. She took his arm and looked him over, eyeing him for wounds. She wouldn't have been surprised if he had a pine tree sticking out of his back.

"Are you well?" she asked Arc, trying to remain calm as she turned her back to the other elves. *Please don't shoot me in the back*, she thought silently, glancing at them. *Or begin a raging battle with Dramour or Arc or both.* "The fall didn't injure you? That seems impossible."

But he didn't appear hurt. Well, he did have a cut on the side of his head that was leaking blood, but it was a minor injury.

Arc spoke and his words stirred Vahly's hair. His eyes held sincerity and amusement. "I'm well and thank you for your concern, Earth Queen."

She raised her head. His mouth was close and his presence hummed in her blood. What would his lips taste like?

"Of course." She stepped back and released his arm.

"I caught the wind on my way down and was able to find a tree."

"Wait. You can fly?"

"Elves do not fly." Vega had her knives out still, but she didn't have them up or aimed at anyone. "We use the wind to lessen a drop."

Arc touched his minor head wound and light spooled from his fingers. He was healing himself.

"No, we do not fly. And we do not use foul magic to deceive one another. That would never happen in Illumahrah. Never. I do not believe this elf's tale." Vega flicked her fingers.

Everything happened at once.

A blinding pain crashed through Vahly's shoulder. She dropped.

Dramour blasted dragonfire somewhere behind her.

Shouts and grunts rose into the air as Vahly rolled to her uninjured side. She worked her sword out, glad the arrow had stuck her in her left shoulder instead of her right.

Leporis, poppy-red hair loosed from its tie, stood over Arc, who had gone to his knees. Leporis spoke in elvish.

"Because we cannot fight the entire elven army and have no wish to," Arc said in dragon with a meaningful glance at Vahly. "We simply need to speak with the King."

Vega had Dramour on the ground, a knife pricking the side of his remaining eye. "If you want to lose the second, try that on me again," Vega said. A bright red burn showed on her forearm.

Dramour glared at Vahly. "Still think this is a good idea?"

Kemen roared in frustration, his talons flashing in the sunlight as he flexed and paced in front of Pegasi and the young elf's shining blades.

Vahly shivered in the grip of pain. "It was a long shot. You know how I enjoy winning against terrible odds."

Pegasi lifted Vahly like she was nothing more than a sack of feathers, and the odd burning cold of a bad injury smashed through Vahly's shoulder. She gritted her teeth and threw her focus elsewhere.

Why didn't these other elves have the strange lights around them like Arc did?

Vega and her cronies walked Vahly, Arc, Kemen, and

Dramour back to where Nix and Ibai waited. The two stood as they approached, smoke billowing from their nostrils.

Leporis gripped Arc by the hair and forced his chin high. Arc's white teeth showed in a wince, but he didn't fight the hold the other elf had on him.

"If you want them to remain alive," Leporis said, "you will come peacefully and allow us to bind you. Only then will you get a word with our King. If not, we will cut these deeply, here and now, then take our chances fighting you to the death as well."

Nix put a hand on Ibai's chest, holding him back. "We agree." Her gaze found Vahly and her lips tucked up in concern. "Although I'm certain King Mattin will simply kill us in a way that is far more creative and painful, we agree."

Pegasi tucked his knives away and snapped the arrow shaft protruding from Vahly's shoulder.

Sweat poured from her face. Pain—burning, consuming—dropped her to the ground.

"We will leave the injured dragon here. She is no threat and we can return if we so choose after speaking to our King," Leporis said.

With quick hands, Pegasi turned Vahly over, cut a slash into her shirt, and then reached inside with chilled fingers to pluck the arrowhead and remaining wood from Vahly's body.

The pain drew curtains over Vahly's consciousness.

CHAPTER TWELVE

R yton led Grystark and a host of sea folk around the northeastern tip of Tidehame. They swam hard, fins slicing through the rough, cold waves, the water pulling at their hair, seaweed clothing, and sharpened coral spears. The ocean was a cacophony of booming spellwork shouted by one of many companies Venu oversaw. The smell of magic pricked at Ryton's gills, masking the other scents of oily breaker fish and the earthblood vents that released bubbles beyond the field of battle.

Their goal today was to extend the flood to the Jades' hunting grounds.

The Watcher had suggested the attack, and Ryton was pleased. This plan didn't call for Ryton's closest friend, Grystark, to lure Jades toward the Blackwater well. The Watcher's strategy was still dangerous, but not as insane.

All cherished the Watcher, an ancient, gnarled female. She could See events in the past, present, and future, making her an invaluable resource in the war. The Watcher had told Queen Astraea that the Jades were the second worst threat to sea folk's power. Ryton and his army had to curtail the Jades' reproduction through direct culling during attacks and by diminishing their ability to find meat. If allowed to thrive, the Jades would destroy all of his kynd's Blackwater sources and drive Astraea and her kin into oblivion.

As to the foremost threat to the sea folk, the Watcher claimed that Fate still shrouded that danger.

Now, a host of Jades flew above the surface, their shadows dark and sinuous among the waves, their flaming maws rippling with fire magic that burned Ryton's gills even as he swam ten feet underwater. Ryton had no more time for thinking of the mysterious threat the Watcher could not yet name.

The Jades were here and he had to fight them now.

"To the right!" he called to Blue Unit. "Spell with speed and accuracy!"

Grystark took off with Blue, as planned, and threw Ryton a nod as he did. He truly hoped that wouldn't be the last he'd see of his old friend.

Ryton kicked and rose, the Silver, Green, and Gold units behind him. A moment before breaking through the waves, they spoke their spells into their weapons, for once they surfaced they'd have no oxygen to shout into air. With their spears, they could throw twenty square feet of spelled water at the dragons. Aside from an expert spear throw to the few sensitive spots on a dragon, water magic was the only way to take the beasts down.

"Touch the sea and turn the tide," Ryton said to his spear. It hummed at his side as he swam up and up and up. *"Water spelled for breaking. Teeth of salt for tearing."*

The rushing, boiling sound of water magic grew louder.

Those beside and behind him spoke the same spells, pushing their will into the spears, using the magic that flowed through their veins. Gills flaring along the sides of their necks, nostrils expelling water, they focused on their approach.

Ryton broke the surface.

Two hundred, maybe more, green dragons flew through the storm-black sky. They shouted in their usual manner, a brutal, guttural sound like a rhythmic growl. The salty air lashed Ryton's cheeks and lightning ripped the sky in two. He raised his jagged spear and threw a column of spelled salt water at the nearest Jade, a large battle dragon with a deep green belly that rumbled with the warning of dragonfire, his fire magic snapping and crackling.

The Jade blasted flames at Ryton just as the spelled water hit the dragon's throat and left wing. Ryton leaped and dove underwater to avoid the fire, his muscles quaking with the effort.

The dragonfire boiled through the leaping waves, its raging orange flames like claws tearing into the sea. The magical fire spread across the surface like a slice of the sun had fallen.

Immediately rising and breaking the surface again, Ryton watched as his magic worked on the vicious beast.

The dragon roared, crashed into one of his allies as the lighting cracked again, then in a circular blaze of flame, transformed into his weaker state before smashing into the sea.

To be sure the dragon was dead, Ryton dove after the beast. It thrashed, bleeding into the water, hair tangling where spikes used to be.

The dragon shouted, face tight with pain, bubbles rising from his mouth. "The Earth Queen rises—"

A spear through the gut cut off his water-muted words. The sea clouded, red and thick, around him.

Grystark swam around the body, yanked the spear free, and nodded to Ryton before shouting commands to his companions.

Ryton shook off his confusion at the dragon's dying words. There was no time for that now. He shouted orders for Silver and Gold to form a line. "Draw up the water!" he called through the tumultuous sea.

The units did as ordered and soon the sea was heaving.

"More!" Ryton added his own will and magic to the force, glad he'd stopped by the Source well before the fight to wash in the salt water-Blackwater mixture that gave all sea folk their power. The magic tugged at his forehead and palms, drawing the energy he'd pulled from the well and throwing it into the rising tide.

The sea folk's power rose to a manic thrum, sounding like the crash of countless waves on endless rocks.

Ryton thrust his spear, and the ocean twisted above his head—a force that uprooted the seaweed from its bedding, shoved the lesser coral and rock into a spinning frenzy, and pulled at Ryton's own beard as it heaved and rushed at the Jades' coastline. Ryton and Grystark raced to the surface to witness the devastation.

Frothing waves sped under the wheeling, fire-breathing dragons and their lightning storm, and then smashed into the rocky shore. The highest of the waves grabbed a score of Jades and thrust them into the depths.

The water crashed over the trees and flooding into the hunting grounds.

Dragons keened and listed away from the successive waves to avoid being caught. One closest bore the blackened marks of spelled water up and down her side. She would die before the sun set on this day and Ryton thrilled to see it.

The trees disappeared under the foam, as did the hills and the sweeping vista of rocky, grassy ground.

Ryton's gills burned. He needed to get back underwater. Grystark pounded a fist into the air, leaping high, his legs thrashing in the sea to lift him.

Then both dove deep along with their companies. The waters of Tidehame enveloped them in salty arms, already healing tired bodies and mending wounds delivered by dragonfire. Those burns were not easily soothed. The fire from a dragon's mouth had a persistent, deadly heat to it, but the sea could ease that pain when one was not too badly burned.

Ryton's mind turned over the fallen Jade's final words. *The Earth Queen rises!* He had called out in sea folk language. The dragon had meant for Ryton and the others to hear it and understand the threat.

But there were no more humans. Ryton's own uncle

had helped flood what the land creatures now called the Lost Valley, known to his own as the Tristura Sea. They had killed every last human.

Ryton shook his head as he joined with his warriors to swim back and report to Astraea. That Jade dragon had only been trying to unsettle the sea folk with his falsehood. It was nothing. The Jades were obviously growing desperate. They were losing and they knew it.

Ryton smiled wickedly. And they didn't even know the worst of it yet.

Three moon cycles past, Ryton had discovered an underwater tunnel that ran the length of the island, from the North, winding under the land and opening outside the Lapis territory. It had taken weeks to navigate and they'd lost two good folk in the effort, but it was well worth the challenge.

With today's major victory for the sea folk, the dragons would unite. They would be foolish not to. Ryton would command the armies of the sea to attack the Jades once more. The fight would draw the Lapis, and then, when most battle dragons were up north, Ryton would lead the Sea Queen's full forces through the tunnel. Without much resistance, they would focus all their power on raising the water and smothering the southern side of the isle with the multiplied salt water.

It would be the end of land and the war.

He couldn't wait for it all to be over.

With the dragons defeated and the world swaddled in salt water, surely Astraea would be satisfied. She would no longer demand the whale's share of Ryton's waking hours. There would be peace, calm waters, time to travel and to dine with Grystark and his wife Lilia. Perhaps even time enough for Ryton's heart to heal so he could consider searching for a mate and creating a family of his own.

That was all he wanted. Quiet days in the sun-touched shallows of the far South, a net of fermented sea apples at his side, and the chance to laugh with a friendly female. His skin prickled as he imagined the warmth of the waters on his face and the caress of a gentle, female hand. Could he find someone with a lovely voice that didn't twist him up with words that sounded like praise wrapped in barbs?

He would be free. If they could just end this Blackwater-forsaken war, he would be free of the Sea Queen, free of the fight, free to find a life worth living.

QUEEN ASTRAEA'S GUARDS, dressed in finer sea cloth than Ryton would ever want to wear, moved away from the entrance to her private chambers as Ryton and Grystark approached.

The queen lounged on a couch of woven salt tulip leaves beneath a bank of glowing nautili, gathered upon their death near Scar Chasm where most of the sea folks's illuminating decor originated. Pearls sparkled in Astraea's braided hair as she tipped her head in greeting.

"I heard we were successful," she purred.

"Yes, my queen," Grystark said. "And the water doesn't seem to be receding from the area either. We now control the northwestern swathe of Jade hunting grounds."

"Ryton, how do you propose we flood the upper reaches, to the East?"

"I don't know if we can, but we'll get the entire area surrounded and won't leave enough land to hunt or survive. We will conquer. And soon."

A smile slid over the queen's lips. "That's what I like to hear. Why don't you stay and keep me company, Ryton? We can let old Grystark here return to his beautiful wife. Give her my love, won't you?"

Grystark looked to Ryton, silently asking if he wanted an excuse to leave.

"What are you looking at him for, Grystark?" The queen rose, her webbed toes a few inches from the sea floor. Eddies pulled sand up and around her tiny ankles. "Get out."

But Grystark stood his ground. She could have him put to death for this kind of disobedience. Ryton had to defuse the situation.

He slapped Grystark on the back. "His head is jumbled, my queen. Took a hard hit today. Please excuse our good general."

Grystark pursed his lips, but went along with the ruse. "Apologies, my queen. High General." He bowed to each in turn, then swam away, giving Ryton one last look before leaving.

He was a great friend, to risk his own life to make certain Ryton was all right. Of course, Ryton wasn't wholly all right with the situation. Far from it. But he could deal with Astraea's advances a little longer.

She only wanted him for his military abilities.

He was not the best-looking male in the sea.

Soon, the war would end and Ryton would be free. There was no need to anger her and risk Grystark's neck as well as his own and whoever else happened to get in the way.

Though he truly longed for bed and sleep, Ryton crossed the room to make the queen a net of fermented tideberries. He uncorked the conch she kept on her coral shelves and then shook six perfect berries into a small net of purple threaded seaweed. Holding them out, he smiled politely.

"Don't give me that look," she cooed before nibbling a berry from its trap.

Ryton rubbed her shoulders. "What look?"

"The one that says you are only here because I bid you to be."

He kept his gaze on his feet and rubbed his neck. "I'm your servant, my queen."

"You are so much more. You are the key to unlocking the treasure of ultimate power. Don't belittle yourself with the term *servant*. It doesn't suit you."

"What does suit me?" His stomach twisted.

"Champion. Conqueror. Blood-spiller."

Ryton was glad she had her back turned because he had difficulty hiding the wince. When had he started wincing at the violence of his life? It seemed like yesterday he'd been more than willing to *slay the day away*, as Grystark and he always put it.

"I haven't conquered yet."

"*Yet.* It will come to pass. And I'd like to be at the front with you when it does. What do you think of that?" She turned under his hands, her skin warm, supple, and shimmering in the dark water.

He studied the slant of her mouth, the edge to her teeth as she bit her lip. "I think you'll do just fine," he said, his voice tight.

She laughed loudly at that, then kissed his ear, taking time to nip the lobe. Moving so that her body lined up with his, she stared into his eyes like she might cast some unheard of spell with only her piercing gaze. He hated Astraea, but he admired her too. If anyone could do such spellwork, it would be her. Running her hands up his bare chest, she grinned. He couldn't hide the chills of pleasure.

Maybe he did love her. He kissed her soundly on the mouth, tasting the tideberries' sour bite. As usual, he forgot about what he should be feeling or what he wanted out of life. He simply fell into their routine and let her drown him in the sense of touch.

Until the words of the Jade dragon flashed through his memory.

He needed to talk to her about what he'd heard of the Earth Queen. But surely it was only the dragon's ruse, a bluff to get one over on them. Surely it was nothing. And if he brought it up now, Astraea would keep him in her chambers the rest of the night, going over strategy and the details of her deal with the King of the elves.

No, he would keep quiet for now, he thought as he bid her goodnight and swam off to his home on the outcropping near Scar Chasm. He could not have stayed alert for another night of endless plotting.

Chasing an errant shark from his front door with a wave of his spear and a touch of tide magic, Ryton took to his home and shut the door on the war if only for a few hours.

CHAPTER THIRTEEN

Vahly woke and thought, yes, perhaps she had died.

No, the pain was still there. Definitely there.

So why was the world like a dream? Beams of golden light drifted through a canopy of oak leaves to touch the exposed roots of trees larger than any she ever could have imagined. Larger than two dragons wide, these oaks spread their limbs over a gently undulating ground of curling ferns, bronze-hued flowers, and carpets of moss thick as winter wool. The air held the scent of sage, mint, and sun-warmed leaves, and despite the pain in her shoulder, drew her into a peace that sang through her bones and told her that all would be well.

She breathed the place in, taking in the smell of forest earth, black and full of last year's autumn. If it weren't for the gaping wound, she'd have been happy to stay in that spot, lying on the ground for eternity.

"Vahly?" A deep voice spoke behind her.

She turned her head, nose swiping a clutch of tiny mushrooms, to see an elf. Something stirred in the back of her mind. She knew him. Didn't she?

"I'm Arcturus. You're Vahly. We came here to find out how you can rouse your powers as Earth Queen. Do you remember? Are you hurting too badly? I don't know why we're here, on the forest floor, beyond the court and alone. I don't recall the circumstances. But I have a mighty knot on my head and I'm guessing we were injured on our way here. I think I came to find you…"

Vahly thought about sitting up, then decided against it when pain lanced through her shoulder. "Yes," she croaked. "You came for me. I found you in the Fire Marshes."

A shock ran through her. She was speaking elvish.

"How am I speaking elvish? I grew up with…" She tried to finish the thought. "I grew up with dragons. Yes, dragons."

Arcturus smiled and put his large, strong hands on Vahly's wound. "You did, yes. And you learned elvish in your studies as a child."

"Of course. Yes."

"I'm trying to heal you, but my own injuries limit me."

He closed his eyes. It was only then Vahly noticed how their outer edges tilted upward slightly and the way a pale purple hue tinged his eyelids. She imagined if she ran a fingertip over the sensitive skin there, it might feel like velvet.

Then his magic began to work.

Pinpricks of heat skipped along Vahly's wound, the sensation oddly pleasant. She looked down, moving her shirt and the edge of her vest aside. The wound was closed, but the skin remained puckered and sensitive to touch.

"Thank you, Arc. The pain is no longer screaming *Toss this human off the nearest cliff please and be done with it.*"

Arc chuckled, a low sound that suited his good nature. "You lost a great deal of blood." He helped her up. "You'll still need to take it easy. We'll hurry to the court and someone there will complete your healing."

"Good plan."

He placed a hand on her arm, and the gentle, intimate brush of his thumb over her wrist threatened to overwhelm her. Her breath hitched.

"You can also ask King Mattin all your questions." Arc paused, his brow furrowing. Pieces of sunlight and small, violet shadows swam around his head and fingers. "I remembered something."

She shook off her strange feelings. This was progress. "Good! What?"

"I'm the King's cousin."

"So you are a royal." He looked the part with his strong features and powerful build.

Ferns and various types of grasses covered the forest floor. Vahly bent to run her fingers over a light green grass soft as feathers. As they walked, the ground rose subtly. Arc held Vahly so she didn't fall when she stumbled, because she was still lightheaded. A circle of shimmering mushrooms and slender flowers gave way to a sandy path of flagstones bordered by what appeared to be an herb garden. Lavender bushes taller than Vahly boasted purple buds, mint reached over earthen pots, and pale yarrow flowered between patches of sturdy rosemary and dusky sage.

Orbs of light floated over the plants, edging every leaf in gold.

It was so lovely that Vahly's pain faded to the back of her mind again.

The path turned beneath more towering oaks. The greenery was so thick, it was like being inside a cave, yet the light was nothing like a cave. Soft and bright at the same time, it limned Arc's hand and forearm as he helped her along. If she'd thought he was beautiful before, now he was beyond words. This was truly his home, where he belonged, and his magic-suffused flesh and bone shone with the truth of it.

"The garden. It's perfect." She paused to pluck a sprig of lavender and inhaled the pure scent. "How do you keep the sunlight here, like this?"

The spheres of light over the garden floated on the breeze like soap bubbles. The outer surface of each orb was clear as glass and each one held a shining sun of its own inside. Once in a while, the contained, sunny luminescence shifted slightly. Miniature rays hit the glassy barrier before scattering into a crowd of tiny, golden stars.

Arc's eyes sparkled, and he graced Vahly with a genuine smile. "Watch this."

He lifted the arm that wasn't holding her up, his muscles churning beneath his seemingly polished skin, and his fingers moved in a pattern that reminded Vahly of braiding. The purple shadows around his thumb and index finger expanded like spilled ink. The tendrils spun through the air, slow and sure, until the shadows from his thumb met up with the ones from his finger. The light faded behind this weave of darkness, and suddenly twilight had descended onto the ancient forest.

Vahly gasped, taken aback by this strange magic. She reached for the mint, beyond where the weaving had stopped, but the plant joined them in the sphere of twilight, or rather, the darkness expanded to include it. Even the insects chirruped inside their nighttime.

"Would you like to embrace the day again?" Arc's eyebrow lifted. He seemed to be enjoying this power of his.

He spread his hands and the purple shadow of near dark reversed itself, drawing back into his thumb and forefinger. Pinpoints of illumination spun from his fingers then and suffused the air. The twilight fled, and in its place, the warmth and ease of sunlight blanketed Vahly's shoulders and head.

She pointed to the half moon, half sun image on his surcoat before continuing their progress, this time on her own and without his aid. "I'm beginning to understand this. What else can you elves manage with your mysterious magic?"

"We hold the power of air and so the wind sometimes speaks to us, tells us stories. If I were wholly well, I could work the wind and ask it to carry me a good distance."

"Great. I'm the only highbeast on land who cannot fly."

"And the only one capable of keeping the rest of us alive to do the flying."

"We'll see."

Arc nudged her gently with an elbow. "During our journey here, you claimed to enjoy making bets. Care to wager on yourself?"

A laugh bubbled out of Vahly. "I'll do that." It was a dark joke, but funny all the same. "I bet one piece of lapis lazuli stone the length and breadth of my palm. Now what exactly are we betting on regarding me?"

The corner of Arc's mouth lifted as he watched the path wind eastward under their feet. "That you will wake your magic and become a true Earth Queen." He met her gaze then, eyes full of mischief, and held out his forearm. "I believe in you."

Vahly rolled her eyes to hide how much his statement touched her. "But if I'm betting on myself, then you'd be betting against me."

"It's not what I would choose," he said, "but someone must spur you to cheer yourself onward. We will make a heart promise of this bet."

"You'd risk your life on a bet? I knew there was a reason I like you."

Arc gripped her forearm.

"Fine," she said, agreeing. "I promise to pay you one lapis lazuli stone the length and breadth of my palm if I don't manage to wake my powers."

He repeated his own version of the promise.

She returned the hold, curling her fingers around his arm. The tingle and sizzle of a promise made warmed her heart.

She held two now.

Both simmered there, deep inside, and if she broke them, they would sear their way into the organ that pumped her Touched blood through her veins and kill her in seconds.

But she couldn't remember what the other promise involved.

Her palms began to sweat.

"Arcturus. I made another promise. I can feel it." Her fingers tapped her upper ribs where the oath sat waiting. "I can't recall anything about it." She shook her head, the ground unsteady beneath her boots.

"You must've made an oath to the matriarch who raised you."

Yes. Amona. Her mysterious injury and the blood loss truly had messed with her head. She'd completely forgotten about Amona.

Breathing slowly to dispel panic, she walked beside Arc and focused on the fact that she would soon get the answers she needed to save Amona and the rest of the Lapis from the Sea Queen.

"How do you think I received this wound? It almost looks like I angered an archer."

Arc nodded. "I don't understand it either. Perhaps you fell from a precipice and landed on a broken tree limb? My mind can't bring it forward. But we'll be at the court soon and we'll get all of our answers from my kynd."

Vahly forced herself to be content for the moment. It wasn't like she had a choice.

The canopy of great oaks clustered even more thickly and shadowed an area bordered by vines. Slim white flowers graced the trailing vines and tangled at the foot of what appeared to be a high-backed throne. The throne looked as though it had simply grown out of the towering oak above it. The tree's gnarled limbs cascaded inward to form a seat.

The light and shadow shifted. A male elf sat on the throne.

CHAPTER FOURTEEN

The elf on the throne had hair that fell to his shoulders, similar in length to Arc's. Eyes like a falcon's stared from his face. His features, sharp as cut stone, twitched at their arrival. A crown woven of tiny, brilliant suns and coiling purple-gray fingers of darkness twisted, ever-moving, around the elf's head. His expression gave absolutely nothing away.

Vahly's first thought was that he would be fabulous at cards. Her second was that this elf had a presence similar to Arcturus. Her skin buzzed as they approached the throne and her stomach dipped like she had leaped off a ledge.

Arc bowed, an arm against his trim stomach. "My King, my cousin."

Vahly echoed the demonstration of submission. "King Mattin."

Twenty or more elves shimmered into view around the dais and throne of tree roots. All were tall and elegant, glowing and beautiful, but none increased that simmering beneath her skin. It seemed one had to have royal elven blood to cause such a reaction in a human. She wondered at the purpose. Was it the magic in their veins calling to her?

A whip-thin female with a head full of thick, pale tresses hurried to greet Arc. She touched his shoulder and smiled like a sister. "Arc. My friend. I'm so glad you are alive."

"Cassiopeia." Arc kissed her on both cheeks.

A shorter elf with acorn-brown hair approached, hands held out. "I knew you had not lost your mind and wandered away. Not our Arcturus." He patted Arc on the back with a force that would probably have brought Vahly to her knees, but merely jostled Arc.

"I hope you didn't injure yourself searching for me, Haldus."

A group of elves calling themselves *elders* came forward dipping their silver, black, and brown heads in greeting.

One barrel-chested male elder smiled at Vahly, but his eyes were cautious and wise. "I look forward to hearing your story, Arcturus."

"Thank you, General Regulus," Arc answered.

The king stood in one quick, graceful movement. "Arcturus. We had thought you dead."

He rushed forward and clasped both of Arc's forearms. Mattin was a few inches shorter than Arc, but they both seemed capable of strong magic. Their fingers and head displayed those barely visible tendrils and pinpoints of shadow and light that were becoming familiar to Vahly.

She knew now how to tip her head and glance at the play of day and night around them to see it more clearly. Her eyes fought to slide off the sight of it, but she kept her attention divided and beat the magic at its game.

The king, resplendent in a silver tunic embroidered with a black half sun, half moon on his chest, returned to his throne, and then accepted a ruby-encrusted goblet from an elf standing to his right.

This king's assistant, or whatever he was, had white-gold hair and a smile like a red wound in his otherwise lovely face.

He was the first elf that got Vahly's hackles up.

But he was an elf. With Blackwater in their very blood, they were inherently good, right? Despite what the dragons thought of them, and the feuds they'd had with the Lapis, elves weren't evil. Arrogant, unyielding, possibly in error when they came up against the dragons at some points in history, but they weren't evil. Except this one elf's presence screamed *I like to cut throats*.

Did Arc feel that way about his king's right hand too? Arc's gaze traveled over the elf in question and his eyes cooled. So yes. Arc was aware of the foul energy that one was giving off.

"Thank you, Canopus," the King said as he flipped the ends of his long-sleeved tunic out of the way and took his seat. "Now, please, Arcturus. Tell us where you have been and who this is."

"Forgive me for not asking for help," Arc said. "The wind told me an unbelievable story. I had thought to prove it true before risking more of my kynd to the dragons' wrath. The wind spoke of a surviving human and that the individual was Touched. This was the tale of the rising Earth Queen, Vahly of the Lapis."

Canopus hissed at the name of the dragon clan. "She is a human? But bonded to dragons? This is foul magic."

He would know, Vahly thought wryly. There was definitely something off about that one. "I have no foul magic," she said. "I have no magic at all, in fact. And that's why I'm here." She rubbed a hand over her Blackwater mark to show the gathered elves that she was indeed as Arc claimed.

"The idea that there might be hope for us in the fight against the sea thrilled me," Arc said. "I headed out to find Vahly, but fell to the evils of the Fire Marshes. The Earth Queen found me though my horse was lost. She believes we have information that will help her find her powers. We headed back, but were injured again along the way, although I can't tell you how for the combination of whatever head injury and noxious gases the marshes inflicted upon us has tampered with our minds. I can't seem to heal myself or Vahly completely."

"Allow me." Cassiopeia set her hands on Vahly first.

A warm breeze stirred the hairs around Vahly's temples and light bloomed along the edges of the female's slender fingers. Relief flooded Vahly's shoulder and energy slipped into her veins, rejuvenating her. As Cassiopeia worked, Vahly explained the circumstances of her upbringing, including how Amona had rescued her from the Lost Valley floods and the teeth of the sea folk. Mattin asked numerous questions, all of which she answered with honesty.

"How was it, living with the fire kynd, with the

dragons?" Mattin leaned forward and propped an elbow on the throne's arm.

"Hot."

The elves' laughter filled the forest.

"Be assured, we won't ask you to live side by side with earthblood vents here. We air kynd do not enjoy such high temperatures."

"That is a relief. I could do without sweating through my clothes during a feast."

"You lost much blood, Earth Queen." Cassiopeia stepped back.

"I feel like gold now though. Thank you."

Cassiopeia bowed slightly and turned to heal Arc.

A steel-haired elf wearing a deep green tunic and brown trousers lifted a hand to Arc. "What answers do you seek, Vahly?"

"Greetings, Rigel," Arc said. "I'm glad to see your face again."

"And I yours, Arcturus."

The sunlight slid through the greenery above and danced over the elves' smooth foreheads, arms, and hands. The scent of lavender and sap floated on a gentle breath of wind. It was enough to make Vahly want to have a seat and live there forever.

"I believe my kynd had a power ritual. Do you know of one?"

King Mattin set his goblet on the arm of his throne and gazed at Vahly with ancient eyes. How long had he ruled here?

"I do," he said.

Hope sang through Vahly's bones. "Truly?" Would it be this easy? "Will you explain the details?"

"Of course. Let us walk." Mattin joined them on the path and they headed past the throne, into the dappled sun of the deeper forest.

The rest of the elves who had gathered faded from view as Arc came up beside Vahly and put himself between her and the King. He didn't glance her way or indicate there was a reason for the physical barrier, so perhaps she was reading too much into it. Her excitement had her nerves twanging like a badly tuned instrument. When Arc's bare arm brushed her shoulder, her skin seemed to wake up, the buzzing his presence brought forth growing stronger.

Mattin raised his chin and closed his eyes as the sun fell over his face. He actually had slight gray circles under his eyes. That had to be a first for the nearly immortal elves. Yes, they aged, but circles? That spoke of fatigue, which she didn't think they experienced often.

"The ritual involved Blackwater. From the spring."

Arc stopped. "One cannot touch the Source's Blackwater. Your flesh would dissolve as soon as you felt its cool embrace."

Mattin touched Arc's arm, then continued down the path. A stag with a wide set of pearly antlers bounded over the sandy stones and into the undergrowth of ferns and flowers. "You are correct. But there is a bowl, crafted especially for the humans' power ritual. Our kynd formed it with magic long, long ago. The magicked stone alters the Blackwater. Diffuses it. The humans, both Touched and not, washed their hands and face in the spelled waters of the Source to raise the powers hiding inside them. Most only possessed simple earth magic."

"But elves cannot use the bowl to wash?" Arc asked.

"No. The result would be immediate death." Mattin rubbed his hands together. "I have the bowl in my possession and we will go now to find it and fill it for you, Earth Queen."

Vahly's heart tripled its pace. "What will happen when I wash in the spelled Blackwater?"

"You will gain your power. Or you will not. Sadly, the last Touched human, supposedly destined to rule the earth and check the power of the sea, had little magic at her disposal."

"I know that story well," Vahly said. "She drowned at Bihotzetik."

"Yes." Mattin's velvet voice held an age of grief. "But now, you have given me hope. Perhaps the magic of earth does indeed hide inside you, strong and willing. We will know when you wash."

Vahly felt like kissing both elves fully on the mouth. This was the answer to all their problems. She would gain her power and save the dragons and the elves and all the land creatures. Well, if her mark wasn't a total bust which it well could be. No, she wouldn't be negative about it. She'd stay positive like...

A familiar face flashed in her mind, the features of a friend, but the image slid away much like the shadows and light around the elves when she tried to see it straight-on.

But Arc and Cassiopeia had healed her. Why wasn't her mind acting like it should?

"Are you certain that Cassiopeia mended me completely?"

Arc frowned and narrowed his dark eyes. "Why?"

"I think I'm forgetting something."

"It's fatigue," Mattin said quickly. "Your kynd consistently struggled with the problem. They slept daily if you can believe it."

"I can and I do." Vahly eyed those dark circles on the King's face. "Do elves not suffer fatigue?"

"Indeed." The king's gaze touched her Blackwater mark, then sank to her throat. "I find myself tired these days. Of course, we have been readying for the autumn carnival. A king's work is never done."

"The sea is rising. And fast. I hate to ruin your fun, but you should be aware."

"If we are to die, then why not embrace every day like it is our last?"

Vahly and Arc agreed, but she couldn't shake the feeling that this king was lying through his nice, white teeth.

A wall of wood rose before them, and Vahly was surprised to realize it was an oak. She'd been so busy trying to figure out the fate of the world, she hadn't noticed they'd come upon the largest tree she'd ever seen. To call it a tree was wrong.

It was a castle built from a single oak.

In the broken and branched off western half of the tree, clean, fresh water had pooled to form a veritable lake. Aquatic plants with bulbous leaves and flat-petaled blooms of violet draped from the sides like waterfalls.

The rest of the tree showed a doorway, not carved

out, but grown into a sweeping arch that led them into a room with a ceiling of thick limbs and shiny leaves. Orbs of light shifted over the growth and lit two long tables that could have seated hundreds of elves.

The place smelled of heartwood and fresh water and Vahly couldn't inhale enough of it to suit her.

A carpet of yellow and green moss brought them into another set of rooms. Four chambers led away from the feasting hall and Mattin waved a hand to a guard standing at the one farthest to the right. The elven warrior —fully armored in green and black overlapping plates of what she guessed was painted steel—bowed and left, heading the way he'd come.

Inside, a sprawling bed had grown out of the tree to support a mattress covered in green velvet and black-dyed linen. Deep shelves lined the towering walls and countless scrolls filled every nook and cranny, their ends like gold coins and their wax seals and shining ribbons like rubies.

What secrets hid in these scrolls? Surely they had to be worth a fortune. Maybe she could pocket a couple when Mattin wasn't looking. The elves could spare them that was certain. They had more in this room than in the entire Lapis library.

The word *secrets* pinched at Vahly. She had definitely forgotten something. Something to do with dragons, secrets, and an ally.

But that could wait.

Mattin opened a massive armoire made entirely of woody vines. The darkness inside swallowed the light in whole and Vahly couldn't see what the King held until he turned to face her. More magic.

It was a stone bowl, large enough to be called a basin. Made entirely of deep blue Lapis, the container showed thick layers of golden pyrite. It wasn't terribly deep and bore no engravings or magical markings, but spellwork hummed from the piece, regardless. There was no doubt this bowl had a powerful kick.

"I present to you, Earth Queen, the Blackwater Bowl." Mattin looked past Arc and Vahly. "Canopus. Would you mind taking the bowl to the feasting grounds? Guard it with your life."

Canopus eyed the bowl like it might breathe flames. "Of course, my King."

Arc watched Canopus go, then looked to Mattin. "Cousin, how does one fill the bowl? What are the steps to completing this ritual?"

"I must carefully fill it at the Source spring."

The white in Arc's eyes showed all the way around. "I'm willing to do it for you, my King."

Mattin smiled warmly, and for a moment, Vahly could see the family resemblance in the way their eyes crinkled at the sides. "I would never risk you like that. Especially after nearly losing you."

"So you can't touch the Blackwater. But I can after it sits in the spelled bowl?"

"Exactly."

"Have my kynd always had this bowl?"

"Always." He waited until she nodded before continuing. "Tonight we will celebrate the changing of the seasons and toast the hope you have brought us all, Vahly of the Lapis. Tonight, we welcome you as a fellow flesh-kynd and a light in the darkness."

Flesh-kynd. She had never heard that term. It made sense. A smile tried to pull at her lips.

A feast with elves. And then, her power ritual.

Everything was coming up roses.

But life had shown Vahly that roses had vicious thorns, and she was having a tough time believing all was as wonderful as it seemed.

For now though, she would squash that doubt and enjoy the night and hope along with the rest of these elves who looked so much like her own kynd. She would embrace their culture and pull their acceptance around her like a well-fitted cloak.

For once, she truly felt as though she was in the right place at the right time.

For the first time, she truly belonged.

CHAPTER FIFTEEN

Haldus, the stockiest elf of the bunch, led Vahly to a room inside Mattin's oaken castle.

"I don't know if I can rest," Vahly said as she followed him into a circular room.

Two chairs sat in front of a fireplace lined in a luminous green stone she'd never seen. A round bed snuggled into a spot to the left of the door.

"You have important business with the King later, if I'm not mistaken," Haldus said. "Don't you want to be at your best? Your body must rest to complete its healing, and then we will feed you to help you regain your strength." The light from numerous candles set in blue-green glass flickered over his frown. Though his words were kind enough, he kept his distance like he didn't trust her.

Vahly's body ached from the journey, her shoulder pulsing with the ghost of her injury. The pain wasn't bad, but as a yawn escaped her lips, she realized grouchy Haldus here had a good point.

Agreeing, she bid him farewell before falling into bed. Satin fern fronds decorated the velvet coverlet, soft under her hands. The fabric cocooned her fingers when she pressed down, and she sighed. It was a perfect place to sleep, but Vahly's eyes refused to stay shut.

The elves had carved words into the strip of wood near the ceiling.

Be at ease. Time is not your master. Breathe in the moment and marvel at all.

Vahly cocked an eyebrow, muttering, "Easy for you to say, woodcarver. You weren't expected to save the world."

Windows lined up along one side of the circular room. The forest beyond the oaken castle showed trees that were larger around than the tunnels of the Lapis mountain palace. Green leaves glowed in the sunlight and waved gently in the breeze. The elves had cracked the leaded glass windows to let in the air. The scent of Illumahrah wafted across Vahly's face—lavender and mint from the gardens, the warm earth of the gently sloping grounds, and the perfume of woodland wildflowers.

A dark wood door stood beside Vahly's bed.

Fidgety and unable to rest, she decided to explore what other elven treasures hid in this amazing place. She turned a blue glass knob and stepped into a room that was much darker than hers. No windows graced this room. Three beeswax candles flickered on a shelf above a tub.

A bubble-covered Arc stood up, water dripping from his body. His black eyes flashed. Droplets fell from his sharp chin, the muscles of his chest, and well, everywhere.

Vahly sucked a breath and averted her eyes in the interest of showing respect. Her blood rushed through her veins like she had eaten one of those purple mushrooms Amona warned her about.

"Arcturus. Apologies." Fighting a wide grin, she kept her gaze on the planks of the floor. She had barged in without invitation, and she wasn't sure elves were as casual about nudity as dragons. "I didn't know this was your room. I'll head back." Body humming like a plucked string, she turned to leave.

She heard splashing and supposed he was getting out of the claw-footed tub.

"No apologies necessary, Vahly. I think Haldus will come for us when the feast is set. Is that satisfactory?"

Stones and Blackwater, she wanted to peek at him, but she stared at the doorknob. He didn't sound ruffled, but still, erring on the side of good manners was probably the way to go.

"Perfect," she said. "See you then. And thank you." She shut the door and leaned against it, smiling.

"For what?" Arc's voice rumbled through the door.

She wanted to say *For the display of male beauty*, but she didn't want to be an arse and make him feel uncomfortable. She pretended not to hear his question and promptly went to her own bed. If he wanted more than a friendship, they could explore that if she lived through the ritual.

Shaking her head at her own hormones, she forced herself to close her eyes. Her mind didn't want to sleep.

The velvet coverlet brought up thoughts of how Arc's skin might feel under her palms. How would mating with him work? What would happen first? A kiss to the mouth? A brush of fingertips over hipbones?

Exhaling to clear her head, she pushed the experience to the very back of her mind. Arc would never consider her as a mate. She was a human. He was an elf. Sure, they were physically compatible, but vast differences in culture and behavior remained. What would King Mattin say if she tried anything with his royal cousin?

Just thinking about Mattin brought up worries about the upcoming ritual.

Vahly trusted Mattin as much as she would trust newly matured dragon Xabier to watch her plate of bacon when she went to the loo.

Which was to say, not at all.

With the face of a card player, King Mattin could hide anything. Everything.

Even if this ceremony and the bowl gave Vahly her earth magic, the whole thing might all end up being an elaborate ruse to take control of her. There was no real way to know. She had to go through with the ritual, playing it roll by roll, hand by hand, until it ended happily or with her as his puppet.

Or worse.

She read the message that ran along the ceiling and decided to take the unknown carver's advice. Breathing deeply of the lovely Illumahrah air, she marveled at the softness of her bed and the moment of peace right here and now.

Outside Mattin's oaken castle, in the emerald-green moss and feather-soft grasses, Vahly, Arc, and the rest of the elves gathered to celebrate what was to come. Scattered throughout the crowd, willow baskets held black cherries, brazenberries, and a leafy vegetable that Vahly had never seen. The elves drank deep red wine from rough crystal goblets and spoke in their soft voices, orbs of light floating around them as they laughed. Their language was so lovely—lyrical and full of sounds that were more music than spoken word. She was glad to understand them.

The lapis lazuli bowl glittered in the fading rays of the sun slipping through the trees.

Arc saw it too and gave Vahly's hand a quick squeeze. She swallowed, admiring the strength in his fingers.

"You are meant for this, Vahly. All will be well," he said.

Vahly took a crystal goblet from an elf with bright green eyes who seemed to be working as a servant. "I sure hope elves are as wise as they seem," she said to Arc, "because I still feel like I'm not the creature everyone here thinks I am." The goblet's base was rock and the crystal sprouting from it hollowed into a smooth cup. The wine tasted like cherries and wood smoke.

"Don't fret. We are the wisest." Arc winked.

"And the most arrogant." Vahly elbowed him gently.

Hopefully, the sleep she'd had during the day had prepared her body for the ritual. Everything had to be perfect. From what Mattin said, one did not repeat this ceremony. Once she'd washed in the spelled Blackwater, that was it. Or so he claimed.

Now, with the sun setting and twilight descending over the forest, a sweet-scented fog drifted through a stretch of papery birches. The fading rays of the sun highlighted the violet flowers that grew beyond the feasting area.

Arc had donned a clean, long-sleeved linen shirt and a new, black surcoat with the half moon, half sun symbol. His hair was tied back, highlighting his jawline and the long column of his neck.

They shared a bowl of cherries with Cassiopeia and Haldus and took turns shooting arrows at a target on the outskirts of the gathering. The target hung from the wide arm of an oak tree, and a symbol marked the center. It was disturbingly similar to the sign of the Lapis—dragon wings over a slitted eye.

Vahly took the bow from Cassiopeia and a green and silver fletched arrow from Haldus's wide palm. "That's not the Lapis symbol, is it?" The target showed wear along its sides and many arrow holes from use that went much further back than today.

Cassiopeia's cheeks reddened. "I didn't even think of removing it to help you feel more at ease."

"Oh, I don't expect you to do that. I'm a guest here. A grateful guest. I was just … curious."

Haldus walked toward the target, then bent to snatch up a blue-tinted fern. He crushed the plant in his hands and painted the bull's eye a deep sapphire color, covering the Lapis symbol. He turned and smiled. "Better? We want you to feel at home here, Earth Queen."

He'd had a change of heart. When he'd brought her to her room, he'd been taciturn and now he was all gracious smiles. Vahly glanced at Arc. Had he talked to Haldus? Arc just nodded his head, mysterious as usual.

"You didn't have to do that," Vahly said to Haldus. "But thank you." She took the bow and shot three times, hitting the bull's eye every time.

The elves applauded her efforts. She handed the bow to Arc. His fingers brushed hers and his gaze lingered on her face. Vahly found herself breathing too quickly for only shooting a few arrows.

"Great shooting," Arc said. "I suppose you are a sharp hunter."

She snorted. "Not compared to dragons."

"Why would you need to compare your skills to theirs? You are not a flying reptile. You are a fleshed highbeast."

"Take it from me. If you ever venture near Lapis lands again, do not let the dragons hear you say that."

Arc chuckled. "I'm only joking. I respect dragons. They are vicious and beautiful in their way."

Haldus sneered. "I didn't realize you had such a soft spot for the creatures, Arcturus."

Cassiopeia touched Haldus on the shoulder, and he visibly relaxed.

Arc aimed the bow, the muscles under his sleeves tensing. With his head dipped down and his gaze so focused, he looked dangerous.

Vahly wondered if she appeared that way to them when she shot. If they thought so much of her, so much more than most dragons did, perhaps they thought of her as capable instead of a waste of breath.

Arc fired the arrows he'd lodged between his finger and they zipped into the target—one, two, three, four—right into the center.

"Nicely done, elf." Vahly patted him on the back, appreciating the feel of his strong back under her hand more than she should have.

After Cassiopeia and Haldus had their turn, Arc walked with Vahly to a spot closer to a river that bubbled along the forest floor.

Vahly leaned on an oak and let out a long, slow breath she'd been holding her entire life.

All around, the elves joked and ate, laughed and competed in archery and knife throwing. Looking at their facial expressions and the way they moved, every one of them could have been human.

Here, there were no blazing vents of earthblood to suffer, no sharp remarks about Vahly's inability to hunt down entire herds of deer or goat. No rituals far away in the sky where she could never join in. These elves stayed on land, lived like humans most likely had, and looked remarkably like Vahly.

Finally, she belonged.

Here, she could fit in. No, she didn't have their magic, but she ate like them, moved like them, lived like them.

Vahly realized Arc was looking at her. "I could live here forever," she said quietly, oddly bashful about the admission.

"And we would welcome you. *I* would welcome you."

Heat rose along Vahly's neck and she remembered how he looked in that bath of his.

She didn't have time for this, but her chest fluttered rebelliously. The fact was, she could think about romance and mating. For the first time, here was a male with whom she was compatible.

He's much more than compatible, her mind whispered. *He pleases you.*

She shook her head to clear it and eyed the nearest basket of food. The elves had sliced a loaf of flatbread into thin wedges. It didn't look like much, but it tasted amazing. Chewy, warm, and perfectly salty.

"Tell me about yourself, Arc."

He crossed his legs and put his hands on his knees. "What would you like to know?"

"I don't know. Whatever you're willing to share. How about you tell me what the story is with you and horses and being able to speak telepathically with them?"

"All elves can speak telepathically."

"I noticed. But can they all talk to simplebeasts in that manner?"

"No. That is a unique skill of mine. Born of my royal blood."

"King Mattin can't do it?"

"No."

"He is the Horse Lord," Cassiopeia said as she walked by with a cloak. She continued past them and placed the thick, black garment on an elf who appeared to be quite old.

"The what?" Vahly thought maybe she'd heard her wrong.

Arc answered. "Horse Lord. It is an old title. The last to hold it lived over one thousand years ago. It is like an affinity for the equine, not unlike the way humans used to be with many types of animals."

Vahly leaned forward. She hadn't heard of this or read about it. "What do you mean?"

"Your kynd always had animals around them."

Vahly remembered the scroll and how badgers, rabbits, bears and various other simplebeasts had gathered around the humans in the drawings. "Were they able to connect with them like you do with horses?"

"Perhaps. I don't know. We can ask King Mattin if you like. He should know. Out of all the elves still living, he spent the most time among your kynd."

"Do you have stables here in Illumahrah or do you focus your talent on wild horses?"

Arc's eyes narrowed. "I … we have stables."

"Are you all right?"

"Yes … I thought I remembered a horse of mine. Etor."

"Good name. It means *steadfast*, right?"

"Cassiopeia?" Arc called out. The female elf had joined in the dancing near King Mattin's tree.

She left the dance, smiling and waving to a friend, then came over. "What is it, Arcturus?"

"Didn't I have a horse named Etor? Forgive me. My mind remains addled from the injuries I sustained during my time away."

"You aren't able to heal yourself?"

"My memory, my power, refuses to be rejuvenated."

"You have never had a horse with that name. Perhaps

you saw into the future days and will find such a steed later?"

"Perhaps." Arc thanked Cassiopeia and she returned to her dancing.

Arc offered Vahly a dubious-looking vegetable. "Want to try one?"

"What is it?"

He tore a bite-sized piece from the plant's long leaf, then chewed it. "It's a bean, but we like the leaves best."

Vahly accepted a second piece. "Ooh. It has a punchy tartness to it, doesn't it? And a sweet finish."

Arc's dark gaze brushed her cheeks and neck. His dark pink lips tilted into a mischievous grin. "I believe I used the same words to describe you earlier today."

Vahly rolled her eyes, but couldn't quite fight off a smile. "To whom?"

"Rigel. He came to my rooms to speak with me. I fear something is wrong with him."

"This place. It's so lovely that I can't imagine anything being *wrong* here." Except for that Canopus fellow.

Though the air was pleasantly crisp and didn't require extra heat, Cassiopeia set up split wood for a fire. She turned to Arc, a question in her eyes.

Vahly thought maybe he was going to use more magic she hadn't known elves possessed, but instead he walked to the fire, and took a flint and striker from a small pouch on his belt. Vahly joined him.

"I understand." He kneeled beside the woodpile. "We are so close to the Source. There is a peace that soothes this forest. But even here, foul magic can take root. It is more easily masked in this beauty." He plucked the thin

191

tips from a bunch of tall grass and tucked it under a split log.

Vahly squatted beside him, keeping her voice low and speaking in dragon. "What do you think is wrong with your friend Rigel?"

Keeping an eye on the surrounding elves, Arc struck the flint. A spark leaped into the tinder. "He has a heaviness to his presence. Like he has suffered a great loss. But he can't recall any event that would mar his energy."

This all sounded much like what she was experiencing. "I didn't want to complain, but I have a similar feeling. Mine is not so much a deep grief, but a worry. A fear."

"And you don't think it's due to your upcoming power ritual and the fear that it may or may not work a change in you?"

The fire bloomed, and its flickering light painted Arc's smooth brow and straight hair with an orange and yellow glow. His long fingers worked quickly as he stowed his flint and striker.

"No. It's difficult to explain. Do you feel as though you are well now? From whatever we suffered?" Only now did Vahly realize they never even attempted to figure out what had happened. "What happened to us? Did you find out anything from your kynd's scouts? Perhaps we should try to trace our steps backwards to learn the truth. After my ritual, of course."

"I don't feel completely healed. But for some reason, I can't worry about it."

"That doesn't seem right either."

Arc's face twisted in frustration. "No, it doesn't." He stood, his surcoat falling in draping folds around his strong legs and tall black boots. "Why don't we do exactly what you suggest and trace the way we arrived? I'm quite good at tracking. The king won't conclude the festivities until after the music."

A group of five elves walked out of King Mattin's oaken castle. One carried a stringed instrument with a long neck like a swan's. The other four elves carted pipes of various sizes and shapes. Some were made of crockery and glazed with blue and green paints, the rest were made of carved wood and resembled large oak leaves.

As much as Vahly hated the thought of missing elven music, she wanted to know what had happened to her and Arc. Whether it had to do with this place or the elves or something she couldn't guess, the answer to their question might prove key in the future.

They left the feasting, music swirling through the night behind them, and headed back the way they'd come. Past King Mattin's throne, along the garden path, and into the wild woods of the Forest of Illumahrah.

Starlight filtered through the treetops and clustered around Arc's head and hands. He looked otherworldly, nearly divine.

Once they reached the spot where they'd awakened, Arc crouched and picked up a broken plant. He studied the area, touching the ground. "This way."

Arc led Vahly down a slope and through a wide but shallow creek that smelled of fresh water and jasmine. She could barely see. Arc's light-colored sleeves helped her follow him in the scant starlight as he hurried up another rise, then through a stand of young birches like pale candles in the darkness. If she asked him, he could call up a light for her, but she was fine, following him like this. Besides, she didn't want him using up his energy with air magic unless it was truly necessary. They had no idea what they might find at the end of this trail.

Panting, Vahly kept up with Arc as best she could. Arc stopped and put a hand on a beech tree. He stood still, head cocked. "Hmm." Crouching, he pressed a hand against a footprint. Then, he took off a quick clip through an oak grove.

She followed, scattering chipmunks and lizards as she tried to step around ferns and through thickets.

Arc halted under a stand of pines that whispered in the breeze.

Leaning on the nearest tree, Vahly sucked deep breaths. "Are you stopping because I'm about to fall on my face or because you actually need to track?"

His mouth twitched. "A little of both." He touched a depression in the damp earth between two boulders. "Do you remember any of this?"

A lump formed in Vahly's throat. She tried to swallow, her stomach twisting. "I don't and I'm thinking that is a very bad thing."

"Agreed." He stood, hair falling from its tie. His face was thunderous, and Vahly was glad his anger wasn't directed at her. He was no dragon but with that look, he would be at least a runner-up in a competition for Scariest Highbeast on the Isle.

He lifted his chin and sniffed the air. "Vahly. There are dead nearby."

Vahly's heart froze. Ice sluiced through her veins. "What do you mean ... dead?"

Murmuring, he crashed through the underbrush beyond her, frightening birds into the air. Vahly didn't want to follow him. But she had to and she knew it.

ARC DREW up quickly at several mounds of freshly turned earth. The ground smelled like rain, sun-warmed dirt, and the over-sweet beginnings of decay.

"Do you normally bury your dead here?" Vahly whispered. "Please say *Yes*." She clasped her own shaking hands to hide the fear from him.

"No." He moved like he was shaking a filthy cloak from his shoulders. "Can you feel the foul magic here? Now, I know for certain someone spelled us."

"I can't sense the magic used, but I feel a distinctly *wrong* kind of energy. How do we discover who is dead under these mounds of dirt?"

Arc put a hand on her shoulder, but didn't look at her. "We dig."

Wind blew through the trees. Overhead, branches scratched together, emitting a creaking sound that send more chills down Vahly's back. "I was afraid you'd say that."

Shutting his eyes, Arc whispered, "We have maybe one hour before the others will begin searching for us. Then someone will grow curious."

Vahly couldn't seem to talk. She followed him to the closest mound and began shifting earth away from the heap, her hands hardly working as they trembled.

Something in the back of her mind knew she was not going to like what they found.

As she dug, dirt pressed under her nails until she was bleeding, though it was too dark to tell for sure and her hands were too numb to feel the injury.

And then, her hands found the tip of a dragon wing.

CHAPTER SIXTEEN

V ahly's memory came racing back.
Her hands couldn't dig fast enough.
"No."

Vaguely, she was aware of Arc speaking in a calming tone, but he didn't stop her from clearing the dirt away from a Lapis blue wing, mottled with splashes of Jade green. Arc joined her in the grim duty, and together, they exposed the side of a scaled body, a neck, and finally, the wide, dead eyes of Kemen.

She remembered him. Fully. Wholly. She knew about the cider house and her many friends there. Her memory knitted itself back together only to rip her apart.

Vahly's stomach seized and she turned to vomit.

Kemen was gone. Her fantastic brute of a friend.

Breathing through her nose, she stared at her fingers in the dirt.

Arc's hands were on her back, and he was whispering, sending warmth and a glow of healing light into her skin.

She touched Kemen's cold face gently.

Kemen, her friend, her cohort in thieving and in dice. The dragon who kept quiet and remained stoic, but had always been there when she needed him.

A buzzing sound filled Vahly's ears. The noise transformed into her own heartbeat and sweat trickled down her neck as she began digging again. Somehow, she knew there was more to find. More horror. More tragedy.

"There is another," she whispered, voice raw. She couldn't look at Arc. She didn't want to see the sadness he might feel for her.

The scent of decay and damp earth hit Vahly's nose again, like it had been saving up for a knockout.

She paused, swallowing bile, then cleared a clump of dirt away to see a leg covered in scales like coins made of emerald and sapphire. Arc swiped an arm over the makeshift grave to reveal the dead creature's face.

Ibai.

Vahly shut her eyes against the flood of tears suddenly overtaking her vision. "My Ibai." She trembled under shock's icy hands. "Do you remember these dragons now?" she asked Arc. "Because I do. I do."

How had they forgotten their entire journey here and what occurred in the Fire Marshes and in the forest that sat between the marshes and Illumahrah?

"I remember." Arc, stiff and slow-moving in the starlight, walked around to the rear of another mound.

He shoveled dirt with his large hands for several minutes while Vahly sat and wept silently, her own body unwilling to follow her commands to help him and to find out who else had been taken from her.

A light wind could have carried her off into the black sky.

Arc stopped, then sat back on his heels. "There is another." His words landed like an axe on Vahly's neck. "Dramour. I remember him."

Dramour's eyepatch and green scales, the black dirt of the mound, the trees—everything turned around in Vahly's head, faster and faster. Dizziness overtook her. She fell onto Ibai's still form and let the tears wash her away. Her fingers gripped the mound. A coolness touched her finger. She raised her head to see the edge of a worn, human coin. The one Dramour and Ibai traded after every bet. Gathering it to her, she rubbed the smooth gold until it was warm, then held it against her heart.

Arc sat in silence, his hand on the ground beside her as if he wanted her to know she could grasp his fingers if she wanted.

Vahly forced herself to sit upright.

Nix had to be here too.

It only made sense.

The elves wouldn't have let her live. It wouldn't have taken much effort to finish Nix off, what with the injuries she'd sustained from the arrow and the fall.

Vahly pulled at her hair, hating herself. How had she forgotten them? Could she have saved them if she'd remembered?

Arc drew her hand away from her tangled braid. "It's not your fault."

Trembling, she forced herself to stand. More mounds. More death. Arc's gentle gaze was like a touch. As soon as she began to dig again, he joined her.

She kept glancing at Ibai, Kemen, and Dramour, expecting them to get up, shake the filthy from themselves, and make a joke. They lay so still. Her head pounded. It wasn't as if she had never seen death. But these had been her friends. So full of life. How could that be them, still and silent in makeshift graves? In her mind, she imagined Dramour saying her name. He would never utter it again. He would never say anything ever again.

Pushing her storm of emotion away, she shoved more dirt away, more, more, more.

But there was nothing.

Hope sparked inside her chest. She wiped her face with the back of her dirt and blood crusted sleeve. "Nix isn't here. We should check that one." Her gaze flitted to the next mound and her stomach tightened, threatening rebellion.

This mound was not as large, but inside, under the earth, among broken bows and arrows, set out neatly— unlike the dragons—the bodies of three elves lay side by side.

Arc sucked a breath and stood in a motion too fast for Vahly to see clearly.

"Rigel's son, Pegasi," he said. "That's what was wrong with Rigel. He found out that his son was dead. He must have. That was the grief hanging on him. But why did he forget? Why did we all forget? Even the others…"

"You told me, in the marshes, that someone had spelled foul magic on you. That you felt it, like a sticky darkness." Vahly choked on a sob and squeezed her fingers into the earth to keep from falling off the side of the world.

"And this is Vega. And Leporis. I can't believe it." Arc shook his head and his throat moved in a slow swallow. "All dead."

"Except Nix. Where is she?" Vahly paced the length of the mounds. "Can you track her? Surely there will be evidence of her escape or her death here."

Arc, his face pale as moonlight, scoured the ground, bending and tilting his head, whispering and frowning. "She was here. Recently."

Vahly was at his side in a blink. The dark of the forest stared at her, its unknown depths pressing against her eyes.

"Nix arrived here after the dead were buried. She may live still. There are footprints over this mound's turned earth. And they aren't ours. She is barefoot."

Barefoot. She hadn't even had time to put her boots back on before her life had veered painfully off course. Vahly's eyes shuttered, scared to the core that Arc might be mistaken that Nix was alive. "Can you follow her tracks?"

He nodded, and they started into an area of oaks growing so close that their branches intertwined to block out what little light had been trickling through the canopy. Arc raised an orb of light with his left hand and released it with a flick of his fingers. The light floated, riding a breeze that was also born of Arc's air magic, illuminating their way. They followed a game trail, its line narrow, obviously not used by large animals. A head-high branch had been broken and Arc gestured to it. She had been here.

Vahly had to talk her feet into walking instead of

running. Nix was out here, somewhere, hurting and alone. But rushing Arc's tracking work wouldn't be a good plan. They had no time to waste on getting lost.

"What kind of animal runs this trail?" she asked.

Arc glanced her way and paused, his lips parting slightly as if he were about to ask why she wanted to know, right now, in the middle of this horror. His gaze lighted over the tears that wet her cheeks, and he held back his question.

"A small, slim deer that keeps to the plateau," he said. "They have one horn in the center of their foreheads and their coats are metallic in look. The hairs reflect and refract light and mimic the look of golden steel."

"Sounds lovely."

They walked in near silence. Arc made virtually no sound as he crossed the ground. Vahly's boots crunched on a leaf or stem here and there, but she too knew how to be quiet when it mattered. Whoever killed the dragons and the elves could still be out here.

"She listed away from the game trail," Arc whispered. "See?" He pointed to a large fern someone—possibly Nix —had snapped along its spine and smashed. "And there is a footprint."

Vahly cupped a hand at her mouth. "Nix?" she called into the dark forest, daring to make a sound loud enough for Nix to hear. "I remember now. We are here to help you. Nix?"

What was Nix going through? Had she been forced to watch Ibai, Kemen, and Dramour die? Had she been witness to whatever foul creature had murdered their entire party?

Vahly drew her sword, the feel of its weight a comfort.

Arc pursed his lips. "Whoever did this is long gone. I don't smell anything but dragon here now."

They stepped around a clutch of what might have been scorchpeppers. The air held the slight peppery scent of them and it reminded Vahly of the cider house.

"Do you have any guesses who did this?"

"It was Canopus," Arc said.

Vahly remembered the elf, tall and fair, with that vicious-looking mouth of his. "King Mattin's right hand."

"The elders reprimanded him for using foul magic in the past. He wanted a maiden for his own and she didn't care for him. She was one of Cassiopeia's nieces. He tried to cast a spell on her while her father and mother were out hunting and gathering. But her younger brother saw Canopus enter through their back door and he ran to the King's guards to get help. Mattin publicly thrashed Canopus, a punishment the King had not carried out in an age."

"Why would Canopus wish to do all of this?" she asked. "What was his motivation? He killed his own kynd and they had captured us. Where was his head in this scenario?"

"Perhaps Vega or the others had information about him," Arc said. "Maybe they knew of a plan of his to gain power."

Vahly frowned. "And when they showed up on the border with us, he decided this was as good a time as any to take care of the problem? With four dragons to deal with too? I don't know. That doesn't sound right. Seems like there would be easier ways to off a group of scouts.

Besides, wouldn't he at least want to know why we, the dragons and I, had come here, to the forest to find elves?"

"He may have questioned the dragons before slaying them."

Vahly tensed, stopping. To think of them being tortured, used against one another. Dizziness took her and nearly threw her to the ground.

"I am sorry for your loss, Vahly of the Earth." The corners of Arc's eyes seem to turn down in his sadness.

Swallowing, Vahly worked to find her voice. "I'm sorry for yours as well. I could tell you respected Vega and Leporis, and that you loved Pegasi like he was your own."

Arc turned away. When he finally spoke, pain cut his words into sharp syllables. "He was a good lad. A strong and good lad."

They stood there, quiet and grieving, with the glow of Arc's magic circling.

Vahly touched Arc's sleeve. "Wait. Didn't Leporis tell Vega and Pegasi to leave Nix because she was injured?"

Arc's face cleared. "Yes. That's why she escaped the massacre. But I do think she is here now. Somewhere."

Arc regarded Vahly, his gaze mournful, before he headed deeper into the wood. Vahly whispered to the Source, her heart aching, begging for Nix to be alive.

CHAPTER SEVENTEEN

Vahly and Arc pressed through the bracken, faces scratched by thorns and branches, and hope dwindling as they failed to find Nix.

"What do we do when we find her?" Vahly said the word *when* like a prayer.

"I'll heal her if I'm able." A branch caught on Arc's surcoat and he brushed it away.

Vahly flexed her sword hand. "Then we confront Canopus."

"Perhaps we should talk to Mattin first," Arc suggested.

"What if they're in it together?" They had seemed close when she'd first seen them at the throne.

Arc blinked, then rubbed a hand over his sharp chin. The orb painted his forehead gold. "Do you truly think they are?"

Vahly shrugged. "Mattin looked exhausted. Bags for days. Isn't that odd for a powerful being like him?"

"It is strange. I thought perhaps he had been ill while

we were away. We do suffer from illness time and again, as humans did. As humans *do*."

"Possible. But I think a straight-on attack in public might be the way to go," Vahly said. "If we expose him, the truth might force the spell from the others."

"All right," Arc said. "It's agreed then." His gaze snapped to a spot on the forest floor, at the silvery base of a towering beech. "Vahly."

Without an explanation, he took off into the brush. Vahly hurried after him.

Arc directed his orb of light over an area of crushed plants.

Nix lay there, asleep in her human-like form, her broken wing at an odd angle.

Vahly hurried to kneel beside her. "Nix?" And then Vahly was crying again. Where had her steely resolve gone? "Nix."

Nix's eyes fluttered open. "Vahly!" She collected Vahly into a hug and Vahly breathed in the rosy scent of her scales. "I thought they killed you too." Holding Vahly at arm's length, she studied her face. "I have terrible news." Nix's eyes tightened and she squeezed Vahly's shoulders, her talons biting into flesh.

"I already know. They're gone. They're all gone."

And then they were embracing again, Nix's sobs causing her body to heave.

"Who did it?" Vahly asked gently. "Do you know?" She didn't want to ask if the murderers had forced Nix to witness the deaths. "When did you manage to climb up the plateau? They had left you in the marshes, right?"

Vahly hugged her one last time and then helped her to her feet.

"Yes. But I followed them as quickly as I was able. I planned to do whatever I could to fight. My wing is broken, but my fire works just fine." Nix seemed to notice Arc for the first time.

Arc bent his head. "I'm sorry."

"You didn't do this crime, Arc," Nix said.

"But it was my kynd, wasn't it?"

"It was your King."

"I knew it," Vahly said. There was no victory in her voice though. It would be nearly impossible to fight Mattin. They had to expose him in front of his kynd and hope the spell on their minds would break, forcing them to band together and overtake the monster.

Arc sat on the ground and removed his boots. He looked positively stricken. Between the death of young Pegasi and the fact that his king was most likely the one who'd spelled him—his own cousin—he seemed about to break. Vahly wasn't sure how to help him. She was still reeling herself.

"What are you doing?" Nix asked, standing with Vahly and wiping her tears with the back of her hand.

Arc offered the black boots to Nix. "Please. Wear these. It's the least I can do. While you put them on, I'll attempt to finish healing your wing."

But Arc's magical strength hadn't changed since the spell dropped away. He was still bogged down somehow and Nix wouldn't get the benefit of a fully powerful royal of Illumahrah.

Nix started to argue, but then agreed. This was a quieter version of Nix, muted in her grief.

After laying hands on Nix and being unable to heal her completely, Arc stepped away and snapped out a phrase in elvish.

Vahly was surprised she understood the curse. She'd have guessed the ability to understand elvish—put there by whoever had spelled her—would have disappeared when the temporary amnesia and false memories departed.

Arc took a deep breath, removed the tie from his hair, and faced Nix. "My power remains stifled by spellwork. Do you have any ideas on how I might rid myself of this curse? I've never seen anything like it. Not in my alchemy work. Nowhere."

"How about we head toward Mattin and see what kind of trouble we can make?" Nix didn't wait for Vahly or Arc to agree. She shuffled into the dark as if she knew the way.

Arc smoothly slipped in front to guide them, and in silence, they trudged back the way they'd come.

Vahly dreaded seeing the mounds again.

Numb, she kept her focus on Arc's back. It was too bad he had taken off his bow and quiver at the King's home. At least he still wore his throwing knives.

Every step closer to the site where their friends had lost their lives felt like a step closer to dying themselves.

Vahly grabbed Nix's arm. "Can we stop? I … I need a minute."

Nix's features tightened like she was bracing for a strike. "Of course. Maybe we should say a few words."

She closed her eyes briefly and shivered, wings quivering.

Arc stood close, forming a circle with them. His glassy orb of light floated above them. "I would like to participate, if that doesn't offend you."

"Of course you're participating." Vahly used her sword to cut a small line in her palm. A few drops of blood dropped to the damp earth. "I bleed for you, Dramour. I bleed for you, Kemen. I bleed for you, Ibai."

Arc obviously wasn't familiar with this dragon tradition of personal mourning. He watched with respectful curiosity as Nix did as Vahly had.

Vahly held her sword out for him and he took it with careful hands.

"I bleed for you, Pegasi." He cut his own palm, not without some effort. Elves' flesh was stronger than Vahly's. "I bleed for you, Leporis." Blood glistened on his shining skin before falling into the dark. "I bleed for you, Vega."

The three of them joined hands and bowed their heads in silence.

"Source keep them," Vahly and Nix said in unison.

"Be of the air." Arc's voice rumbled in his chest and his fingers twitched against Vahly's. "Be of the light and the shadow. Never forgotten."

The wind stirred Vahly's hair and slid across her face, drying the last of her tears. They stood there for a while and Vahly was in no hurry to let go of Arc or Nix. Both were a comfort, a balm against the raw pain of loss.

Nix finally broke the silence. "We need to solve this problem or our friends died in vain."

Arc politely gestured to Vahly's fresh wound. She gave him her hand and he held it softly, his thumb dusting over the back as he poured magic, warm and sure, into her cut. When it was healed, his gaze flicked to her face. She stared into those glittering black jewels, wondering how she'd been so Blackwater blessed to find this ally. This friend.

Next, Arc took Nix's hand. Her eyes narrowed as he began his work, but she remained still and thanked him genuinely at the conclusion.

Vahly started down the path, Arc beside her and Nix just behind. They passed the mounds and remained quiet until the place was well behind them.

"How did Mattin act?" Vahly asked Nix gently. Then she turned to Arc. "Do you have any idea why he would do this?"

Nix gripped the front of her dress, her hands shaking. "He came with only one other elf."

"A fair-haired male wearing a vial around his neck?" Arc asked.

"Yes. They had magic I've never even heard stories about. Not only light and shadow and wind. It was ..." She stumbled a step and shuddered.

Vahly put a hand on her forearm. "You survived. You are strong. And we will annihilate Mattin and Canopus. Just you wait, my friend."

"Mattin spread his arms, whispered elvish spells, and then Dramour, Ibai, and Kemen fell on their own swords."

The words were a hit to Vahly's back. She nearly

dropped, but Arc caught her arm. She squeezed his elbow and steadied herself. "That bastard."

Nix walked on as if she were afraid to stop. "He did the same to your kynd, Arc. But he told them to cut their own throats."

The wind gusted as if it could sense Arc's growing rage. "We will avenge them all." His words were steel, sharpened to a deadly edge.

"Wait," Vahly said, realizing their mistake. She felt foolish about not thinking of it, and also hesitant to bring it up, but… "What if we pretend we don't know and I go through the power ritual. Then, hopefully I'll be far more capable of helping to bring down Mattin. He's most likely lying about the entire ceremony, but that bowl has power."

"It does." Arc's gaze grew distant.

A few steps ahead, Nix twisted and put a hand against a young oak. "So the elves did know of a human power ritual?"

Vahly nodded. "There is a lapis lazuli bowl. Mattin said he used to fill it with Blackwater from the Illumahrah spring for the humans. They would wash their hands and face to wake their powers, both Touched and not."

Nix inhaled slowly, a sound almost like a hiss. "Where is this bowl? Can any elf fill it for you? Or must it be an elf of royal blood?"

"I have royal blood. I would fill it for you, Vahly," Arc said. "Mattin has the item at the feast."

Nix kept an eye on the forest. With her dragon eyes, she could see far past both Vahly and Arc. "Could we grab this sacred bowl and get to that spring without Mattin knowing?"

"We'll run a nice little con on him," Vahly said, anger rising in her and cloaking her grief. "We've done them together many times, Nix. We can do it again now."

"A con?" Arc's eyebrow lifted in question.

"A confidence trick. We shower Mattin with praise, distract him by pretending we are a couple," Vahly said, wanting to grin at him, but not quite able to make eye contact.

Nix snorted. "Pretend."

Vahly ignored her. "Then we'll nab the bowl. The bowl might be a trick. It might curse me. But I have to give this a try. I don't have any other options. But we can't trust that Mattin will actually let me go through with the ceremony, if it even is a power ritual. It probably isn't. It's most likely all a lie. Do you have any idea why he would do all of this? The spellwork on everyone's minds? The killing?"

Arc shook his head. "It makes no sense. We should all be as one, united against the coming flood."

"Nix, are you willing to head to the Source's spring on your own? That way if we need backup when we arrive, you can bring on that dragonfire of yours."

"Oh I'll be more than ready to roast elves. Sorry, Arc."

"Roast away," he said, his voice tight. "I'll drive Mattin and Canopus right into your flames if I have the chance."

"I just wish we could get you back to your full strength," Vahly said to Arc.

"We will make do with what we have," Nix said. "There is no other choice."

"True." Vahly embraced her.

Arc looked into the night. "You'll need to head northwest. Can you use the stars to guide you?" he asked Nix.

"If your fancy trees don't block the constellations the entire time."

"The Source's spring pulses with all four magics. Air, water, earth, and fire. As a highbeast and a worker of fire magic, you will feel the Blackwater as you near it."

"That sounds ominous." Nix winked at Vahly and began to leave. She glanced over her shoulder. "Don't worry about me. I'll probably smell the fancy magical pond. This thing is the stuff of legends." She touched her nose.

Vahly nudged Arc. "She knew I was bonded to Amona when none of the other Breakers realized it."

"Good. She is enlightened, and that is one more tally on our side of this coming fight."

Once Nix seemed to have her bearings and disappeared from view, Vahly and Arc headed straight for Mattin.

Vahly's heart beat so loudly she could feel it in her neck and at her collarbone. She wanted revenge, and by the Blackwater, she would get it.

CHAPTER EIGHTEEN

W hen they returned to the celebration, the elves had replaced the baskets of berries and vegetables with long, wooden slabs covered in silver platters. Each platter held slices of venison dressed in mild blue peppers and pearl onions. The elves were seated on the mossy ground, chewing and talking companionably.

Around them, the forest sang. Glowing distura birds chirped like perfectly tuned woodwinds, a warm breeze rustled thick leaves, and the pool of fresh water inside the oaken castle gurgled.

Vahly sighed and said a silent prayer. She hated that Mattin and Canopus tainted the beauty and peace of this place.

Arc talked to Vahly as if they had never left to find their kynd slaughtered in the forest. He asked her about her preferred bow and what instruments she played.

"The biggest one I can pull and no instruments at all," she said.

"Funny, because you look like a music sprite."

Vahly glared.

Arc chuckled, but the joy of teasing her didn't reach his eyes. Anger and sadness warred in those dark depths.

"My King," he called to Mattin.

The elf sat on the raised root of an oak, a cloak of silver and black sliding over one shoulder and down his back. A clasp in the shape of a fist held the garment against his neck. His crown of light and shadow remained in place, churning and spinning when Vahly watched it from the corner of her eye.

"Yes, my dear Arcturus?" the King answered. "Did you and your Earth Queen enjoy your solitude?"

So he had noticed their absence. Even in this crowd.

"We did." Vahly linked her arm in Arc's. His muscles tensed beneath his linen sleeve.

The elves' light orbs twinkled among the many trees, hanging in limbs and along bunches of dark leaves.

Vahly nodded toward a pitcher of deep red wine. "Great king, perhaps your cousin here would like to brag about his conquest over a cup?"

Mattin sniffed, the corner of his mouth lifting. "Indeed? That would be most unlike our Arcturus."

"Love does strange things to us, does it not?" Arc said, taking up the ruse. He accepted a crystal goblet from a serving elf and raised it to Mattin.

The word *love* widened Vahly's eyes and she had to recover with a cough. She knew well he did not love her. But they had formed a friendship. A sad smile crossed her face. She hurried to broaden it into the one of a new lover for the benefit of their con.

The king lifted his cup, echoing Arc's gesture. Mattin drank his cup dry, then wiggled the goblet at a servant who stumbled over himself to refill it.

Did any of these elves realize their King had spelled them and that their minds weren't fully their own? Well, it was better that they remained ignorant if she was going to nick that bowl from under Mattin's nose.

Arc broke away from Vahly and slid up next to the King. He raised one eyebrow and whispered into Mattin's ear. The elven king barked a laugh and shook his head.

Vahly pretended to be keenly interested in a dessert platter a servant had laid down on the outskirts of the feasting area. She took one of the tiny, silver spoons sitting beside a bowl of nutmeg-and-vanilla-scented pudding and enjoyed a mouthful.

Canopus walked out of the dark and stood beside Arc. The creepy elf kept an eye on Vahly.

She lifted a second spoonful of the pudding. "So good. I had a dessert much like this one back at the Lapis palace. I do think they considered stirring me into the mix though. Well, Lord Maur did anyway. This recipe is much better. Or perhaps I only think that because my own self wasn't considered as a potential ingredient?"

Canopus's face gave nothing away. He seemed bored with her, which was exactly her goal.

Rambling quietly about various desserts, Vahly ate three more helpings. Once Canopus found another target for his gaze, he moved away from the King. Vahly went around the clutch of oaks behind Mattin and Arc to listen.

Arc was still chatting with Mattin. Vahly watched him from the Y in the oak that hid her from view. Arc made eye contact with her, laughed at something Mattin said, and then let his hand stray to the bowl near the King's right leg. Arc's fingers braced against the lapis lazuli, then he slipped the bowl behind his back. It was a good thing he was a large elf because that bowl would have shown behind Vahly's smaller form.

"One moment, my King," Arc said, eliciting a bored wave from Mattin, and in a flash, he was beside Vahly handing her the bowl.

They walked away from the gathering, into the starlight, so they would not be heard.

"Nice work, elf." Vahly clutched the bowl to her chest. The magic in it hummed against her breastbone.

Arc glanced over his shoulder to see if anyone had followed them. "Head northwest. There will be a path of wildflowers. They grow year round because they bloom so close to the Source's waters. You will know you have gone too far if you come to a clearing. I'll meet you at the spring."

Giving Arc a quick nod, she turned.

And ran directly into Canopus.

"Apologies. Where are you headed, Earth Queen?"

Arc's lip curled. "Wherever she wishes."

Canopus lifted his chin. "King Mattin," he called out. "I think we need your wisdom just now."

Mattin rounded the tree and approached, his movements quick and his face in shadow. "Why do you have the bowl, Earth Queen? I thought I had set it next to me. For safe keeping."

She wasn't sure whether to expose the fact that they were no longer spelled or to play along.

"I would like to go forward with the ritual," she said. "I've waited my whole life for this. I tired of waiting."

Canopus, fingers lighting on the tiny, stone vial he wore on a string around his neck, glanced at Arc, but Arc gave nothing away.

Something about that vial tugged at Vahly's attention. It was made of rough-hewn lapis lazuli and definitely worth a week of meals and several hands of cards, but it wasn't any more valuable than other pieces she'd seen.

The elves left their feasting and gathered around to see what was afoot.

Mattin's fair eyebrows lifted as he studied Vahly. "That seems fair. You have waited years since maturity. Far longer than your predecessors. I understand that you would be eager to begin your true life as Earth Queen." His gaze flicked to her Blackwater mark. "Let us go now." He plucked the bowl from Vahly's grasp, then spun, smiling at the crowd. "Follow us to the Source spring to witness the last of the humans take part in the ritual of earth magic."

Vahly forced a smile and nodded in thanks. A bead of sweat rolled down her temple and she wiped it away quickly, wishing she could speak telepathically with Nix. She looked to Arc. He nodded and curled his hand so his fingers looked like claws. She had to assume that meant he was thinking the same thing, to warn Nix telepathically.

Delighted gasps and grins greeted Mattin's news. The elves walked in pairs and small groups behind their King as he led Arc and Vahly toward the spring. Luxurious cloaks brushed over fallen leaves and excited looks danced across the elves' faces. General Regulus spoke of a time when he visited Bihotzetik and the humans there.

"Their art was unparalleled. You should have seen the murals painted on their walls. With such short life spans and their lesser ability to heal, they suffered more than we elves can imagine. But from that suffering, beauty flourished. They valued the simplest flower, a touch from a child's hand, a fine song. I liked the humans." He glanced at Vahly. "And I have to say, I like you, Vahly of the Earth. Do you know what your name means?"

She swallowed against the sudden tightness in her throat. *"Blooded for the battle."*

He raised a hand. "Indeed. If all goes well this day, I do believe we have a fight ahead of us that does not seem quite so hopeless."

Fists bunching, Vahly let her anger for Mattin and Canopus rise. These kynd were faithful and kind. How could their King treat them so?

Just as Arc had described, a trail of wildflowers marked the path with petals of moon white, deep red, and onyx. Mattin and Canopus traded whispers, their smiles as fleeting and disconcerting as the darkness of a solar eclipse.

The elves wove orbs of light in their hands, then tossed them into the air.

The group passed the stables, a long building made of curling roots the size of a dragon's tail. Horses much like Etor stood in the high stalls, their nickering blending with the sound of night insects and the elves' conversations.

Arc's gaze drifted to the horses, worry lining his brow.

He spoke a quiet word to them, and they turned as one to regard him, liquid eyes trusting.

Vahly hoped Etor had found a safe place to graze in the forested borders of the Red Meadow.

A creek slipped and shushed over round pebbles that lined the waterway's bed as well as much of the path.

Arc pointed out an owl to Vahly as the winged simplebeast flew in silence overhead.

She jerked at his sudden movement. Her gut knew Mattin and Canopus had something up their sleeves. But she had to play along and see how this panned out.

"The owls in Lapis territory have brown and white feathers. Is that one silver?" The bird landed on a high pine branch. Its tail reflected the moonlight, looking like fish scales.

"Yes," Arc answered. "It's a male. Their fine plumage draws potential mates. The females do all the hunting. Females do love beauty." His eyes twinkled.

She wished with her whole being that they were truly flirting instead of trying to stay alive while carrying grief like baggage. If only life were so simple.

"Your plumage isn't what lured me in," she said.

Mattin was watching them. Vahly felt his stare like a brand.

"Oh no? I have always believed I am somewhat handsome. Perhaps I have been misled. I blame sweet Cassiopeia."

Cassiopeia looked up from her conversation with General Regulus. "You are as lovely as the dusk before a storm, Arcturus." She grinned at Vahly.

"You aren't bad on the eyes, but no. The plumage

wasn't it. The respect you showed … " Ibai. Kemen. Dramour. Nix. Their names burned her tongue. He had been honest, forthright, but also respectful to them. Even when they insulted his kynd. He had shown a humility she had not known elves possessed. "Your respect for me and who I'm trying to become, that's what drew me to you." That was true as well.

Arc's throat moved and he blinked, all teasing gone from his eyes. He opened his mouth like he wanted to speak, but instead, he turned his face away.

The trail wandered around twisting pines and through a tumble of boulders over which a few lizards and mice scurried. A gentle breeze stirred a thick stretch of ferns that grew hip-high and the scent of pine resin, fallen leaves, and wet earth rose into the air.

Still no sign of Nix. Good. She had taken to the forest to remain concealed.

Ahead in the scattered starlight, five stones like guards fashioned of thick rock stood around a place that had to be the spring of Blackwater, the one place the Source existed in its pure state, untouched by magma or salt water.

Vahly couldn't tear her gaze away from the holy heart of her world.

Her blood rushed through her veins, urging her forward, closer. A burning touched her eyes and she lifted her hand only to realize she was crying.

Beside her, Arc was likewise touched. His eyes were wet with unshed tears and his entire demeanor held a reverence close to what she had seen in him during their mournful bloodletting.

She walked closer, whispering, as the rest of the elves came along slowly behind, their voices quiet. "Arc, do you think this," she pointed toward the spring, "might affect them?"

Would he understand she meant that perhaps getting close to the Blackwater would break the spell that still held the rest of the party in its grip?

"It's possible and—"

A wind gusted from the East, roaring through the forest.

Branches snapped. Dirt and rocks hit Vahly's raised arms, biting at her skin.

Shouts rose as Vahly and Arc bent to lower their center of gravity, to keep from pitching over onto the ground.

"What kind of insanity is this?" Vahly shouted into Arc's puzzled face. The wind tore Vahly's braid free and set Arc's surcoat to flapping against his legs.

A great cracking sounded in front of them, near Mattin and Canopus.

The odd windstorm died.

Beside a rocky outcropping, the lapis lazuli bowl lay in pieces.

Vahly's mouth fell open, shock holding her in a vice-like grip.

"You dropped it?" Arc's voice was a whip.

Mattin winced and shook his head. "That wind. It plucked the bowl right out of my hands. I didn't expect it and … " He gestured to the remains of Vahly's hope.

Desperation and anger warred inside her.

Anger won.

She charged Mattin, raising her voice. "Elves are strong. Wildly strong. You can't tell me you didn't do that on purpose. What game are you playing, King Mattin?"

The elves grew silent, watching the exchange.

The king put a hand on Vahly. The hairs on the back of her neck lifted and she involuntarily took a step back. Pleasure gleamed in the King's eyes.

"Earth Queen, I am sorry. But don't fret. We can fashion another in less than a week's time. Come, let us return to our feasting and I will ask our craftsfolk to begin work immediately. I have a piece of the fabled stone in my own things. I happily give it to you in hopes you will help us defend ourselves from the Sea Queen."

The elves visibly relaxed, their shoulders under their fine and sparkling clothing easing and their conversations returning to mundane chatter as they turned to leave.

Arc remained, jaw set and hands fisting at his sides.

Mattin steered Vahly back down the path. "Come. All will be well. And once again, I apologize for my grave error in not securing the bowl."

Numb, Vahly let herself be led, but her mind chittered like a thousand little birds inside her head. That wind wasn't natural. He'd called it up. Or Canopus had. But what was his end game? Why wouldn't he want Vahly to help him save his people? It made no sense.

The realization swept over her like a deadly wave.

He had made a deal with the Sea Queen.

That was the only lens that clarified Mattin's bizarre and criminal behavior.

Vahly nodded to Arc as they passed him, silently urging him to go along with this for now.

But what was Mattin's agreement with Queen Astraea? She was going to flood every inch of the land, leaving no place for elves to live.

Unless she didn't flood the plateau.

Perhaps the sea folk's magic was so controlled that they could feasibly overwhelm the high mountains in the Lapis and Jade territories, but preserve this plateau. That would be worth a promise, seared to the heart.

What might the King have sworn to give in return? To delay any potential threat to the sea's advance? Or was this specific to Vahly? And when was this promise traded? During this age or the last? Mattin had been around for a long while.

The trail of wildflowers gave way to the moss and grasses of the feasting grounds. The king and Canopus left immediately, presumably to talk to their craftsfolk.

Vahly grabbed Arc and dragged him behind the nearest oak. "I think Mattin is working with the Sea Queen."

"He called up that wind as an excuse to break the bowl, to be sure. But why would he deal with the sea folk?" Arc asked. "Their goal is to end all of us on land. Elves included."

Vahly shrugged. "What if they promised to protect the plateau in exchange for Mattin's help in curtailing any threat from potential Earth Queens?"

"So this began long ago?" Arc tapped one of the throwing knives at his belt, his gaze beyond Vahly, watching his kin as they danced and smiled in their ignorance.

"It's my guess, anyway. But why did he allow the

humans before me to use the bowl and gain their powers? Why break it now and not sooner to keep his promise to the sea folk?"

"I think perhaps this agreement between Mattin and the Sea Queen is new. That falls in line with his actions. Only now is he driven to destroy any chance you have to gain your powers. He won't allow the craftsfolk to finish a new basin for the Blackwater. He'll delay and delay until you die of some strange accident."

"Great." Vahly chewed the inside of her cheek, thinking. Was Arc right? Was any of this right? There was no way to know if Mattin had a promised agreement with the Sea Queen nor was there any certainty about the Blackwater bowl.

If she went to the spring herself, without the bowl, she would at least find out whether the bowl was truly required. She would find a replacement basin. Another rain-hollowed rock. A wide leaf. It was a huge risk. If Mattin had been telling the truth, the ritual required the bowl's magic. But Mattin had lied about everything thus far. What if the Blackwater was safe for Vahly, a Touched human, as long as she used a natural item to draw from the spring?

Arc couldn't be a part of this wild plan forming in her head. She couldn't put his life on the line for a reckless guess.

Of course, if she died, the Sea Queen would win anyway. With her dead, would the sea folk let Arc live, even though he'd befriended an enemy to their cause?

The dragons would die for certain. They had no deal with the salt water demons.

ALISHA KLAPHEKE

But there were no other options that could possibly lead to Vahly's power and a check to Queen Astraea's magic.

"Arc. I need a minute to think. Alone. Can you keep everyone distracted for me?"

His eyes narrowed. "I suppose. But don't do anything rash, Earth Queen. I've grown used to having you around."

He brushed his fingers over her wrist. She shivered with pleasure, looking into Arc's proud face. His lips parted like he might say more, his tongue touching his teeth.

Vahly swallowed, then laughed off the serious nature of the moment, her mind and heart warring. "Ooh, write that line down. *Grown used to having you around.* That'll get you all the elven maidens."

Arc didn't seem fooled by her false levity. He pressed a kiss to her temple, quick and warm, before leaving her in the shadows of the forest. Her fingers went to the spot he had kissed and she wondered if anyone had ever exploded due to experiencing too many feelings at once.

Grief. Joy. Rage. Fear. Pure, unadulterated happiness.

Before said explosion could ruin everything, before anyone could call her back, she slipped into the night, praying the starlight would be enough to get her back to the Source spring.

CHAPTER NINETEEN

A scream jerked Vahly to a stop, her boots sliding in the pebbles and scattering debris into the wildflowers. Her heart beat hard against her ribs. Who was that? A female. That was certain.

Holding her breath, she listened.

Arc called out, his words unintelligible and twisted with pain or terror or both. His voice lifted again. "Go, Vahly!"

Sweat poured down Vahly's neck.

Mattin must have figured out Arc was no longer spelled. He would have Canopus kill him.

She had to keep going.

But this was Arc. Never before had Vahly considered a mate, but with Arcturus …

A sob caught in her throat. She squeezed her hands into fists and her nails dug into her own flesh. Her feet began to run back to Arc, but she pulled herself to a stop, tears rolling off her chin and down her neck. This is what it meant to be Touched. To save everyone, she had to sacrifice. She had already lost so much.

But she had to lose him too, to give up her chance at love and a family of her own. A shudder shook her hard.

To be a queen, she had to fight on.

The night swallowed her up as a rise in the ground brought her past the place where Mattin had broken the bowl. Pulse knocking furiously in her throat, she hurried forward. A root tripped her and she landed on her palms. Rocks bit into her skin. Jumping up, she finally saw the stones that stood guard over the Blackwater.

She never should have gone on without the Lapis. This was a mistake. A horrible string of deadly errors.

Amona? she called inside her head, trying to use the Bond with her mother. *Mother? I lied. I'm sorry. I need you. I'm in the Forest of Illumahrah. If you don't come quickly, this may be the last you hear from me. I love you.*

No answer came. The breeze turned cold and goosebumps ran over Vahly's arms.

"Nix?" Vahly's voice spilled into the night. "Nix, things didn't go as planned. As usual." Her throat seized up as she forced herself to keep going.

But there was no answer.

Slowing, she approached the spring. As she crunched over the rocks and across soft, damp ground, her heart eased into a peaceful rhythm despite all of the day's horrors. The air was holy, perfumed with jasmine, clean water, and a scent that reminded her of beeswax candles.

The tall stones, fashioned with rude tools and chipped at their edges, cast shadows over the spring. Leafy vines and moss in varying shades clung to the pool of sparkling Blackwater.

Arc had told her this spring was the origin of all creation.

Stay alive, she thought. *For me, Arc.*

The depths of the spring were still as glass, and flecks of sapphire, ruby, and amethyst refracted the starlight, drawing Vahly closer. A shiver danced over her shoulders, then down to her fingertips.

She kneeled and breathed in the power of the place. Eyes closing, she felt its effect immediately. Her muscles relaxed and her stomach tightened, not with fear, but with excitement.

She'd hoped there would be something near the spring that she could use to ladle the Blackwater out, but there was only a scattering of pebbles and a fair amount of large, flat rocks. Perhaps she could use one of the leaves from the vines to draw the Blackwater from its bed.

Leaning over the spring, she plucked the largest leaf she could find and bent it to create a dipped space in the middle. The Blackwater slipped over the leaf's edge in fingers of glittering black that reminded Vahly of Arc's eyes. She trembled, half expecting the leaf to burst into flames and take her along for the ride. But the Blackwater remained in the leaf, shaking slightly from Vahly's nervous grip. She lifted the leaf, then tipped the contents to pour the liquid into her cupped left palm.

As the Blackwater left the leaf's surface, it shimmered into nothing. Not a drop made it to her hand. Ice filled Vahly's stomach.

ALISHA KLAPHEKE

There was a sound to her back, on the trail leading away from the feasting grounds.

She froze, leaf still lifted, and listened.

Only the night insects and a gentle breeze greeted her ears. Where was Nix?

Turning toward the spring again, she set the leaf near her knee. She just had to do it. To plunge her hands into the Blackwater and pray the Source blessed her instead of wiping her off the face of the world.

The guard stones watched her, silent. What had they seen here over the eons? The creation of this isle, Sugarrabota, and all of its dragons, elves, humans, and simplebeasts too. From this very spot, the entire world had spilled into being.

Vahly wished Nix were here. She wished Arc were here.

The names of the ones she loved flickered through her mind.

"Amona. Helena the healer. Nix. Dramour. Kemen. Ibai. Arcturus. Baww." She whispered their names like a chant as she reached her fingers toward the shimmering surface of the Blackwater.

The water cooled her fingertips. It wrapped around her palms. Cloaked her wrists and forearms.

There was no pain. No dissolving. Only the beat of her heart echoing the lapping of the Blackwater against its borders. Her mind stilled, cleared.

Breathing in the perfumed and holy air, she cradled the Blackwater, lowered her face, then poured the Source of all creation over her brow, cheeks, mouth, and chin. The cool liquid smoothed its way down the column of her throat and seeped into her clothing, wetting her collarbones and dampening the loose strands of her hair.

A rush of pure joy suffused Vahly.

She opened her eyes. The Blackwater disappeared from her arms and hands. Touching her face, she realized her cheeks and chin were clean too. Had her body absorbed the Blackwater?

A strange sound washed through the night.

A quiet, but pervasive thudding.

Vahly put a hand to her chest. It sounded like a heartbeat, but it wasn't her own. She moved, readying to stand, and placed a hand on the ground.

The drumming intensified.

She slammed down both open palms, her own pulse rate climbing.

The thudding remained constant, vibrating into her hands, and suddenly she knew.

This was the earth's heartbeat.

A tear escaped her eye and ran down one cheek. She could feel the earth's life under her hands. The Blackwater had not killed her. It had changed her.

Standing, head spinning, she listened to the world for the first time.

The slow scrape of leaves growing. Creatures digging through the dirt beneath her feet. Trees reaching thick boughs toward the blue hint of dawn.

She could hear the earth and everything in it.

Now, what could she do with this ability? Did she have any chance of fighting Mattin and Canopus and saving everyone from whatever dark magic they possessed?

Another scream ripped through the early morning. There was shouting and suddenly a crowd of elves rushed at Vahly.

Nix crashed out of the forest into the clearing beyond the spring. "I'm going to shift!" she shouted before calling up her fire.

Mattin appeared over the rise, the last of the night painting his face a pearly gray. He held out one hand, cloaked in purple shadows. The darkness stretched above the heads of all, and inside its swirling depths, Arc thrashed, two flashing knives drawn, but useless in the murky magic.

He lived.

Walking beside him, Canopus also held a captive in a hovering cloud. Cassiopeia.

Behind them, the rest of the elves wore faces of fear and rage. A wall of twisting darkness held them so they could not strike out at Mattin or Canopus who were outside the barrier.

Haldus, along with several others, shot arrows that bounced off the spellwork boundary. Then Rigel, Pegasi's mourning father, and Haldus, Arc's sturdy friend, both drew throwing knives. The blades flew, but connected with the barrier and fell to the leaf-strewn ground. General Regulus's face reddened as he tried his own air magic against the wall, light and shadow peeling away from his scarred hands and shaking Mattin's barrier.

Vahly's hands trembled violently as she drew her sword and stood her ground. Nix rose onto her hind legs beside Vahly, dragonfire rumbling and ready in her throat.

"Mattin!" Vahly's voice was strong despite the fear lancing through her heart. "Why do you fight us? We are all on the same side against the sea. Why wouldn't you want me to gain what power I can to help you and your kynd survive? It makes no sense. Have you spelled your own mind with this dark magic you've wrought?"

Mattin thrust a tendril of the shadow holding Arc to Canopus who grabbed the tether. Canopus thrust the haze to the ground. Arc fell, his head banging sharply against the earth. Vahly felt it in her own neck and temples.

Rigel pounded fists on the magicked barrier, his gaze on Arc's limp form.

King Mattin sneered. "Listen to the human with her arrogance. Your kynd always believe they are the answer to everything. We elves were the first kynd, the purest kynd. Our blood flows with Blackwater. Well, you were easy enough to fool. The lot of you. I have diluted the Blackwater your kynd used in their power ritual for generations. I was tired of your presumptuous behavior, your lording about as if you were the first instead of us."

What was he admitting? He had weakened the earlier Earth Queens by twisting the ritual? "Is this about the bowl?

"Of course it is, fool. I spelled that bowl to diminish the Blackwater's effect on your kynd. I all but eliminated its ability to alter the Touched as well as the less magically inclined. I tired of you traipsing through our lands like you owned the world. You made all the rules and used our Blackwater spring as if it stood in your home and not ours. We were first. And all I wanted was peace!" Never had the word been uttered with such malice.

Nix roared. She was ready to roast him, but Vahly needed to understand what was happening. What if he could trap Nix too?

"Didn't you realize you were aiding the Sea Queen by weakening us?" Vahly asked, her voice raw. "You are to blame for the rising seas. You are the reason no recent Earth Queens have had the ability to shake the earth and change the tides, to drive the waves back."

Shame washed over his features, but he schooled them into a mask of vanity and rage. Vahly thought perhaps he hadn't realized what powerful results his actions would have on his own kynd's future. Only out of desperation, had he made his oath to the Sea Queen. At that point, he had known it was too late to revive the power of the humans.

And the Sea Queen hadn't known what he did with the bowl and the Blackwater. She had still feared the earth's power.

But Mattin knew the truth. He had ruined the line of Earth Queens and only a deal with his greatest enemy, the sea, would save his kynd.

"Enough talk." Mattin raised his hands, bunched his fingers, then released a thousand tendrils of purple shadow.

CHAPTER TWENTY

Today, the Watcher would meet with Queen Astraea and Ryton had been called to attend the report on her visions as she scried in her great bowl of volcanic rock.

Despite the acid rising in his belly at the thought of what the queen would learn—and how he might very well be strung across the chasm to die for not telling the queen what he'd heard from the dying Jade during the recent battle—Ryton finished his breakfast of sliced eel and breaker fish that he'd boiled in an earthblood vent outside his back door.

He enjoyed large breakfasts that were more akin to dinners. Hearty helpings, high in protein, with a fair-sized net of fresh sea apples to top it all off. There were days when he had no time to eat after he'd left his home, days of endless strategy meetings, training, or warring. So bolting down what sustenance he had on hand before he left was only sensible.

Ryton's home was not much more than three spaces

and a few tunnels hollowed from the teal green rock. He had built a hammock for sleeping, a few cabinets for storage, and braided a seaweed rug for each room. Windows with proper shell shutters could be opened to allow clean currents to sift through on days when the weather was good—calm waters and comfortable temperatures. The table beside his hammock held a carved image of his brother and sister, back when they were children together. The smiles on their faces, happiness ruined by the dragons, pushed Ryton to train harder and fight with passion. The image was the only sentimental item in the whole house.

Sitting on the edge of Scar Chasm, Ryton's place did not look welcoming. But he liked it that way. He did not care for visitors. At home, all he wanted was peace and quiet.

Upon leaving, he didn't bother locking his stone door. Only those folk whose job it was to harvest glow creatures dared the Scar Chasm's electric eels and lanky sharks. And honestly, if they wanted to steal Ryton's manuals on battle strategy or his stash of food, they were welcome to it. Blackwater knew they weren't paid enough for the risks they took so everyone could have light in the darkest reaches.

And if the queen, displeased that he'd been too much of a coward to risk telling her what he'd heard from that Jade, decided to break down his door and destroy his home, no lock would stop her rage.

The murky waters of the chasm and its bevy of illuminated longfish, nautili, and jellyfish faded as Ryton passed a human shipwreck. The masts had long broken free of the main ship, and they shifted in the pull of the sea like an old giant's fingers, ready to grab unsuspecting sea folk. Ryton would never stop being amazed by the talent and daring of the long dead humans. Yes, they had been terrible and his sworn enemies, but they had stones. He could not deny it.

As he swam into the populated areas of Tidehame, the pathways straightened. The city planners had brought in white sand to line the pathways and tied glowing nautili along their borders. Most of the sea folk lived in group homes like the one Ryton passed now.

Bright purple and black striated rock stretched from the ocean floor to the moon-touched upper reaches of the water. Doors and windows showed families dining, some sleeping already, and one group of younger sea folk playing instruments.

Outside a ground-floor window the length of a full grown bull shark, Ryton slowed to enjoy the music. He was stalling, but would never have admitted that.

A dark-haired female turned the steel handle of a *winding wail*, her other hand pressing the strings down in varying patterns. A melancholy tune poured from the shell attached to the end of the four-foot instrument.

Beside her, a male with an impressive chin knocked a hammer against a set of brass hardbells, adding percussion to the song. Another male—too young for fighting but not far from it—sang along, his voice carrying with his water magic through the pull of the tide to reach Ryton's ears.

Pushing away from the song, Ryton kept on, toward Álikos Castle.

He had a job to do, and honestly, he had to be there when the Watcher announced what she saw. If it was nothing, he would need to placate Astraea so she didn't fall into a rage and slaughter the nearest guard. If the Watcher saw the falling Jade or heard his words about an Earth Queen, Ryton would need to call Grystark and Venu and begin discussing strategy with the queen. If it didn't come out that he'd heard such news already...

INSIDE ASTRAEA'S CHAMBERS, the Watcher had already set up shop. And the queen had called her other two generals, Venu and Grystark, already.

Ryton fought to keep his stomach from emptying right there on the mosaic-shell floor.

Venu nodded in greeting and Grystark smiled, a gesture that was more pain than happiness.

"Get on with it." The queen swam back and forth behind the Watcher.

The Watcher's hunched back moved in a deep breath as she reached her veiny hands over her bowl of volcanic rock to grip the sides. Her cloak of salt tulip leaves slid away from her forearms, showing fins that were surprisingly firm and shining. There was power in her still.

"I must wait for the feel of it, my queen." The Watcher's head lifted and she turned to Ryton, a smile stretching her wrinkled mouth. "High General Ryton."

He bowed to her even though she had no eyes to see it. Somehow she saw everything in both the physical and metaphysical world. "Honor to you, Watcher," he said quietly after bowing deeply to the Sea Queen.

Old stories claimed the Watcher clawed her own eyes out when the Sight came on her. She couldn't stand seeing double when the visions came. Ryton had always wondered if she regretted that hasty action, but of course, he would never ask. That would be horribly rude.

Besides, she most likely knew he was curious about it.

She couldn't see everything in the great world, but she saw many things and was keenly perceptive when it came to those around her regularly. Last year, she'd told Grystark to remove the growing lump on his thigh fin before it killed him. He did as she instructed and the healers confirmed the fin was eroding with blueeater, the disease that tended to take down sea folk if one lived long enough.

Now, the Watcher leaned over her bowl and peered into its empty depths. She said the shape of it, the hollow of it, helped her to focus.

"I see a storm," she mumbled, wiping spittle from her mouth.

"Where? Near the Lapis lands? Or in the North?" the queen asked.

"In the far, far south. Southern hemisphere."

The queen waved the information off. "Move on. No one cares about the desolate southern realms."

"I see three Jade younglings."

Venu snarled quietly and his hands became fists. The general, second to Grystark and Ryton in rank, traded a look with Ryton that reminded him of how many he'd lost to the battle with the green dragons. Ryton shuttered his own eyes halfway and gave the male a nod of acknowledgement. He too mourned those new recruits, lost too young to the vicious Jades and the dragonfire that bled into the waves themselves. Such abominations dragons were.

"What is so special about these young ones?" Astraea demanded, her sharp teeth flashing like pearls in the light of the nautili along her walls.

"They were born in the far, far North. Not here."

"What of it?" The queen raised a hand like she was about to strike the Watcher.

Ryton swam to her and gently took her fingers, then kissed them. "She'll tell you, my queen. She will."

The queen glared, but allowed him to keep caressing her hand.

"I see … I see that these three Jade younglings, born in the far northern edges of the island, under the cold sky's flurry of color, will rise to be the strongest of all."

Did she mean strongest of the Jade territory?

"If we don't drown them as eggs." The queen crushed Ryton's hand in hers.

"I'm not a dragon," he whispered into her ear, going for a teasing tone and wincing at her strength. He was no shrimp, but this Queen was Touched, imbued with water magic he couldn't dream of. Her power went far beyond muscle and bone.

She threw his hand and swam to the far end of the Watcher's bowl. "What else do you see? Anything we actually need to know?"

Ryton knew Astraea worried that the dragons had learned about the underwater tunnel.

The Watcher shook her head, her hood sliding away from her straggly white hair. She sat straight up and slammed her hands onto the sides of the bowl. "By the Blackwater."

The queen yanked her away from the bowl and gripped both of the Watcher's arms. "Tell me. What did you see?"

The Watcher swallowed, her leathery throat moving in successive swallows. When she finally spoke, the normally deep and confident timbre of her voice went reedy and thin. "The Earth Queen. An Earth Queen. She has washed in the Blackwater of the elves. She begins her journey."

Ryton's heart hung in his chest. It was as the Jade had said. There was a surviving human. And she wasn't only a regular human. She was an Earth Queen.

The room went hazy, and Ryton put a hand on Grystark's chest to steady himself.

Astraea dropped the Watcher's arms and swam backward slowly, her eyes widening and the veins at her temples pulsing. "That can't be. I killed them. I killed them all."

"This can't be true," Grystark said, allowing Ryton to keep his hand where it was. "We annihilated the last of the things at Tristura. None of our scouts—"

The queen flew at Grystark, clawed hands out and spells drumming from her lips. Before Ryton could fully process what was happening, he had flung out an arm and spoken a spell to throw the queen back.

Shocked, she stared at Ryton.

Grystark and Ryton both went to their knees, sand and shell grinding against their flesh.

"My queen," Ryton said. "I was mistaken. My body acted before my mind could catch up."

"A warrior's mistake." Grystark looked up warily. "Punish me as you see fit. Have mercy on your true servant, Ryton."

The queen huffed and turned away. "You don't matter. What matters is this new truth the Watcher has brought us."

The Watcher stood over her bowl again, her head bobbing like she could see movement. "She did this without the elves to see her," the Watcher whispered.

"Interesting," the queen spat. "So Mattin may live another day. But how? How did this human live through our flood? And how did she discover how to wake her latent powers? Did the elves instruct her at all? Do you see anything that points to such an event?"

"No." The Watcher's head swiveled like it might come off.

Ryton and Grystark stood. Ryton's heart hammered his ribs. He'd almost struck the queen. If he hadn't bitten off that spell...

The army would have been leaderless right before their final war. They would have to wait for another Queen to rise. Their magic would weaken, for hers strengthened all of the sea folk's power. They were linked through the water. And he nearly ruined everything for which they'd fought.

Ryton could tell Grystark was bursting to say something to him, but he knew he'd barely escaped one situation with the queen. He was wise enough to hold his tongue for now.

"The dragons!" The Watcher whirled and lifted her chin to the queen. "The Lapis aided the Earth Queen."

"The dragons? They hated humans."

The Watcher went back to her bowl and began humming a tune that was disturbingly similar to the one Ryton had heard from the window on his way here. She twisted her head toward him like she could read his thoughts, then she smiled, a quick lift of one side of her aged lips. Before he could question her, she turned away and fell quiet.

Had the grin and her humming only been products of his ravaged nerves?

"They most likely hate the idea of drowning to death more than they hate humans," Grystark said.

Ryton began to cover for him and his attitude, but it seemed the queen's entire focus appeared to be on understanding this catastrophe, which was wise. If this was indeed what the Watcher thought it was, the war was about to take a sharp turn in the wrong direction.

"Forgive me, Watcher, but could you perhaps be wrong?" Ryton eyed the bowl as if he might be able to see what she did. But there were no images, no sounds, nothing.

"I see what is, what was, what will be."

Ryton rubbed the back of his neck. "What exactly will we be dealing with if this human worms her way through the power ritual's steps? How many steps are there anyway? Who is our expert on this subject?"

The queen was swimming back and forth and back

again, behind the Watcher. Everyone stepped away to give her space. She stopped, crossed her arms over her pearl and salt tulip tunic. "The Jades would never consider the possibility that after all this time an Earth Queen of any repute could rise. But the Lapis are different. Well, even if this human does have power, who is to say how strong she will be? No one knows. Unless you see more, Watcher? Do you see her rising against us in a way that does more than inconvenience me?"

"I only see the woman. I see her washing in the Blackwater, in the Forest of Illumahrah." The Watcher glanced at Ryton and he nodded politely, not sure why she was looking at him. "There is a shadow in her life," the Watcher added, "but I cannot see it clearly. I do not know what it means."

"So this Earth Queen might not even be a threat?" Venu finally spoke up, violet eyes hopeful in the dim light.

Astraea shrugged. "She still must find her familiar, speak the spell at the place of her birth, and visit the Sacred Oak before she'll be capable of doing much of anything. This human only completed the first step. By the time she begins the next, she will be dead, along with the rest of them."

"Her familiar?" Ryton hadn't heard much about human power rituals.

Humans had guarded their ceremonies and kept them secret, holy. And in the passage of time, during their diminishing strength, those secrets had become mostly forgotten. Only a few living today knew of them. Ryton had heard Grystark mention them once.

"She'll need to follow her magic to a simplebeast who will aid her in her journey," the queen said, looking distracted. "That is the next step after washing in the Blackwater."

"Will the elves and dragons help her find this familiar?"

"I doubt they even know she needs to do this. She most likely doesn't know. How would she? She was probably hiding in some rotten cave when we finished off her kynd. She is most likely ignorant of her own capabilities."

"But she made her way to the elves and their Source spring." Grystark kept his voice respectful.

"She did." Astraea eyed Grystark. Her gaze held a warning. "But King Mattin promised me. She must have acted without his knowledge. He'll find out about this and strike her down." The queen's face broke into a wide grin. She tapped Grystark on the chest. "Indeed. I don't think we have much to worry about. But to be sure, we will send our spy to our contact within the ranks of the elves. We will find out everything and we will be ready if this Earth Queen does indeed prove to be worth our time."

"Our inside contact is alive still?" Ryton knew of the gray-haired elf who had turned on his own kynd in exchange for a rare sea tuber that gave elves an exhilarating high. The elf had an illness that would take him before Astraea flooded the land so the elf saw no problem with the deal.

"I believe so. We shall see."

The queen began to throw orders. Ryton was to

organize the meeting with the spy and gather any further intel possible. Grystark and Venu would develop additional training drills to combat an Earth Queen's ability to shape earth, call up creatures of leaf and stone, and all manner of horrors. Astraea sent the Watcher away with a guard holding the great bowl. The queen commanded her to continue Watching with only a few hours of rest at night.

Everyone swam away to their duties, leaving Ryton alone with the queen. He paused at her door, drumming fingers on the archway. He had to ask about the strategy she had suggested, the one where Grystark's units took the brunt of the dragonfire in a reckless, full front attack.

"I know what you're going to ask me, Ryton," the queen purred from across the room. She turned her back to him, her skin showing, smooth between the two flaps of her elaborately designed tunic. "Don't bother. I'll either use that strategy, or I won't. You know we mustn't put our hearts in the way of a win. You know better than to think for even one moment that I care whether Grystark lives or dies. I don't want him wasted though. He is valuable. At least take comfort in that."

Grystark was valuable. She could never understand exactly how valuable he was to Ryton. Astraea knew nothing of friendship. Ryton's heart pinched and for a fleeting moment he frowned, pitying her.

"Yes, my queen."

CHAPTER TWENTY-ONE

"**N**ow!" Vahly yelled to Nix.

Nix blasted Mattin with dragonfire. The elf stumbled backward, his shadows reeling around him, protecting him. But then the shadows faltered under the onslaught of the orange-red flame and his face streamed with sweat as he fell to his knees.

Nix couldn't strike out at Canopus because he held Cassiopeia close.

Cassiopeia's rage showed in her eyes as she struggled against the shadow's hold, floating just above his shoulder, her hands gripping a bow and a nocked arrow.

The barrier holding back the crowd wavered and thinned. The elves called up blazing flares of sunlight and spinning lengths of purple shadow, but it was nothing compared to the strength of Mattin's darkness.

Rigel broke through and ran at Mattin before the wall reformed.

Vahly joined him. "Hold, Nix!"

Nix ceased the stream of fire aimed at Mattin, then

lashed out at Canopus with her spiked tail. The elf leaped to avoid a hit, but landed hard on his side.

The spell holding Cassiopeia broke, and the sun-haired elf immediately fired at Canopus, nailing him to the ground with a shot to the heart. Dark red seeped into the ground around his body.

Vahly feinted a horizontal slash with her sword, then flipped her wrist at the last second, slicing the blade diagonally at Mattin. The steel edge fought through the shadow, the weapon trembling against the magic, and managed to cut across Mattin's chest. His surcoat fell open. Blood spooled from his pale skin.

From behind, Rigel hit Mattin between neck and shoulder, but the wound was shallow.

The king raised his shadow shield again and there was no getting through. He looked to Canopus, eyes wild, and threw darkness toward the vial at Canopus's neck. Tendrils of dark magic curled around the vial, quick as a breath, and brought the container to Mattin's lips. He drank, shuddered, and bent double.

Arc rose. His voice broke through the chaos. A stream of ruby blood streamed from his head, but he held his daggers ready. "Cousin!" His face twisted like he was in pain as he watched Mattin finish the contents of the vial. "That's Blackwater. Why?" It was obvious Arc thought the act an abomination.

"It should kill him. Shouldn't it?" Vahly looked to Arc, then Cassiopeia, then Rigel. They only stared, mouths agape and faces pale.

Nix roared, and Vahly backed up, motioning for the others to do the same.

Dragonfire skirted over Mattin's darkening shield, not injuring him, but igniting the wildflowers, trees, and vines.

Vahly raised her hands, the urge to use this new sensation rushing through her body. She could feel the earth, the very dirt, waiting for her command, longing to smother the fire eating at its growth. But nothing happened. She had no power to do such a thing.

Eyes fierce, Arc raised two blinding orbs of light and flung them at Mattin's shield. The shadow blinked on contact, but held its shape. Mattin straightened, his face slack with the nausea that came with drinking the Blackwater, and shoved a churning cloud of inky darkness toward Arc. At the same time, Mattin drew up a wind.

The gust threw Vahly, Arc, and Cassiopeia down, then knocked Nix backward into one of the guard stones near the spring.

Tail slashing, Nix exploded with rage. Her dragonfire blazed toward the canopy.

On the ground, Vahly stared, unable to pry her head away from the earth, as Nix struggled to aim, fighting the elemental force, the muscles in her neck straining.

All of them fought against the wind, but Arc was the only one making any headway. His lights shone on, even as he lay on the ground, hitched up against a boulder. The shadows that slipped around his light only caressed him like fingers, their movement unwavering despite the wind.

I didn't drink Blackwater and Mattin is strong. I won't last more than a few more seconds, Arc said into Vahly's mind.

You are changed. I feel it. I smell it. Throw your will toward my light and let us see what might happen. Trust your friend the alchemist.

But I can't do anything. It didn't work.

It will. Just try it.

Tears pricked Vahly's eyes. She looked to Nix, who broke away from her pinned position to breathe fire over Mattin once more. He trembled as if he might feel the heat of it, but still his shadows and his elemental wind crushed her and the rest. Arc's nose began to bleed and his eyes rolled like he was about to lose consciousness. Mattin's gusts blew Nix back. Her head slammed against the tree where she was pinned. She roared in pain, throat trembling.

This was it. Mattin would kill them all. The Sea Queen would flood the land and every hawk, sparrow, stag, fawn, steed, and dragon—all the creatures, simple and high—would perish in the crashing waves, burned by spellwork or ripped to pieces by the sea folk's teeth.

Only Mattin and the elves he chose would live on. An abomination, their magic twisting the way the world was meant to be. This beautiful place, the Forest of Illumahrah, would crack and decay would seep into its emerald glens and lofty towers of oak. All would be ruined.

Pull yourself together, Vahly, she told herself. *You won't go down like this. Fight for Kemen. For Ibai. For Dramour. For the innocent elves, Vega, Leporis, and Pegasi, who died by the hand of someone they trusted. Fight. Fight. Fight.*

Taking a deep breath, she opened her senses to the earth, to the tree roots, to the vines and to the rocks. The ground cooled her cheek, its touch like a friend's hand. Not at all sure what in the world she was attempting, she poured her will toward Arc's light.

Bind, she thought. *Join and grow.*

The ground between Arc and Mattin churned. Then the earth rose into a mound as if a wild, crazed animal crawled under the surface. The earth burrowed straight toward the King.

Vahly's lungs squeezed and she sucked a breath, already exhausted. Her temples pounded with the effort. Sweat rolled down her face, her limbs shaking with the effort. Her control began to slip.

The earth reared under Mattin's feet and threw him to the ground.

His concentration broke just as the sound of a hundred dragon wings filled the air.

I am here, Amona said into Vahly's mind.

Vahly's concentration broke. She lost her ability to move the earth, but happiness soared inside her, regardless.

Amona! she shouted through the bond. *Only torch King Mattin. Trust me. Please!*

The Lapis' great bodies appeared above the canopy, their scales like glittering water in the dawn light and their talons long and fearsome. The elves cloaked in the shadow barrier shrieked in anger and terror both, their hands drawn up to cast light and dark.

"No!" Vahly ran toward them and Cassiopeia joined her. "The dragons will save us. Don't hurt them, and they won't hurt you!"

Cassiopeia bent her head, and Vahly guessed she spoke to her kynd telepathically.

The dragons circled but only one breached the forest ceiling to blow fury down. The massive stream of dragonfire roared with the strength that could only come from a matriarch, enveloping Mattin entirely. Nothing of him or his shadow work remained visible. The ground bubbled under the heat of Amona's flames.

Vahly, instinctively knowing what to do, whispered to the ground. The earth rolled up and over the fire that reached beyond Mattin, suffocating the errant blaze.

Arc was standing now, beside Nix and Cassiopeia, and the Lapis landed one by one in a clearing beyond the spring.

Amona ceased her dragonfire and eased her way to stand beside Vahly.

A pile of ash was all that remained of Mattin's body. Vahly blinked, realizing Amona had also obliterated Canopus's body.

Arc's gaze latched onto Vahly's. A sad smile lifted one side of his mouth, and he bowed his head to her. *Our friends did not die in vain,* he murmured gently inside her head, his deep voice soothing and genuine.

Vahly wished she could speak alone with him right away. What had they done, combining their magic like that?

The wall Mattin created shivered and fell away, a sign that his soul had fled the remains of his body. A few elves raised their weapons at Amona and the Lapis approaching from behind her.

Vahly sheathed her sword and put a hand on a hip.

"Truly, elves? They fly in here and save you all from your own problem and you're going to fire at them?"

Most had the grace to look ashamed as they tucked their knives and bows away. Some muttered and disappeared the way they'd come.

Vahly turned to Amona. *Thank you. Once again, you saved my life.*

I don't know. You seemed to have things under control. But I didn't want to miss a chance to roast an elf. What was wrong with him?

He drank Blackwater.

From the Source spring? How did it not kill him? All the stories claim that would end him.

He diluted and spelled it. It turns out, he had been diluting the Blackwater my kynd washed in as part of their ritual for generations. That's why the last few Earth Queens were so weak and why so few had even been born.

Why would he do such a thing? Oh. Never mind. He is an elf. And a royal one at that. They thirst for power more than life. It has ended many of their kynd. You must continually be wary of the royal line of elves.

Vahly glanced at Arc who was deep in conversation with Cassiopeia, Rigel, and General Regulus. Perhaps she'd bring up royal-blooded Arcturus and their burgeoning friendship on a day when Amona hadn't had to fly so far to burn a foul elven king to the ground.

So you found a way to wake your powers here? I was wrong?

I realize that's surprising.

Amona gave Vahly a look.

I'm no Earth Queen. Not yet anyway. But I sense the earth

now and all the growing things. I can hear the earth's heartbeat and shift the ground when Arc helps me. Vahly put a hand to her mouth. Whoops.

Arc?

I don't know when I'll be a full Earth Queen or if indeed I ever will grow into powers that will be fit to fight the sea. I do know the ritual must include more steps for completion. I feel an undeniable urge to travel to the area near Bihotzetik.

Vahly hadn't realized the strength of this new feeling until the words had come out of her mind.

We searched the caves there, Amona said. *It is a desolate place, full of sadness and nothing else.*

You may be right, but I feel this longing just the same, and I must follow my gut.

As long as it leads you away from the elves, I approve.

They aren't all bad.

A growl rumbled in the back of Amona's throat.

Fine. Be angry now. Close-minded. Someday, I'll get you to believe we're all on the same side.

I know we are. And that is why I commanded all the Lapis to meet in the Red Meadow and sent a message to the Jades to come as well. You are going to address every dragon on Sugarrabota, and every elf if they'll join, and tell us what you think our best strategy is against the Sea Queen.

I don't know anything about that. Just because my powers are stirring doesn't mean I'm suddenly the answer to our survival.

Doesn't it? Amona glanced at the dragons gathered behind them. *If you aren't the answer, Vahly of the Earth, then we have no hope at all.*

So I'm supposed to fake it and keep everyone from crumbling into despair.

I think your Call Breaker friends call that a con, yes?

Vahly wanted to laugh. She tried. Dramour would have loved hearing Amona's words. But she could not bring herself to smile again. Too much sadness surrounded the name of her cider house cohorts. She told Amona as much through the bond.

Amona turned her head. *They died? But Nix...* Amona's reptilian gaze found Nix where she was talking with Arc and a few of the elven elders.

Nix survived. Ibai, Kemen, and Dramour did not.

My condolences. Amona extended a wing, and Vahly closed her eyes for a moment inside the familiar comfort of her mother's shadow as they approached the other Lapis.

The sun poured rays of gold through the trees and outlined patterns of oak leaves across the dragons' backs. At Amona's arrival, they sat back on their haunches and tucked their wings submissively.

"Lord Maur?" Vahly couldn't believe he had come.

Distaste filled his eyes, but he dipped his head respectfully.

Of course he came along. I commanded him. Do not for one moment, Amona said silently, now addressing the entire group of dragons plus Vahly, *think that any one of us will ever stand in your way again. No matter what wild scheme you believe might help you fight the sea, we will support you in full. Every Lapis. We will have your back, Earth Queen.*

Vahly thought maybe this would be a good moment to show off her new abilities. If she could manage it. She focused on the vines surrounding her place on the path. The plant snaked up her legs and sprouted new leaves when it reached the tips of her fingers. Her head ached with the effort. With a whisper, she released the vines and they returned to the ground.

It wasn't much, but it was a start.

The Lapis, including Maur, bent their heads as Vahly began to tell them the entire story of an elven king lusting for power, an oath he had made in a time of desperation, and how the Blackwater had changed everything.

CHAPTER TWENTY-TWO

R yton swam through a school of striped redfish and they scattered, dashing toward the distant surface of the sea. He had no time for beauty, or breakfast. Echo had reported that the gray-haired and diseased elf who'd turned on his own kynd was on the coast, ready to talk.

Jaw tight and gills flaring, Ryton couldn't swim fast enough. They needed to know everything about this supposed Earth Queen.

Hopefully, the elf would tell them Mattin had killed her. If not, well, this might be the day Ryton killed his first elf.

The elves had once warred with his kynd, but they'd given up fighting the sea before Ryton's birth. Their air magic did little against crashing waves. True, the spelled salt water did not affect them as it did dragons, but they could drown like the humans had. The elves had powerful flesh, but if a sea warrior sharpened his coral spear correctly, the elves' bodies split beneath the weapon's edge with only a dose more strength behind the blow.

Ryton's curiosity begged him to get a closer look at an elf. He hadn't seen one close up and wanted to know how they moved and spoke, what their mannerisms were and how they differed from sea folk. Of course, elves had no fins along their skulls, arms, back, or legs. But more than the obvious contrasts, he longed to see how they gestured when angry and how they behaved in greeting.

Once he reached the end of the more sandy run beyond Tidehame, Ryton increased his speed further. His body was warmed up now and he could move more quickly than most. His sensitive sea folk eyes told him the light above water had moved and it was nearly time to rendezvous with the scouts.

A verdant forest of panypsila fykia told Ryton he was getting closer to the edge of the mainland where the Forest of Illumahrah and the elves' plateau held fast to the ocean floor. The wide leaves of the seaweed forest waved gently, brushing his beard and shoulders like hands.

He left the green-black of that place and swam toward the wreck of another human vessel. This one was far older than the one near his own home. No masts remained, only a portion of the ... hull. He recalled the word from his school years long ago.

Wishing he had time to scour the place, he began to glide past, but a glint flashed from the sand near the last section of the hull. It was something made of silver, that material the humans loved almost as much as their gold.

As he dug around the object, trying to free it, sand billowed around his fingers. It was a human coin.

Blackened nearly to the point of being completely unreadable, the disc had two crossed lines across the side that was less damaged by age and water. The lines divided the coin's face into four sections, with a few squiggly marks directly in the center. Ryton tilted the silver piece this way and that. He rubbed it with a thumb, but he still couldn't quite tell what the symbols in each section were. Maybe a flame at the top right?

Ryton tucked the coin into the sealinen bag attached to his shell belt and kicked away from the wreckage. Later, he would study the coin in the privacy of his own home, away from the queen's prying eyes. He knew exactly what she would do if she noticed his interest in a land artifact.

Astraea's two scouts floated above an algae-covered outcropping along the edge of the island. Still underwater, their dark clothing and blue-black hair twisted in the tidewater, both sets of their arms crossed. They weren't happy about this mission. Never had been.

The most experienced one, Calix, wore a look of resignation. He never could hide his emotions. Face like an open book. He ran a hand over his high hairline, then saluted to Ryton.

"The elf should be above now, waiting for us, High General."

Echo, the second scout, saluted more sharply than Calix. The sun pierced the few feet of seawater above them and glowed over her short hair and her hands, hands that seemed a little too large for her frame.

Ryton saluted in return. "Do you have the tuber for him?"

Echo lifted a sack of the sea plant that the elf wanted to relieve himself of pain, and possibly of life. Because of the elf's fatal disease, he traded information for the tubers.

Ryton reached his arms wide, swimming toward the harsh light. "Then let's get this over with."

At the surface, the sea folk moved their second eyelids over the first to lessen the light and placed tympanic leaves over the gills along their necks. The air eased through the porous, water-soaked leaves and allowed their bodies to continue to process oxygen in the same manner as they did underwater. It wasn't comfortable, but in order to speak and stay above the waves for any length of time, it was necessary.

Pale sand stretched from the water to a spit of land covered in grasses and small trees that looked like diseased coral branches. The elf crouched at the end of the isle, his face drawn and whiter than the beach. His sickness was most likely to blame for his pallor. The wind kicked up, and he pushed a strand of gray hair behind one pointed ear. His sleeve fell back to show a forearm missing any type of fin. Ryton couldn't help but think this creature looked naked without the translucent fins that ran along everyone else's arms.

Ryton swam closer as the elf called out in greeting.

"Good day, sea folk," the creature croaked. The elf glanced over his own shoulder, toward the forest. Most likely he was merely making certain he hadn't been followed, but Ryton readied his spear just in case an army of elves came out of the coral—*no, the trees,* he reminded himself.

"Please." The elf reached a shaking hand over the water, his eyes wide and focused on the bag of tubers that Echo had brought up.

The elvish language was old and all sea folk were taught to read and speak it, along with human and dragon too. Though most sounds were incredibly difficult to produce, a lack of education simply wasn't tolerated.

"Please give me the plant," the elven spy said. "I'll tell you all. There has been a great disturbance here and it will prove important for your kynd."

Ryton kicked his feet and rose higher, the harsh air biting at his chest. "You will tell us what you know, and then, only then, will you receive the amount of plant we decide you deserve. Or Echo can simply toss it back into the sea. You are welcome to swim down here to fetch it." Ryton grinned like a shark.

The elf paled further and drew back. "It's the King. He's dead."

Ryton rubbed at his ears. "I heard you wrong."

"King Mattin is dead. As well as his right hand, Canopus."

Ryton swam close and stood on the sandy ledge above the outcropping. The ocean lapped against his calves. The world listed to the side for a moment, mostly because he'd never been so far out of water, but also because this information, well, this changed everything.

His dense body weighed too much out of the water to move properly, so Ryton cupped a handful of the sea and whispered a spell. The sound of water magic bubbled and rushed past his ears. His bones and flesh grew lighter and he was able to take a confident step forward.

Ryton's mind raced. King Mattin's promise to Astraea had somewhat protected them from an Earth Queen. But if he was dead...

Frustration seared Ryton's veins. He gripped the elf's cloak and lifted the frail creature high. "How did he die? Did the new Earth Queen kill him?"

"The dragons," the elf choked out, his spindly fingers winding around Ryton's grip, "joined with the potential Earth Queen and one of our own who rebelled—they came together and took him down."

"And your kynd didn't rise up to save him?"

"Mattin was bent, wrong, foul. He had been drinking Blackwater."

Ryton dropped the elf.

He splashed into the water, hissing and moaning. He managed to get himself up and onto the beach.

Ryton's mind could not wrap itself around what the elf had told him. Drinking Blackwater? He swallowed disgust. To take the Source's blessed waters into one's own filthy mouth? Horrifying.

"The Blackwater didn't injure him?"

"It gave him great power. Enhanced his ability to wield air magic. He could twist minds and turn memories away."

The elf shuddered, and for the first time, Ryton was in tune with the land creature. What Mattin had done, it was unthinkable.

"But the Blackwater did take a toll. It tainted the crown he wore, making it possible for him to hurt his own royal blood, albeit indirectly, through his cohort Canopus. And I think drinking the Blackwater wore on the King's own mind as well. Now, I have told you plenty. Give it over. Give over the plant."

"Where is this potential Earth Queen now?" Ryton demanded.

"The dragons and elves banded together and made an oath to her. The Lapis matriarch claims she is in their palace, arranging strategy to fight you, but the wind says otherwise."

"Don't speak in riddles, elf."

He swallowed, gaze too wide and focused still on the bag. "The wind has told many of us that she travels to the place where the humans once reigned."

"Toward the Bihotzetik ruins?"

"Exactly so." A line of drool ran from the corner of his mouth.

Echo wiggled the bag and lifted her eyebrows, urging the elf to tell Ryton more.

Ryton scratched at the tympanic leaves lying on the gills at his neck. He stepped back into the water, letting the sea come up to his shoulders. "But why would she dare to enter the ocean?" he asked, talking more to himself than anyone else.

"That I do not know. Now fulfill your end of the bargain and I'll listen further for you." The elf's voice cracked with want. "Did you know Mattin had been diluting the Blackwater we gave the humans for a long time? To weaken them?"

Ryton had no room in his mind for more information. He waved at Echo and she tossed the bag of tubers to the elf. Despite the creature's obviously diseased and skeletal limbs, the elf leaped and grabbed the sack from the air.

Echo and Ryton dove back into the sea, leaving Calix above water for a moment to be sure the elf returned to his plateau and brought none else to the water.

"High General." Echo swam beside Ryton, her spear catching a bright beam of sunlight through the shallows.

Ryton stripped the leaves from his neck and relaxed as much as one could knowing what he did. That there indeed was an Earth Queen and she had already slain one of Astraea's allies.

"High General," Echo said again.

"Yes?"

"If the Earth Queen heads into the water, won't we simply kill her? I don't understand your anger. Please forgive me if I'm overstepping, sir."

"Because when a mission or a duty appears easy, simple to solve, it absolutely never is. You will learn that when you've spent year after year after year at war."

"But hopefully I won't have to."

Ryton smiled briefly. "Indeed. I do hope you don't have to learn and that we find peace. We can win. But I don't have any illusions about how difficult it will be to finally claim the last of the land."

Especially now, with all the creatures on the island joining forces. There was no way to fully predict how this development would affect the war. What would dragons and elves do together in a battle against them? They'd always faced the creatures separately, with the elves hardly putting up a fight. Their magic didn't work well against Ryton and his kynd, thank the Blackwater. But could they use their shadow, light, and air to aid the dragons?

OUTSIDE ÁLIKOS CASTLE, Calix gave Ryton his full report. The elven spy had returned to the forest and would sink a rock-filled red cloak when he had more information.

Ryton's mind wandered to past battles and long ago losses as he dismissed Calix and Echo and swam through the emerald coral and yellow fish in the castle's courtyard.

Queen Astraea herself appeared at the outer castle door, flanked by four guards.

Pulse tripping, Ryton bowed low. She must have been too eager to wait for him in her chambers.

Whispering a spell, she raised her arms, pearly skin shimmering in the glowing lights set above the red coral archway. A membrane of turquoise flowed over her body, then stretched to envelop Ryton. The guards stood outside the membrane, eyes wide with panic. They remained where they were and did not act rashly. They knew their Queen well enough not to act without being ordered to do so.

"None can hear us. Now. What did you learn?" Astraea's voice was dangerous, her eyes half-lidded. The sea lifted the edges of her blue-green sea tulip dress and tossed her long hair. A crown of scarlet coral nested in the braids over her ears.

"Mattin is dead. The Earth Queen is headed for Bihotzetik."

Astraea's eyes closed and her hands fisted. "Go, High

General Ryton." Her gaze flashed open and bright, power surging from their depths. "Go and slay our enemy. If you fail, do not return."

So this was to be a quiet mission, completed on his own. A chill traveled the length of his spine and the fingers gripping his spear tightened out of reflex to a threat.

Heart thudding, he thought of what Grystark would say. *Run, friend. Run to the South and pray to the Source the queen is too busy to find you.*

Ryton's brother would order the opposite. *Go, brother. Avenge our sister and destroy the one chance the dragons have to live a life our Selene never had the chance to live.*

But Ryton was no coward and he did intend to avenge Selene.

He alone would face this Earth Queen, the one born to destroy Ryton and every last one of his kynd.

Or he would die trying.

CHAPTER TWENTY-THREE

A natural wind gusted over the Red Meadow, below Vahly's perch on a western outcropping. The tiny flowers moved like ruby waves among the vast crowd of jewel-toned dragons dressed in their finest.

"So many rings and necklaces," Vahly said wryly to Arc and Nix, who stood beside her on the high rock. "Sparkling like sand on the beach."

"Your lot look like sad little leaves next to mine," Nix teased, jabbing Arc with an elbow.

She was decked out as well, dressed in a new quadrant-cut cloak in the darkest green can be before it becomes black and a split-leg dress to match, embroidered with the symbol of the Breakers. The flame over the talon glittered a deep gold in the sunlight. Her red hair was knotted at the top of her head and her bright eyes scanned the distance like a true predator.

Arc wore a black linen shirt beneath his usual black

and silver surcoat. Fully released from his evil cousin's spellwork, his magic twirled about his head and hands in purple tendrils and gold circles. His straight black hair hung loose at his broad shoulders. The breeze tousled its ebony length, and for a moment, Arc appeared bed-rumpled and vulnerable. But his gaze remained hawk-like, and it held Vahly's attention for reasons she wasn't ready to think about.

He was pretty much breathtaking, Vahly had to admit. Not that either of them had the time for romance. There was so much to do and they had no time to do it.

She knew for certain the earth was telling her to visit the region near Bihotzetik. But she had no idea why. Arc and Nix had agreed to accompany her there.

Vahly decided they would tell the world they were busy in meetings with Amona, deep in the Lapis mountain palace, but truly they'd be on a quiet mission to discover the secret her magic was desperately trying to tell her.

Below them, in the meadow, the elves stood well apart from the dragons. They had chosen to gather on the Lapis side of the meadow. A smart choice. The Jades were not yet sold on this idea of including them in the war against the sea. Their Matriarch, Eux, paced the grassy area. She appeared ready to explode in anger at any second. Vahly couldn't see her orange and slitted eyes from here but she would bet all of last season's gambling haul that they were darting from Amona to Cassiopeia with complete and utter loathing.

Cassiopeia stood, willowy and grim, before the host of

elves. From the small pool of elves with royal blood, the elders had crowned her the new ruler of Illumahrah. And she looked every inch the queen. Her crown of spinning light and curling darkness was visible even from this distance if Vahly titled her head the right way and slid her gaze side to side. The peaks of the magical diadem stretched higher than Mattin's ever had. She couldn't trap anyone with a massive barrier wall or bend minds like Mattin had. Her magic was true. But she could do enough damage with her own elemental wind, piercing light, and controlling shadow. Arc's power was the only one of their kynd that was nearly equal to hers now that she wore the crown.

Nix raised an eyebrow at Vahly and pointed down to the Jades. "I think you'd better speak up, Queenie Vahl. If they're bunched up together for too much longer, it's not going to be pretty."

Arc grinned and glanced at Vahly from the corner of his eye.

Vahly stepped forward. "Wish me luck, you two. Because if I go down, you'll likely be salted right along with me."

"I don't like my odds against Eux. Or Maur for that matter." Arc's eyes widened as he gazed at the dragons.

Vahly waved him off. "You'd give them trouble before you died."

"Comforting," Arc muttered.

Nix smiled. "Our Vahly isn't known for coddling or mincing words, Arcturus."

"I thought you wished to call me Arc."

"Well, now everyone is using the nickname," Nix said. "It fails to be rebellious at this point. I'm going back to Arcturus."

The ghost of Dramour drifted through the conversation. Vahly could almost hear his laugh and see him adjusting his eye patch. She gritted her teeth. She couldn't break down again now. That would have to wait as well.

After a meeting with the elves and their elders, Vahly, Arc, and Nix had brought together every elf and dragon who wished to mourn the lost. They'd all visited the burial mounds in the forest and set flowers and pine boughs over the graves. More tears had been shed and none had argued when Arc, Vahly, and Nix joined hands in silence there, as they had before.

Grief had bonded these three and Vahly was so glad to have them. She never could address this crowd without them by her side.

She belonged with them, her small band of Breakers.

Spreading her hands, she spoke as loudly as she was able to the legions of dragons and elves.

"We are united in our fight. From this day forward, we are never enemies. If we fight amongst ourselves, we will fall and fall quickly. For the Sea Queen prepares for the final flood. Her forces are visibly stronger, raising massive waves and churning whirlpools, in the waters off the Lapis territory as well as in the Jade. Her army has grown in power and ability for they practice their maneuvers in many places at once now. Scouts from all corners of our island have reported increased activity and sea levels surpassing every high water mark.

Matriarch Eux's scouts reported an unusual tide this morning. This is unprecedented. We must unite. As the hopeful Earth Queen, determined to wake my powers in full, I ask that, today, all highbeasts take an oath to defend and fight for all others in our midst. That Lapis will support Jade. Jade will back elves. That all will fight together, as determined and led by our strategists, Matriarch Amona, Matriarch Eux, Queen Cassiopeia, and me."

The dragons lifted their heads and blasted dragonfire into the sky, Nix doing the same at Vahly's side. The flames crackled and snapped as the elves wove light and dark into spinning clouds like windstorms above their own congregation.

As one, the highbeasts spoke in dragon, the chosen tongue for discussions of this sort. "We promise to fight as one, to respect the wishes of the strategists, to unite against our common enemy."

The magic of the promise felt like a quick burn of a too-bright sun as it seared the hearts of every intelligent creature gathered in the wide meadow. The red hat flowers danced in the wind, oblivious to the serious nature of the moment.

As if on cue, the dragons and elves began to stream out of the Red Meadow and back to their assigned positions on the isle. Some to scout or begin planning attacks and defenses. A good many to test the new talents of the sea folk army in the North. Groups to gather supplies and move young and old to higher elevations. Battle dragons, both green and blue, shifted and flew into the skies to run drills.

"Ah!" Nix pointed high. "Euskal and Miren are there. With those Jades!"

Sure enough, the cider house Call Breakers had joined up with a unit of Jades and were practicing quick dives and flying rolls. Their bodies reflected the sunlight and were nearly too bright to look at.

"This would have pleased Dramour to no end," Nix said quietly as Arc and Vahly followed her off the rock and down a winding path bordered by wide, low-branching oaks that humans had pruned for centuries for charcoal.

"And Kemen too, I think." Vahly braided her hair tightly.

"Ibai would've hated it," Nix and Vahly said in unison.

They shared a sad kind of laugh as they took their satchels from Arc, who'd retrieved them from their hiding place behind a cluster of rocks.

Nix strapped a large, brocade bag over one shoulder and buckled it neatly beneath her wing joint. Her wing had not yet recovered enough for flight, but she didn't seem overly bothered by pain or discomfort. She had also taken up a long stick that she claimed General Regulus had taught her to use in fighting. Seems they had been busy while Arc and Vahly were meeting Cassiopeia before her coronation. Who could have guessed that a dragon and an elven general could become allies in such a short time? Not Vahly. Surprises, some wondrous and others gruesome, now filled her life. And it wasn't going to get any easier.

Arc wore a satchel strapped to his back, bow and

arrows sticking out from the top near a rolled up sleeping mat. His knives gleamed from where they hung on his wide, black belt. He'd met privately with Vahly last night, during a bonfire to celebrate the coronation. With his hand in hers, he'd sworn full allegiance to her, saying that Cassiopeia had insisted upon it. Arc, royal-blooded elf that he was, had embraced the ceremony of the situation, going to his knee and presenting his knives to Vahly, hilt first. The gesture was not lost on Vahly. She had kissed his head primly and raised him up, accepting his fealty with pleasure.

"So. Are we ready?" Vahly's veins pulsed with the beat of the earth's heart as she looked over her two closest allies.

"We have no idea what we're looking for," Nix said, raising an eyebrow, "and no idea what we'll face when we get there, so—"

Arc interrupted. "Of course we are." He glanced at Nix and winked.

And so the Earth Queen and her Band of Breakers headed into the wilderness, following the whispers of the world.

GRAB THE NEXT BOOK IN THE DRAGONS RISING SERIES, BAND OF BREAKERS HTTP://HYPERURL.CO/BANDOFBREAKERS

WANT A FREE BONUS SCENE ABOUT ARCTURUS SWEARING ALLEGIANCE TO VAHLY?

THEN SIGN UP FOR ALISHA'S FANTASY FANS NEWSLETTER BY VISITING ALISHAKLAPHEKE.COM TODAY.

YOU'LL ALSO RECEIVE UPDATES ON THE NEXT BOOK IN THE SERIES, BAND OF BREAKERS, AND TWO OTHER FREE BOOKS FROM ALISHA.

CAST OF CHARACTERS

Humans

Vahly—twenty-three years of age, the only survivor of her kynd

Lapis Dragons

Amona—Matriarch of the Lapis Clan

Maur—male noble warrior, daughter in line to be next Matriarch

Helena—female healer

Ruda—female youngling

Linexa—female who cares for younglings

Xabier—newly matured male warrior

Elixane—deceased Matriarch with legendary hoard

Lys—female librarian

Draes—male librarian

Eneko—male noble

Rip—male palace guard

Ty—male palace guard

Jade Dragons

Eux—Matriarch of the Jade Clan

Zarux—male noble warrior

Call Breaker Dragons

Nix—female smuggler, spy, and owner of cider house

Dramour—male former warrior who is devoted to Nix

Ibai—male healer

Kemen—male healer and muscle

Aitor—male spy and thief for Nix

Euskal—male former warrior

Miren—female former warrior

Baww—male who manages cider house

Elves

Arcturus—royal male alchemist

Vega—ancient female guard

Pegasi—young male guard

Leporis—male guard

Mattin—King of the Elves

Canopus—the King's right hand

Cassiopeia—royal female strategist

Regulus—elder and warrior

Rigel—male scout

Haldus—male host and warrior

Deneb—female devoted to the King

Gruis—male courtier

Ursae—female courtier

Sea Folk

Ryton—male consort to the Sea Queen, High General

Astraea—the Sea Queen

Grystark—male General

Venu—male General

Sansya—young female warrior

Echo—female scout

Calix—male scout

Selene—deceased female warrior, sister to Ryton

Lilia—female craftsfolk, wife to Grystark

EXCERPT FROM WATERS OF SALT AND SIN

(WATERS OF SALT AND SIN IS THE FIRST BOOK IN ALISHA KLAPHEKE'S BESTSELLING UNCOMMON WORLD SERIES)

The air, raised by the Salt Magic, shushed gently past my face, and the boat lurched forward. Calev slipped, and I caught him, hearing a thud from the tiller.

Oron had rolled off to one side. He swore as he righted himself. "My mother's third—"

"Where did you learn to talk like you do?" Calev's knuckles whitened on the boat's side, but I didn't think it was from Oron's foul mouth. His chin lifted as he scanned the thankfully empty night sky.

"Watch our lean, Oron," I said. We were heeling to leeward. A little more and we'd be thrown into the water.

"I was raised in a roadside brothel by a mother who fancied traveling theatre players," Oron said to Calev, his words whipping toward us as the wind rose even higher, and we sped forward. "I speak the tongue of the wicked and witty."

To keep our conversation off what had happened, to keep myself from jerking the tiller from Oron and turning us back and raging toward the oramiral to battle for my sister and lose, I picked up the distracting thread of talk.

"Surprised you never heard that one," I said to Calev. "It's his favorite line."

Moonlight slipped over Calev's hair. It rolled down his skull and sat on his broad farmer's shoulders like a death shroud. I tightened my sash's knot and pulled my sleeves lower on my arms.

"I'll take the tiller now." I moved to aft.

Asag's Door was quieter, though white caps still curled around the bases of the rocks. With the gusts and Oron at the sail, I pulled the tiller and guided us through the Spires. It was low tide now. The boat responded to me, shifting under my body like a horse. The sea had listened and sent us wind and soon we'd be home. If the Salt Wraiths let us be.

Calev came to the tiller with me and Oron moved to watch at the bow.

Calev tried to laugh. "Oron and I haven't had the opportunity to talk as much as I would like."

This was ridiculous, us trying to be brave and making jokes. Black shadows and streaks of moonlight used my imagination to turn the water and rocks into a slithering beast waiting for us to make one wrong move.

"He has the best foul language. I could pick up some tantalizing bits from him to shock Eleazar," Calev said.

I tried to smile, but all I could think was right now Avi was being led up the steep side of Quarry Isle. They would fit a bell contraption around her waist.

How were we going to persuade Calev's father to use his influence to get her back? Old Farm had never interfered with the oramiral. At least to my knowledge. It hadn't come up. Being people of the land, all Old Farms, except their full ship kaptan, stayed clear of the sea. Similar to my aunt's people in Kurakia, across the Pass.

Avi. My brave little Avi. How are we going to rescue you?

A grin trembled on Calev's lips but fled when Oron made a choking noise near the mast. We jumped up.

"They're here." Oron pointed to the western sky.

All the blood in my head drained into my feet. Salt Wraiths.

I whipped my flint and dagger out of my sash. We had to get the lantern lit. Now.

Calev held the Wraith Lantern's miniature door open. My flint sparked onto the wick, but it didn't flame.

A swooping noise like a tree limb swinging through the air stung my ears. The sparkling white of one Salt Wraith whisked between the moon and us, but far enough away that we could barely see it. Its soul-and-mind-possessing shadow didn't touch us, but it soared closer. I dragged the flint over the dagger again. The wick caught fire and blazed bright. Calev slammed the opening shut to keep the wind from putting out the strange flame.

Seeing the orange, black, and silver flickers, the wraith reared and disappeared in the distance.

Hanging the lantern on the mast's hook, Calev sighed. "That was too close."

"It might come back." As I made my way back to the tiller, I studied the fire encased in the glass. A flash of silver rose and fell, then a glint of orange.

"We need to squeeze into the hull." Feet first, Oron lowered himself through the square opening.

"We won't all fit in there." I raised my gaze to the sky.

"I told you we needed an on-deck compartment for ropes and water," Oron called out of the space. "If you'd let me buy the wood to build one, you could've tucked me in there. Being lesser in stature might be an advantage. Who knows? In one hundred years, we small people might be the only ones left."

A look dark as the Expanse's greatest depths crossed over Calev's face. "Let Kinneret in there first, coward."

I looked at Calev's hands as he stood beside me. "You're trembling too," I said. "I wouldn't cast labels around so easily."

"Courage isn't not being afraid," Calev said. "It's standing and fighting through your fear. Protecting those you love." His eyes softened. "Not that I have to tell you."

My heart skittered through three quick beats, and I looked away.

"I'll go down if I think it's necessary," I called out to Oron. "Someone has to get us home."

Whispering the sea's words over and over again under my breath, I worked with the magic to veer and tug, push and pull our craft toward Tall Man, toward home. Calev stayed by my side. The lantern's sunset light flickered over his cheekbones and his forearms. He looked made of flame.

Stars pierced the velvet sky. The moon watched, its candle-white glow melting onto the sea. Eventually, Oron climbed out of the hull. Calev stared at him, eyes slitted.

"Oron, will you see to the prow?" I asked. The tiller vibrated against my hand, a current fighting our direction. "I want your eyes on the waters."

Rubbing his small hands together, Oron nodded but didn't exactly hurry to his post.

"In case you decide to condemn me for cowardice, you should know I witnessed a wraith Infusing an entire full ship's crew," Oron said to Calev. "And yes, I can feel that scornful glare through the tunic on my back."

"What happened?" Calev asked.

The sail billowed in a gust and the ropes pulled against the blocks. The pulleys knocked against the mast like hammers.

Staring out at the sky, Oron crossed his arms over his chest. "A flock of nine came."

"Nine wraiths?"

Nodding, Oron said, "They spun around the vessel like the skin of the moon had been peeled away and tossed into the wind. The emotions whisked over me though I was a good league away on another boat. Rage, the desire to inflict control...it was..." He bent his head. "When the wraiths left, I watched their Infusion lights leave the sailors' mouths and leak back into the sky. We boarded their ship—I rode with a fishing crew then— there was nothing left alive. Men had hung themselves from the boom, their bodies swaying with the movement of the sea, their tongues swollen, eyes popped clean out. Blood covered the decking. I slipped in it. Drew up against a pile of men who'd either fallen on their own yatagans or been murdered by their Infused crew mates."

He ran a hand over the fat tangles of his hair.

"So when I go to the hull, you'd be wise to follow. We should all squeeze in there like happy sardines."

The whooshing sound returned. Calev looked to me. Oron swore. Another wraith.

The whispering began. Hissing, sighing, moaning in my ears.

I covered my head with my hands and the remainder of the salt I'd used rained onto my face and hair.

Oron was already back in the cabin. Calev grabbed my arm and dragged me toward the tiny space. We'd never fit. Besides, someone had to make sure the lantern didn't fall over or go out. If it did, the wraiths would swamp us and cover us in their whitewashed shadows—their way of possessing mind and body—and it'd all be over. We either had to be under the shadow of a solid roof in the hull or swamped in the Wraith Lantern's light.

I snatched the lantern and crawled into the hull behind Calev. Turning, he pulled my back against his stomach and wrapped his arm around me to help me hold the lantern up. His fingers lay on mine, his hips pressing into me. Both of us were shaking against one another as the sounds increased. Oron had to be suffocating behind us. The air was hot and moist with our breath. Our feet stirred up the pungent scent of old lemons and last year's barley, remnants of the shipments we'd made over our lifetimes.

We lifted the lantern as the wraith came screaming toward us. The light spun a web of colors over my forearms, but this creature was strong and some of its power crept under and over the flickering orange and silver. Emotions flooded my mind, rushing in like boiling waves, filling in every crack of my thoughts, my heart.

Check out Alisha Klapheke's other fantasy series today.
  Waters of Salt and Sin (Uncommon World Book One)
  The Edinburgh Seer (Edinburgh Seer Book One)

Made in the USA
Columbia, SC
06 January 2020

86457445R00176